Five Steps to Celestia

by

Terry Segan

The Wild Rose Press, Inc.
PO Box 708
Adams Basin, NY 14410-0708
Visit us at www.thewildrosepress.com

Publishing History
First Edition, 2024
Trade Paperback ISBN 978-1-5092-5512-2
Digital ISBN 978-1-5092-5513-9

Published in the United States of America

Dedication

This book is dedicated to Lyn and Wilson. There are mystical forces at play every day. It's these forces that bring amazing people into our lives. You are two of them.

Chapter 1

"Suzi, are we done yet?" Joy pleaded more than asked. Aimlessly, she wandered the aisles, enduring yet another gift shop on their road trip up the Oregon coast. The overpowering scent of freshly baked cookies from a row of candles gave her hunger pangs.

"Almost. Look at these glasses." Her friend held one up, enamored with the design of a grape vine etched around the top. She studied it as if she'd found the Holy Grail. "Aren't they cute?"

Suzi had been like that for as long as Joy could remember. Everything fascinated the woman.

"Adorable. You've touched everything twice. Can we go now?" Her tolerance waned as her eyeballs rolled back into her head.

With her traveling companion in the middle of a messy divorce, Joy wanted to be supportive. Their friendship spanned almost two decades, and it was Suzi who remained constantly by her side when Drake had died in a car accident two years earlier. At only forty-four, Joy's hope of growing old with a wonderful man got destroyed by a patch of black ice on a cliffside road.

The loss of a spouse, no matter the method, takes its toll. Despite using these distractions to camouflage her emotions, Suzi couldn't fool Joy into thinking the split didn't terrify her. Pushing sixty and about to be on her own again had to have an awful feel to it. Not that it hadn't happened before, this being her fifth divorce.

Glancing at the man leaning on the front counter, Joy did a double take. She'd caught a glimpse of a purple vial on a chain peeking out from the neck of his button-down shirt.

Since she stood before a seed display, Joy snatched a packet labeled *Five Steps to Celestia*. She had no interest in plants or anything else in the store, but it would do as an excuse to get a closer look at the necklace. The wooden floorboards creaked at her every step. Showing him the paper envelope, she asked, "What kind of plant is Celestia?"

He stared for a long moment, stroking the point of his gray goatee, as if deciding whether this customer was worthy of an answer. Scratching his chin one more time and swiping a hand over the top of his bald head, he said, "You have beautiful eyes. That's quite a rare color." He pointed to his own, which bore the same shade of violet. "I'm Pete, by the way." He thrust out a hand.

Joy robotically grasped it. "Um, nice to meet you." Pete kept a firm grip, leaning his head forward. "Oh, yeah…um…I'm Joy." Still not receiving freedom, she added, "And she's Suzi."

Pete turned Joy's hand sideways. He shifted his gaze to her wrist, then back to her face before placing his other hand on hers. "Truly a pleasure, Joy."

Earning her release, she narrowed her eyes and nodded once as Pete relinquished his grip and launched into a sales pitch. "I can tell by your discerning eye, little baubles and trinkets aren't your thing." He spoke like a carnival barker working a booth, as if he expected his audience to ooh and aah before continuing.

"No, not exactly. You have a lovely store, but I'm not one for knick-knacks."

He nodded toward the packet. "So, gardening is more your style?"

"Well, no. Actually, I have what you would call a black thumb. Leaves quiver when I walk by." She chuckled.

Pete smacked the counter as he laughed; the crinkles around his eyes deepened.

It was a small lie on her part. She was quite skilled in gardening but didn't feel the need to offer up her life's story.

He paused, as if once again deciding her worthiness of more information.

She waited.

"To tell you the truth, Joy, this store is a bit...well...packed with a few too many useless odds and ends. It's my wife's passion. She's the real connoisseur of *treasures*, you could say."

She grinned. "So, in other worlds, you're just the hired help?"

"Other worlds?" He tilted his head.

"Pardon?"

"You said 'other worlds,' but I think you meant to say, 'other words,' " he offered.

"Did I? Sorry. Guess I tend to mix up my nouns once the eyes glaze over in boredom." His dwelling on her slip of words reached a rating of obnoxious.

Pete placed his hands flat on the counter and leaned in conspiratorially. The gold-braided chain slipped out of his shirt and the vial hung loose, emitting a vibrant hue. "In my wife's words, I'm only the counter boy, but after forty-eight years of marriage, I'm used to it." He shrugged and smiled. "In answer to your question, I really can't answer your question about the seeds. Maybe you should buy a packet, and see what you end up with?"

While not intending to purchase anything, the mystery intrigued Joy for some unknown reason. She eyed the vial as it dangled from the man's neck.

"Perhaps you should buy two, and give one to your friend? Make it a bit of a game to see whose plant may or may not survive." Pete straightened his stance, and the chain nestled back on his chest.

He may be *only* a "counter boy" in his words, but he was a good salesman, she thought. "How do I know how to care for this thing if I don't know what it is? For all I know it could grow to be a twelve-foot tree."

"It looks like there's information on the back. That should tell you everything."

The tag didn't offer much. It stated there were five steps to Celestia yet only listed one.

Step 1: Plant.

Nothing more.

Looking at her new best friend, Joy asked, "The instructions are a bit vague, don't you think, Pete?"

He spread his arms wide. "But that's the beauty of it. Get a pot of dirt and give it a whirl. For a dollar ninety-eight, what've you got to lose?"

"Okay. I'm intrigued—I'll take two."

"Good choice!" He winked while giving a slight nod.

As he made the gesture, light shone off the glass vial. The purple substance inside glistened with familiarity.

Pete asked, "Everything okay? You

seem…perturbed?"

"No, I'm…a…well." Suddenly she couldn't string words together to form a whole sentence. Good grief! "What I mean to say, it's just—"

"You appear to be in a bit of a quandary. Let me help you. No, I don't believe we've ever met."

"How could you know what I was thinking?" Joy didn't recognize him, but the question covered her awkward pause.

"Not a far stretch," Pete said. "I get that all the time. I'm sure it's the uniform."

"You're wearing an apron."

"*Exactly*."

She waited a moment. Nothing. His explanation complete. *Okay, moving on.* Returning to the display, Joy grabbed two more packets and strode back to the counter. "I think I'll go wild and buy three. You never know when you might have a seed emergency."

He chuckled. Winking again, as if it were a twitch, he said, "A wise choice, madam. There's always room for one more."

An odd comment, but Joy refrained from asking about it. The explanation might be more daunting than the plant discussion. "That's an interesting necklace. Quite unique. Where did you get it?"

Pete rested it in his hand. "This old thing? I've had it for years." He rang up the purchase. "Thank you for your patronage. It truly was a pleasure meeting you, Joy."

She feared her hand might be lost to his grip once again. Thankfully, he kept his arms at his sides. While she wanted to ask more about the jewelry, she found his comment dismissive. Looking to make an exit, she scanned the store.

"Over here!" Suzi waved from the front door. "Just waiting on you."

Joy playfully glared at her blonde-haired companion as they walked outside. This detour was almost painful. She hoped they wouldn't see another store full of *treasures* for several miles.

****

"Was it her, Pete?" The plump woman's eyes were glued to the exit as she shuffled through the office door behind the counter.

"It's been twenty-two years, Tessa."

"I know." Her voice quivered as her eyes met Pete's. "Was it her?"

"Yes, but she doesn't remember. And her symbol has faded."

The woman broke her gaze and looked at the floor.

Pete reached over and wiped at the tears rolling down his sister's face. "She'll find her way back," he reassured, tucking a stray silver hair behind her ear. Slipping an arm around her shoulders, he pulled Tessa close in a hug.

Leaning in, she looked up into his face. "How can you be sure?"

"Couldn't you hear from behind the door? It's already affecting her. Out of all the things in this store, she chose the one that would help her remember. She'll recall in time." What Pete wouldn't voice aloud was the question forming in his mind—once she remembered, would she *want* to come back?

Chapter 2

Back on the road, the women hummed along in Suzi's red SUV. Make no mistake, she scoped for additional distractions—translated to gift shops.

As they drove the winding highway up the Oregon coast, Joy took in the breathtaking scenery. A huge formation of boulders off the shoreline looked to be strategically placed by the gods. She had seen the coastline a million times, and it still awed her.

"So, what did you buy?" Suzi asked.

"I didn't think you saw me, as you were on your third lap around the store," Joy poked.

"I may *appear* distracted but notice plenty. I'd say you were flirting with the cashier, but he was wearing a wedding ring."

"Alas, he was quite the prize, wasn't he?"

A moment went by before they burst into giggles. This was how their road trips usually went—lots of laughter. Joy loved seeing a genuine smile on her friend's face.

Suzi's mood darkened as she glanced in the rear-view mirror. "Get off my ass!"

Joy didn't turn around. "Maybe you should move over to the right lane."

"I'm going the speed limit. They can go around me."

That was Suzi's usual stance. The other drivers

were under the delusion they could intimidate a woman driving a vehicle with a license plate sporting DAISY. They were wrong.

After several minutes, the tailgater passed them.

Suzi was a pro at holding exactly to the speed limit and not giving ground—no cruise control needed. Personally, Joy wished she would speed up or move over. Her driving did add a little spice to their trips though.

"What did you buy?"

"Oh, just a couple packets of seeds. Probably weeds. I couldn't leave the store without *some* prize, could I? I see you managed to escape without a purchase."

She sighed. "I'm trying to downsize. My buying needs to be selective."

"Great. So, we can skip the next one?" Joy grinned.

Suzi glanced at her and not the road ahead. "Heck no. I can still look."

"It was kind of weird though."

"What was?"

"That guy. Little odd, wasn't he?"

Suzi's focus returned to driving. "You mean the cashier?"

"Yeah. Didn't you think so?"

"No. But I didn't have quite the personal encounter you did." She smirked. "He looked a bit old for you, but those summer-winter relationships are in these days, right?"

"Really?" Sarcasm dripped from her tongue.

"Kidding. You know I'm kidding. Honestly, I didn't look too closely at him. Was too busy enjoying the merchandise. They did have some great stuff. You know, we could turn around and go back if you wanted another look."

Clutching the door handle, Joy shouted, "Don't you dare. One visit per store is enough."

"Maybe he recognized you from the winery. He and his wife might have been in for a tasting. You do meet a lot of people while pouring at Mystic Swirl."

"Maybe." Joy's thoughts drifted to Pete's necklace—until she got slammed into the back of her seat then jerked forward as brakes screeched. Her hands braced against the dashboard.

"Sorry. I was admiring those pretty, blue flowers lining the road. Didn't notice the semi slowing down." Suzi shrugged, as they sat bumper-to-bumper with the tractor-trailer ahead of them.

"Um, Suzi, remember the part where you're the driver?"

She chuckled. "Yeah, I forget sometimes. I'm working on better focus." As the truck pulled ahead, they were off again. "And are you deciding about the winery?"

"Whatever do you mean?" Joy asked, hand to her chest.

"You said you'd figure it out in two years, girlfriend. Time is up."

"I wondered when you'd bring that up. Though, you're a little off. It's been one year, eleven months and twenty-three days. I have seven more to decide."

"Grace's husband is *not* managerial material, and you know it."

Joy sighed. "Yes, I do. Putting that man in charge would be wrong on several levels. Grace may say she doesn't want Mystic Swirl, but I believe it's because she wants to boost her husband's confidence. Both you and I know his ego doesn't need any more stroking. He's an arrogant jerk who treats her like garbage!"

"Thank you for admitting it out loud. He *is* garbage, and there is no way you should give him control."

"That's why I won't," Joy told her. "Like it or not I'm naming Grace the sole heir to the kingdom. What she chooses to do afterward is up to her. Hopefully, she'll see there's a reason I gave her control and not her man. I know Drake would have wanted his only child in charge."

Suzi gripped the wheel. "She's your child too, you know. Just because you didn't give birth to her, you still raised the girl since the age of four."

"I know. Grace is my daughter too, and I'm her only living relative. I didn't mean it that way."

The blonde sat up straight and squared her shoulders. "Do you want me to talk to her about taking over? She's always considered Aunt Suzi a very important person in her life."

"Thank you, but no. I need to impress upon her how monumental a decision this is, and if I choose her to run the winery, it's because I feel she's the best candidate."

Shaking her head, Suzi said, "You know she'll defer to that awful husband of hers anyway."

"Yes, but if I get the legal eagles to word it correctly, Grace will realize everything is up to her and only her. He'd run it into the ground, and her father would roll over in his grave if we were to lose the winery because of mismanagement."

Suzi looked at her passenger a moment. "Joy, are

you truly ready to retire? You're only forty-four, give or take a year or two, and have plenty of time left to run the winery and still enjoy a long retirement. What's next for you otherwise?"

"Funny you should ask—" Instead of finishing the statement, Joy screamed.

Returning focus to the road too late, the older woman slammed on her brakes. Rather than careening into the pick-up ahead of them, their angle was enough to skid past the truck and onto the shoulder. After several feet, the vehicle skidded to a halt, a rock wall inches from the passenger side window.

Joy sat motionless, until she felt something poking her in the arm. She turned to her left, where Suzi held out the car key.

With a sheepish grin, she suggested, "Maybe you should drive for a while?"

Facing forward, Joy rested her head back against the seat, hands covering her face.

Chapter 3

"Michael," Joy screamed, clutching at the man in front of her. Her mouth formed his name again, but no sound emitted. Sensing weightlessness, she no longer felt the bike beneath her. As her body flew, she saw clouds, trees, dirt—it all spun. Cold air rushed past as she soared. She glimpsed Michael still clutching onto the handlebars of the motorcycle, as he flew over the cliff and was gone.

The impact jolted the back of her head. Pain coursed through her shoulders and hips. Then everything went black.

"Joy! Wake up! Joy!" Suzi stood by the bed shaking her. She never looked so scared—or so ridiculous in a baggy T-shirt and penguin pajama pants. With her blonde hair wrapped in pink curlers, she looked even more comical. Suzi continued shaking Joy even after her eyes opened. "Joy. You're dreaming. Wake up!"

"I'm awake. What? What is it?" Joy, confusion tightening her jaw muscles, wondered why the woman woke her. "What's wrong?"

"What's wrong? What's wrong?" She heaved for breath. "You were screaming. It must've been a nightmare. Are you all right?" Her body trembled. "Oh God, I need to sit down." Shoving Joy over, she collapsed onto the bed.

More concerned about Suzi, she asked, "Are you all right?"

"I'm fine. What happened?" Suzi asked, still visibly upset, her face flushed.

Joy couldn't remember anything except being shaken awake. They had hit the wine bottle (or two) hard before bedtime.

"You were calling out."

"What?"

The older woman put a hand to her heaving chest. "You were yelling. Who's Michael?"

How bizarre, Joy thought. Why would she ask her about a man who wasn't her deceased husband? "I give up. Who's Michael?"

"You called his name. Hell, you screamed his name. He was either in danger, or you were having wild sex." Suzi's breath still came in gasps.

"I don't remember the dream, but I doubt it was the latter."

"You sounded terrified. Can't you recall anything?"

"I...I don't know. I called him?"

"Yes."

"Did I say anything else?"

Someone banged on their hotel door. "Security! Everything okay in there?"

Both looked at each other, eyes wide. Slowly, Suzi arose and walked to the entry. Checking the peep hole, she hesitated before unlocking the bolt. Cracking the door, she said, "Yes. Everything is fine. Why?"

"Well, ma'am," came a voice from the hallway, "someone called the front desk and said they heard screaming."

Suzi turned her head, looked at Joy, then back through the opening. "Sorry, officer." She lowered her voice. "My friend tends to have…ah…erotic dreams. It's a rare condition with some long medical name I can't pronounce. I'm sorry if she disturbed anyone. Her therapist is working on an experimental treatment, but it still has a few kinks to be smoothed out."

No response for several seconds. "Well…ah…ma'am, maybe she could try to keep it down? People are trying to sleep."

"You bet, officer. I'll make sure she keeps it to a PG-13 rating."

"Ahhhh…thank you, ma'am. Um…appreciate your cooperation." He remained shuffling his feet on the carpet.

Suzi stared a moment longer. "Thank you, officer." She shut the door. After a few beats, she turned around.

"Erotic dreams? Rare medical condition? That's the best you could come up with?" Joy held her hands up in the air.

"He bought it. I think."

Neither could contain their laughter.

Falling back on the pillows, Joy stared at the ceiling. "I can tell breakfast should be either interesting or awkward tomorrow morning. You couldn't have said I had a nightmare? People do have those, you know."

"How boring. Come on, he's a hotel security guard in a sleepy little seaside town. That should keep him going all week with stories."

"You are such an angel brightening the lives of those hopelessly trapped in boring jobs. Who's next on your list, toll booth attendants?"

"Nah, there aren't any toll booths in the area. I

checked." Suzi smirked. "Seriously, Joy, whoever Michael is, or was, you sounded gravely concerned."

"I told you, I don't know."

"Has anything from the dream come back to you?"

"Nothing."

"Well, it must've been a doozy. Look what you've done to the bedclothes."

The blankets lay crumpled on the floor and the sheets pulled apart. Joy breathed deeply, as if hyperventilating.

"It's okay, honey. We'll put it back together," Suzi said gently.

After the bed was fixed and she'd crawled under the covers, Joy stared at the ceiling. This wasn't the first time she'd woken up to a disheveled bed. Sometimes she remembered bits and pieces. The sensation of falling nagged at her. She suspected the cause, but without her memories from before she met Drake, how could she be sure?

Sleep eluded Joy until the light of dawn crept through the curtains, and it felt safe to drift off.

Chapter 4

Arriving home in Huntsville the next day, Suzi swung by the Royal Doggie Hotel and picked up Jester, her puggle, on their way to Joy's. After an embarrassing reunion scene, for the dog not Suzi, she dropped Joy off at the main house of the Mystic Swirl Winery. They declared their road-trip a huge success before the older woman continued to her own small cottage at the edge of the next winery.

Joy carried her suitcase to the master suite and tossed it on the bed. The comforting scent of roses seeped from the sachet on her nightstand. She immediately unpacked, then stowed her luggage in the bottom of the walk-in closet.

Back in the bedroom, she approached her jewelry box on the dresser. With shaking hands, she opened the side panel holding her necklaces. Dangling from a brass hook was a glass vial pendant—identical to the one Pete wore. She wanted reassurance it still hung there.

Years ago, Joy had met Drake, the physician on duty, in the hospital. Her memories of the week spent in Bonner Medical Center were hazy at best. The doctor told her she had survived a horrible accident. With no memory of the event, it took a while to believe him. Everyone said how lucky she'd been being thrown from the motorcycle. The young man she rode with hadn't been as fortunate. His broken body lay on a slab in the morgue. Obviously, her nightmares stemmed from the crash. He must be the young man from her dreams, but who was he? Boyfriend? Brother? Stranger?

The hospital staff referred to her as Jane since she had no identification or memory of who she was. The dead man had nothing on him either. Drake said she was a true *joy* with her upbeat attitude, and the name stuck.

Staring into the dresser mirror, Joy placed the gold chain around her neck. Her thoughts flitted back to the grizzled hands of the hospital volunteer who'd put it on her the first time. The man had slipped the delicate chain around her saying it was a gift for all those who needed a memory or two. She couldn't recall his face. He never returned to visit again. The nurses she'd questioned about him didn't know who she talked about. Why had she forgotten that until this moment?

The doctors said she would recover her memories in time. Joy never did. There was no medical explanation for the permanent loss. Amnesia didn't work that way, yet here she stood, twenty-two years later with a name given to her by the doctor, now her deceased husband.

Joy wrapped her hand around the small vial begging it to conjure the memories promised. Loosening her grip, she stared into its depth. A purple haze glistened from within. The thickness of the glass obscured its true form; she could never tell if the substance inside was powder or liquid. Whenever she gazed into the tiny receptacle, she felt at peace. Maybe that's the purpose of it—simply to soothe the wearer.

She hadn't worn the pendant since Drake had asked for her hand in marriage six months after they met. For some unknown reason, she couldn't bring herself to put it back on afterward. Maybe she had feared if she remembered the past, she wouldn't get to stay in her present. Now that he was gone, perhaps it could give her guidance as to which direction her life should take. Maybe the time had come to search for her past. Reaching around to the back of her neck, she meant to unhook the clasp, then changed her mind and left it on.

****

Joy met Suzi for lunch the next day at the Wandering Vine Café. Both arrived at the same time. Once inside, Suzi strode to the podium to arrange for a table near the window overlooking the vineyard.

They followed the hostess to a table. Pungent aromas of garlic and oregano teased Joy's taste buds.

Suzi wiggled her hips and tugged at the side and back of her pants as she walked.

"Do you have a rash?" Joy whispered.

"No. The damn elastic in my granny panties just gave out. They keep sliding down my butt." She made no effort to be discreet.

A couple sat with a young boy at the table next to theirs. The mother flashed Suzi a disgruntled look, which was lost on the older woman.

Joy covered her mouth, stifling a laugh. She never knew what thoughts would come out of her friend next—one of the many reasons they'd bonded shortly after meeting.

Both thanked the hostess as they sat and were handed menus. Suzi continued to squirm.

"Perhaps, you should go to the ladies' room and straighten yourself out," Joy suggested.

"I guess I'll have to, or the waitstaff may think I'm having convulsions and call the paramedics. Though a little mouth-to-mouth from one of the handsome servers would be fine with me." She laughed. "Order me a glass of the house Pinot Grigio." Suzi got up and hurried to the restrooms at the back of the restaurant, pulling and tugging the whole way.

After a few minutes, their waiter approached the table. "Hello. My name is Charles, and I'll be your server this afternoon. Did you want to order a beverage, ma'am, or would you prefer to wait for your dining companion?"

Joy looked up from the wine list. "She'll have a glass of your house Pinot Grigio, and I'll have the Syrah, please."

"Good choice. This current vintage of our Syrah is particularly bold, with a hint of nutmeg in the finish. Quite unique."

"Sounds delicious."

Suzi passed the waiter on her way back to the table. Thankfully, her fidgeting had subsided.

"All secured?" Joy smirked.

"Yup. I'm going commando." She raised her arms in victory.

Joy looked over her friend's shoulder where the young mother furrowed her brow.

"Mommy, what's *commando*?" asked the little boy.

"Never you mind!" She said, spewing daggers Suzi's way.

Putting her hands over her eyes and shaking her head, Joy wished she could be as oblivious to those around her. "Don't ever change, Suzi."

"Don't plan on it. Why?"

Thankfully, Charles arrived with their drinks, so Joy wasn't forced to answer.

"Cheers." Suzi raised her glass.

Joy returned the sentiment, and they clinked glasses.

Once they had ordered, Suzi broached the reason she'd asked her to lunch. "Joy, are you going to tell me what that nightmare was about and who Michael is?"

Her first urge was to say it was nothing, but Joy knew better. And she knew better than to lie to Suzi. Despite her hazy demeanor, the woman wasn't dumb. In fact, she was one of the most perceptive people Joy had ever met.

"Okay. To tell you the truth, I don't know who the man is in my dreams, but it's happened before. Ever since Drake…" Despite being two years, the words still stuck in her throat. Taking a deep breath, she continued. "Ever since Drake died, I've been having nightmares. I don't remember much, but the state of the bed linens tells me I'm actively participating in whatever is going on in my head."

"Every night?"

"No. A few times a month. It kinda scares me since I never had them before he…before his accident. Now they're occurring more frequently."

Suzi reached across the table and placed her hand on Joy's. "Why haven't you said anything?"

"Because I didn't know how to broach the subject. What could I say? Hey, Suzi, I've been dreaming about falling off a motorcycle?"

Suzi pulled her hand back and put it to her mouth. After taking a gulp of wine, she asked, "Is that what's happening?"

Joy sat up straight with her fingers pressing onto the table, veins popping in her hands.

"What is it?" Suzi asked.

"Until this moment, that's the first time I remembered I was on a motorcycle in my dream. Or falling off one."

"Any idea who the man is? Sounds like you were riding with a guy and, what…you tumbled off?"

Joy sat back and thought a moment. "I remember…falling. The landscape spinning around me."

"What else? What does Michael look like? How old do you think he is in your dream? How old are you?"

"Stop!" Joy said, much louder than intended. She glanced at the family seated next to them. The husband threw down the bill folder as he stood. Joy shrugged. She had bigger issues to sort out than disgruntled diners. "One question at a time. Not sure I can answer all of those."

Suzi took a bite of her pasta primavera. Chewing the noodles, she opened her mouth to speak, then closed it again. Swallowing, she asked, "Do you think he's someone from your past?"

She was one of the few who knew Joy's true past and how she'd met Drake. The exception was that Suzi didn't know the accident was on a motorcycle or that the guy she was with had died. Most people bought the story she'd told them of her growing up in Southern California and having no living relations. No need for constant explanations. "It's possible. Remember how I'd told you the accident that landed me in the hospital was a road accident?" Joy fiddled with the glass vial hanging from the chain. She hadn't taken it off since yesterday.

"Uh-huh." Suzi nodded.

"What I haven't shared is that I'd been riding on the back of a motorcycle. From what they told me we'd gone off the road while on Bellington Mountain. I fell off, which is what saved my life. The young man I rode with went over a cliff with the bike and didn't survive."

Suzi put down her fork. "Hello, Captain Obvious! This isn't a mystery, it's a search party to figure out who you were riding with." She almost sounded disappointed. "How come you never mentioned these dreams to me? We both know they're clues about your life before Drake."

The waiter approached the table. "Everything all right, ladies?" He eyed Suzi's empty dish. "May I take your plate?" he asked.

"Yes, thank you."

"I'm done too." Joy put her fork down in defeat. Her appetite had disappeared.

"Was there something wrong with the ravioli, ma'am? I could bring you something else if it wasn't to your liking."

She always appreciated the excellent service here at the Wandering Vine. "No, Charles, it was excellent. Guess my eyes were bigger than my stomach today."

The waiter smiled. "Shall I box it for you?"

"Yes, that would be great." Maybe she'd feel hungry later.

Looking at Suzi, he asked, "Dessert, ma'am?"

"You bet your sweet ass!" She shifted sideways, enjoying the server's backside.

Joy stifled a chuckle as the young man's face

reddened.

"Um, certainly, madam." He stumbled over his response. "Shall I bring you the dessert menu?"

"No need." She waved her hand. "I'll have the Napoleon."

The dishes poised in his hands, he recovered enough to say, "Very good, madam." Looking toward her dining companion, he asked, "Anything for you, ma'am?"

"Coffee, please."

He turned away, taking the dishes to the kitchen.

"Notice how you remained 'ma'am', yet I turned into 'madam' all of a sudden?" Suzi giggled.

"Funny how that happens. Perhaps it was your comment about his sweet derrière?"

The two laughed.

"Seriously, Joy, those dreams must be about the accident you were in years ago. Since you had no identification nor memory, that means your early twenties. How did you end up with a July 25th birthday?"

"It was Drake's idea. Obviously, we needed something to go on when guessing my age, so he went with 'Christmas in July' to stick with the 'joy' theme."

Suzi smiled. "Clever."

They were quiet a moment while the server placed a huge dessert in front of Suzi and a steaming mug of coffee by Joy. He set a small pitcher of cream along with a container of sugar next to her cup. "Anything else, ladies?" he asked, not looking at Suzi.

"We're good, thank you," Joy answered.

Her friend dug into her Italian pastry. After wolfing down a few bites, Suzi asked, "What's that necklace you're wearing? Did you pick it up at that shop we stopped in?"

As if guilty, she stopped fingering the vial. Joy wasn't sure how much to share but decided she couldn't stop now. "No, it's old. I'd forgotten about it until yesterday when I saw Pete wearing the same one."

"Pete? You mean your new best friend at the cash register?"

"The very same."

Suzi was homing in on the finish line with her dessert. Fork poised for the last bite, she asked, "He was wearing something similar, that jogged your memory?"

"No." Joy held out the container far enough for her to look at, and the purple glowed a little brighter than yesterday. "He wore the exact same thing. That's what made me think of mine."

"Where did you get it?"

Sipping her coffee, she said, "Some old man gave it to me in the hospital. After putting it on yesterday, I've been remembering snippets of my time there."

"Like who you are and where you really come from? And who the guy on the bike was? Who was the man that gave it to you?"

"I'm not certain. I can't even remember his face. Just a pair of grizzled hands, rough like someone who does hard labor, yet they were as delicate as silk when he put this on me."

Scraping the last bit of sweetness from her plate and licking the fork as if it were her dying effort, Suzi set the implement down. "This is getting stranger by the minute. You didn't remember any of this before yesterday?"

"Nope. After putting it on, I recollected what the man had said to me as he placed it around my neck. He said it was a gift for someone who needed a memory or two. Strange, huh?"

"Maybe you could go back to the hospital and see if he still works there?"

Joy shook her head. "He never returned to my room the whole time I was in the hospital. I asked the staff about him, and none of them knew who he was. Not one of them."

"Wow. Do you remember anything else?"

"That's it so far."

Charles approached with the bill. Before Joy could grab it, Suzi scooped it up. "This one's on me."

Once the tab was paid and they walked out of the restaurant, Suzi said, "Sounds like we have some sleuthing to do."

"I'm not sure where to start. Besides, after all these years, what would be the point?"

She stopped and turned to Joy. "The *point* is there may be family out there looking for you or the guy you were with. Aren't you the least bit curious about your home?"

"Actually, it's all I've thought about since yesterday. But if there were, why hadn't anyone come looking for me? Maybe they don't want me found."

"That sounds a bit ominous. This mystery is getting thicker all the time." Suzi rubbed her hands together as if about to dig into something messy. "You've been wondering what to do with yourself, especially considering retirement. Sounds to me like it's staring you in the face and screaming to be heard."

Yes, that's what frightens me.

Chapter 5

Grace arrived for dinner at six o'clock—alone as requested.

"What's going on, Mom?"

"I wanted a girls' night. We haven't had one in a while. Owen didn't mind too much, did he?"

"Not at all. He practically pushed me out the door. His buddies wanted him to meet up for beers anyway." She followed Joy into the cavernous kitchen, their steps echoing on the tiles.

Copper pots hung from a large rack above an island. Miles of counter space filled the edges of the room on either side of the stove and double steel sink. The tantalizing aroma of roasting chicken filled the kitchen.

Joy held up a merlot from the Burning Axe winery. "This one okay?"

"Start pouring!"

Opening the bottle, Joy set it on the counter to breathe.

Her daughter grabbed stemmed glasses from the cabinet and set them by the wine. The stool scraped on the tile as she pulled it out and sat, placing her elbows on the counter with her chin in her hands. "Okay, Mom, spill. What's really going on?"

"I could never fool you, could I?"

"Nope." She brushed her long dark hair behind her

shoulders. "Usually, the dead giveaway is when you send in Aunt Suzi. Guess you're going solo tonight?"

Joy smiled, poured the wine, and set one glass in front of her stepdaughter. Perching on a seat next to Grace, she asked, "Am I that predictable?"

"Uh-huh."

She sighed. "You're right. I have ulterior motives. It's about the winery. Short version is I've decided to retire and want you to take over. There. It's out. I want you and *not* Owen to run the place. How do you feel about that?"

Grace squared her shoulders. "I refuse. What're we having with the chicken?"

"Hold on. You can't turn me down and move on to the menu. What do you mean you *refuse*?"

"I don't want the winery. Did I stutter?" She arched her eyebrows.

Joy fussed with the dinner plates and silverware while processing what her daughter had just said. The steamed asparagus smelled done, and she turned off the burner beneath them. She gave a final stir to the hollandaise sauce with a wooden spoon, then extinguished its flame as well.

"Grace, you know your dad would want you to run the place. And I'm sorry if you think Owen should be the chosen one, but I don't think he's capable of handling the business end. He makes rash decisions with no serious thought involved. Drake felt that way too. I know Owen's your husband and you love him, but your father never would have approved, and I intend to honor his wishes."

Grace grimaced. "Like I said, no thank you. I don't want to talk about it anymore. Can we simply have dinner and enjoy each other's company?"

Joy sipped her wine while trying not to show distress at Grace's answer. She never expected that response but had to respect her daughter's choice. "All right."

"Tell me about your road trip with Aunt Suzi. And where did you get that necklace? It's amazing." Excitement punctuated her voice.

"The trip was full of laughter."

"And the necklace?"

Joy wrapped her hands around the vial. Looking down, she said, "I haven't worn this necklace in a long, long time. Someone gave it to me at the hospital—" she looked into her daughter's face "—where I met your dad."

Grace narrowed her eyes. "At the hospital?"

"He never told you how we met, did he?"

"What do you mean?" Grace asked.

Joy twirled her glass by the stem, staring at the crimson liquid as it swirled up the sides. "I guess I always assumed you knew, but you were so young when we got married. I wasn't sure."

"He said he met you at work."

"Yes. I was a patient."

"Dad mentioned that," Grace said. "I didn't think anything of it. Why?"

"I couldn't remember anything, but I was told I'd been in a horrible accident."

"What! He never said why you were there. I thought you were getting a check-up or something. What kind of accident? How bad was it?"

Joy took a deep breath. She'd hoped to avoid this conversation but needed to come clean. "I'd been in a motorcycle accident where my driver was killed. I couldn't remember the accident, let alone my own name. Nor the name of the man I rode with."

"You rode on a motorcycle?" She smirked. "Sorry, Mom. I can't picture you on the back of a bike."

"Guess it is out of character for me now. As a younger woman I must've been quite the daredevil." She made a revving gesture as if she clutched handles.

Grace put her hands to her forehead. "Still can't picture it." She let out a chuckle. "So how did Dad convince you of who you were? Or did you get your memory back?"

"No, I never got it back, nor did I have any identification on me. He made one up."

"Your name really isn't Joy? And what do you mean you had no ID? Everybody carries something with their name on it."

"Your father christened me. He said I was a 'joy' to be around and decided it was a better choice than 'Jane Doe.' I had to agree."

Grace drank. "Dad always looked on the bright side of things, didn't he?"

"Yes, he did. More people should be that way." Joy's lips curved up into a sad smile.

A comfortable silence descended on them.

Swiping a hand over her eyes, Joy broke the quiet. "I didn't mean to make you feel sad."

"It's not your fault. We'll never forget him, so why can't we reminisce?"

She placed a hand on her stepdaughter's. "You're absolutely right. There are plenty of happy memories we'll always hold dear. We shouldn't shy away from them."

Grace brushed away a tear. "Who was the man you rode with?"

"I don't know. Apparently, we weren't local since nobody recognized us. He didn't have identification either. Seems odd, doesn't it?"

"In this day and age, yes. It's hard to believe someone would be walking around with no license or credit cards or *something* with their name on it, even twenty-two years ago."

Joy nodded. "It distresses me that the young man I rode with lies in a grave marked 'John Doe.' If he had a family, they'll never know what happened to him."

"Have you tried to find out who he was or where you came from? What if he was your family? Could you have been married?"

With a deep sigh, she feared many of those questions might never be answered. Joy owed it to the unknown man, and herself, to find out who they really were. "You know, I've been trying to figure out my next move in life. Perhaps I should pick up the trail, despite how cold it is, and seek my past. I thought I'd need direction once I passed on the winery…"

"You're relentless, you know that?" Grace laughed. "I'm not taking the reins. You'll have to get over it, Mom."

"So, guilt isn't working? Not even a skosh?"

"Nope."

Joy snapped her fingers. "Dang it. I thought I might slip it in, and you'd agree."

"I think the chicken is done. The timer went off two minutes ago." Grace pointed toward the clock on the stove.

"I believe you're right." Grabbing the hot dish

pads, she pulled the pan from the oven.

They spent the rest of the evening speculating on how Joy could find out about her past. The list included digging out the police report she'd received before leaving the hospital. Maybe she could visit the scene of the accident. It might be traumatic but could inspire a memory.

Before leaving, Grace asked, "Mom, do you have a small suitcase I can borrow? Rosemary and I are leaving for an overnight to Portland, and I can't find mine. Probably stuffed away in the attic or basement."

"Sure. I'll grab it from my closet." Joy walked to the stairs.

She returned with the small rolling bag she'd used on her recent trip.

"Thanks. I'll return it next week if that's okay."

"Of course." Joy threw her arms around her stepdaughter. After a moment's embrace, she said, "Thanks for coming. You know you're not off the hook for running the winery."

Grace pulled away. "Yes, Mom. Let's leave it be. Okay?"

"Okay—for now." She walked her daughter to the door. As Joy waved from the front steps, she thought back on her daughter's response about not wanting to take over. Grace loved Mystic Swirl as much as she did. There had to be more to her refusal. But what?

Chapter 6

The next morning Joy stood before the bathroom mirror examining the pendant around her neck. Was it her imagination, or did the color appear more vibrant? Probably a trick of the light's reflection, she thought, before removing it and stepping into the shower.

Toweling herself off, she found a pink rash forming on the inside of her right wrist. The spot didn't itch, but she couldn't figure out what had caused the discoloration. Without hesitation, Joy grabbed the gold chain and hooked it in place.

After breakfast, she walked the short path to the tasting room where she'd spend the day. One of the perks of owning a winery was meeting the patrons who visited. When she and Drake had gotten married, Joy didn't know much about producing wine. As she learned the process and different varietals it offered, she grew to love the Mystic Swirl Winery.

They opened at ten, and she arrived just after nine. Once inside, she admired the side walls lined with dark, wooden racks. Bottles filled every spot, ready for purchase. Along the right were all the reds, while the left held the whites. Tables and lower shelves beneath held glasses, openers, and other related merchandise for sale.

Grace, who'd beaten her in, hummed with energy as she set up a whiteboard listing the day's samplings.

With her dark hair pulled back in a high ponytail, it bobbed as she moved. "Hi, Mom."

"Hi, sweetie. What're we featuring today?"

"I thought we'd push the Syrah, since it's finally ready, along with the cabs and merlots. The whites are good to go with the usual line-up."

Joy pulled glasses from the dishwasher in the back room and placed them upside down on trays. She carried a load up front to the counter.

"Mom, I found these in the outer pocket of your suitcase." Holding three seed packets, Grace extended her hand.

"I'd forgotten about those when I unpacked."

"Did you buy them on your trip with Aunt Suzi?"

"Yes. They were a souvenir I bought at our last stop. You know how much Suzi loves those trinket stores."

Grace went back to complete her notes on the whiteboard. "I do. It's amazing you survive those crusades. I know how much you despise knick-knacks and whatnots."

"Well, with her latest divorce, she needed to go to a happy place. And that happened to be every hundred miles or so." Joy chuckled.

"What kind of plant is Celestia?"

"I asked the proprietor the same thing. He didn't know." Joy hesitated, thinking back on the purple vial necklace peeking from his shirt.

With her brows furrowed, Grace placed a hand on Joy's arm. "Earth to Mom?"

Joy focused on her stepdaughter. "What? Oh, yes, sorry. Senior moment."

"You are *not* old enough to use that excuse.

Agreed?"

She nodded. "Agreed."

"So, what are the seeds for?"

"Something to do. The vague description was intriguing. Guess I'll plant them and see what I get." Joy stuck the packets into her back pocket, then walked into the storeroom to retrieve their featured wines of the day. Returning with a box of Syrah, Joy stopped just before the doorway as she found her son-in-law standing at the counter in a heated discussion with Grace.

"I told you the boys wanted to go drinking at Logan's Tavern, and I got too wasted to drive. Jimmy let me crash at his place." Owen slammed his hand on the counter. "These accusations are getting tedious. Call Jimmy if you don't believe me."

Grace leaned closer toward her husband, using a controlled voice. "Should I ask him what kind of perfume he's been wearing lately?"

"Damnit, when are you—"

"Everything okay?" Joy stepped into view.

The couple exchanged fiery glances. Owen massaged the back of his neck.

"Everything's fine, Mom. Just *fine*." Grace set out glasses. She tucked her yellow T-shirt neatly into her jeans when the tray had been emptied.

Joy set the carton on the counter, not taking her eyes off Owen.

"Sorry for the ruckus, Joy. Like Grace said, everything's fine. A lovers' spat, nothing more. I'm sure you and Drake had them too." He grinned.

Her hands tightened around the bottles as she pulled them from the box. "I'll have to admit, we never spent the night apart without the other knowing. No need for unnecessary worrying, wouldn't you agree?"

His eyes smoldered while a grin remained pasted on his face. "I didn't want to disturb her by calling so late." Owen's gaze rested on his wife as she shook her head. Looking back at his mother-in-law, he continued. "Anyway, I didn't come here to air our domestic issues. I wanted to discuss a deal I have going with a new distributor."

Joy stopped unloading the wine. "We aren't in the market for a new distributor. Things are fine with Jackson and Company."

"Yes, but the contract Drake made with them is years old. This guy is offering a much better deal than what Charlie and Dave are giving us. He's willing to take a smaller cut."

Grace spun to glare at her husband. "As Mom pointed out, we've been working with Charlie and Dave forever. Both parties are making a nice profit, and like I told you a few days ago, you are *not* in charge. You're supposed to be running the warehouse not meddling with sales."

"Thanks for pointing that out—again. I'm only trying to enlighten your mother about other opportunities. With Drake gone, I thought she could use some help with the business."

Exhaling loudly, Grace stomped into the back room.

Owen continued working on his mother-in-law. "Peter Brach is his name. Can I set up a meeting for this afternoon so we can discuss a contract?"

"No need." Joy kept her tone light. "I know Peter. So does every vintner this side of the Rockies. He's a shyster."

"How can you say that?" Owen's voice escalated.

"My husband may have handled the business end of this winery while alive, but we discussed everything before he made any major moves. Peter Brach swindled Marcy at Buttercup Winery, and she would have lost half her inventory had her lawyers not gotten involved. You tell your distributor buddy if he so much as sets foot on my property, I'll have him arrested for trespassing. Now if there's nothing else, I need to finish setting up. I believe you're late for preparing today's shipments, so I won't delay you any further." Her voice remained even.

Fuming with displeasure, Owen pounded across the tiles to the door. It slammed closed, startling Joy.

Grace returned with a case of Chardonnay. "Sorry, Mom. I told him not to get involved with that man, but he ignored me."

"Don't worry about it. I don't remember putting him in charge of sales anyway." Joy smirked, making her daughter laugh. Placing a hand on her shoulder, she said, "What does concern me is the conversation going on when I walked in."

Grace's jaw tensed. "I'd rather not talk about it. Besides, we've got our first customers rolling in early. We better finish setting up."

A minivan came to a stop in the parking lot.

Glancing through the window, Joy said, "I'll put those in the cooler. We need more merlot and pinot."

"I'm on it." Her daughter disappeared into the storeroom.

Joy's shoulders slumped. Sadness wrenched at her heart knowing the unhappy relationship her daughter endured. If Drake were alive…she halted those thoughts immediately. *He's not, and it's up to Grace to choose her own path.* Standing up straight, she finished setting out the water pitchers, providing a stack of paper cups beside each.

The two women unloaded the wine cartons. When all was ready, fifteen minutes remained before tasting hours. Joy turned the sign in the front window to Open anyway, allowing the van load of people to wander inside. With a steady stream of tasters throughout the morning, neither had time to revisit the awkward conversation.

A few minutes before one, a young woman wearing jeans and a blue and red paisley blouse arrived alone. She flicked a wind-blown strand of golden hair away from her face as she entered.

"Right on time, Harmony. Come meet Mom."

The newcomer strode to the counter.

"Mom," Grace said, pulling her mother by the arm. "This is Harmony, our new tasting room associate I told you about."

Harmony extended her hand. "A pleasure to meet you, Mrs. Harper. I'm *so* excited to begin working here."

Joy locked onto the young woman's face. Something stirred inside of her. Recognition? The sensation coursing through her body was confusing. The small hairs on the back of her neck prickled. Recovering, she grasped Harmony's hand in both of hers. "Sorry. You look…sorry. A pleasure to meet you." She lightly squeezed, feeling a warmth generate up her arm. "I hope you'll enjoy working here." She released her hold.

"I'm sure I will, Mrs. Harper. It really was a stroke of luck, my running into your daughter at the coffee shop. Being new here and looking for work isn't easy in a small town like Huntsville."

"No, I imagine it's not. Please, call me Joy."

Harmony smiled.

"Come to this side of the counter." Grace gestured with her arm. "I'll show you around."

Joy watched Grace lead her into the back room, overhearing the new employee say it shouldn't be much different than when she worked in a wine shop.

The hackles on Joy's neck relaxed as she wrapped her hand around the purple vial hanging from her neck.

Chapter 7

Joy left the training of their new attendant to her daughter. She went to the house and made herself a lunch of chicken salad slathered on sourdough bread. After squeezing lemon into a fresh pitcher of iced tea, Joy poured a glass and sat down, then immediately stood back up. The lump in her back pocket turned out to be the seed packets her daughter had returned.

She laid them out on the table and studied the large nub in each of the three clear wrappers. Flipping one over, she read the directions again, "Step 1: Plant." A chuckle spilled from her lips remembering the total lack of help the shopkeeper offered. Picking another one up, she fingered the hard pod enclosed in plastic, its rough edge almost cutting through the bag. It was the oddest seed she'd ever seen, almost like a broken piece of root. A faint musty smell seeped from a hole in the side.

When she'd cleaned up lunch, Joy went out back to the garden shed. Removing three pots from a stack in the corner, she grabbed a trowel and went outside to fill each with soil. She carried them back to her kitchen. Since there were no specific instructions, Joy poked a hole in the center of the dirt and submerged one seed into each then covered it up. Pulling three chop sticks from a drawer, she intended to tape each packet to one as a label and add them to the pots.

Joy flipped the first one over and froze. Blinking in

disbelief, she picked it up and checked the front of the label. While it still read "Five Steps to Celestia" spread over two lines, the back instructions had changed. She was sure there'd been only one step listed, yet now it said, "Step 1: Plant. Step 2: Nourish." Maybe the one packet only had the first step, while she'd missed it on this one? Slowly, she reached for another and flipped it over. Two steps.

Her legs gave out, and she fell more than sat onto a stool. *How can this be?* With a quivering hand, she turned over the final label. It also had two steps.

A bead of sweat dribbled down her forehead as she stared at the three sets of instructions lined up side by side on the table. There was no way she'd missed those directions on all of them. Her gaze moved to the pots. *What the hell had she gotten herself into?*

While the situation made her nervous, curiosity kicked in. She might as well be all in on this venture and see it through. Finishing the placards, she stuck one into each pot and carefully placed them on a tray on her kitchen windowsill. With a glass from the sink, she filled it with water and generously *nourished* each seed.

After one more glance at her little garden, she tore herself away. She was never one for whimsical fancies, yet there was no rational explanation for what had appeared. Clutching her necklace, Joy wondered if life would ever be the same. First the shop, then the necklace, and now these plants, which made no sense. A rush of warmth flooded through her as she remembered the face from her dreams. That same face of a man lying on a metal slab, his body covered with a sheet. The man's eyes were closed, as if in peaceful slumber.

Tears slid down her cheeks and dripped onto the counter. Wiping the moisture with the back of her hand, Joy arose from the stool. Grabbing her car keys and purse, she drove to the local market and busied herself picking up groceries.

****

Joy was working in the kitchen cooking dinner when her daughter came in. She remained a little distraught over her episode with the seed packets but did her best to shake it off. The last thing she needed was Grace being concerned about her mental state. Her daughter had enough problems going on at home. Mustering a smile, she asked, "How did our trainee do today?"

Grace perched on a stool at the counter. "She's a natural, Mom. Her customer skills are excellent. The specifics about our vintages will come soon enough."

"Great. We need qualified help. Anybody can serve a glass of wine. The difference is in the gab with the patrons."

"She definitely has that down. I'm sure she can fill in for me this weekend while I'm in Portland. I do have one question though."

Joy joined her at the counter. "What's that?"

"Well, you had a strange expression on your face when you met Harmony. Did you recognize her from somewhere?"

Joy hesitated. How could she possibly describe her feelings? She didn't even know what to make of her reaction. "It felt like I'd met her before, but I don't know where. Maybe I saw her in town. When did she move here?"

"Only a couple of days ago. I ran into her yesterday

when I stopped for lunch at the Huntsville Café."

Joy's brow furrowed. "She looks familiar, but I can't place her." She got up and stirred the chili simmering on the stove. "Stay for dinner?"

"Thanks, but I need to get home. Owen and I need to talk through some things." Grace got up and kissed her mother on the cheek. "See you Monday when I get back. Harmony will be here at nine-thirty tomorrow."

"Have a safe trip." She remained at the stove so her daughter couldn't see her face. The thought of being alone with Harmony unsettled her. But why?

****

Joy had the tasting room set up by the time Harmony arrived the next morning.

"Good morning, Joy. You should have waited for me to help you."

"Oh, don't worry. There'll be plenty of opportunities for you to do this. What did you think of your first day?"

A huge grin spread across her face. "I loved it. It was like I was meant to do this."

"I'm speechless. And *very* glad you like being here. You wouldn't believe how hard it is to find just the right person. There's more to working the counter than simply pouring samples."

"I imagine that to be true. Even working in a wine shop, it was more than ringing up sales. If you don't love what you do, it shows."

Joy put a hand on Harmony's arm. Before she could agree, a jolt ran through her body. A memory of being on the back of a motorcycle flashed through her mind. The man seated in front caressed her leg as they rode. His touch sent a tingle of excitement through her.

Snapping back to the present, Joy backed away until hitting the counter.

"Mrs. Harper…Joy…what's wrong?" The young woman stepped closer.

"Don't." Joy jumped away with her hands up. "Please, don't touch me. Who are you?"

The surprised look on Harmony's face suggested the young woman had no idea what she'd done to Joy. Obviously, while Joy felt a bolt of energy run through her, Harmony experienced nothing.

"I'm sorry. I don't know what you mean."

Joy forced a smile. "No. It's fine. I don't…you…I'm okay. Why don't you grab one more box of Zinfandel from the back room? That seemed to be the popular bottle from yesterday's sales."

"Are you sure you're okay?"

"I'm fine. Let's finish prepping the room."

Harmony nodded and walked into the back room.

The first customers started trickling in twenty minutes after opening. Joy observed how polished Harmony acted with the patrons. The young woman listened attentively to their comments while engaging the quieter tasters in lively conversation. Her genuine laughter enchanted many, and they joined in. Subtle hand gestures and touches eased the men into purchases Joy knew they hadn't intended to make. Sales soared higher than they'd been in weeks, and the run lasted throughout the weekend.

Joy refrained from standing too close to the young woman, not wanting to experience the same occurrence as Friday morning nor the memory flashes. Still not sure what exactly happened, she wanted to finish the weekend and take a couple of days off. On a break, she called Suzi and arranged to meet her at the Wandering Vine for lunch on Monday. Maybe she could help sort out some of the odd events of the last few days.

Chapter 8

Joy waved at Suzi from a table by the window. As her friend sat down, Charles, their server from the other day, arrived with two glasses of wine. An almost imperceptible grimace flashed across his face as he glanced at Joy's dining companion.

"Thank you, Charlie," Suzi said as he set the Pinot Grigio in front of her.

"It's *Charles*, madam," he said curtly. Setting the Syrah by Joy, he sloshed a few drops of the red wine on the table. Mumbling an apology, he walked away.

Suzi grinned. "I do believe he remembers me fondly."

"I'm sure he'll be trying to conceal his derrière from you." Joy snickered.

"Damn. I was hoping to get another gander. Am I that obvious?"

"Yes."

Suzi placed her hands flat on the table. "You know you could have hesitated a moment before answering."

Joy tilted her head. "Really?"

"Okay, you're right. Now, what's going on with you?"

Taking a deep breath, Joy organized the details in her head. "We have a new tasting room attendant. She's sending shocks through my body and inspiring memories I didn't know I had. The seed packets I bought now have two steps printed on the instructions instead of one. Oh, and Grace thinks Owen is having an affair."

Suzi took a swig of wine. "Really, don't hold back. Tell me everything."

Joy smiled. "I love you. You know that don't you?"

"You must. Nobody on the edge of 'I tolerate you' would put up with my crap. Let's start with the new employee. Who is she, and where'd she come from?"

"Grace met her at the diner in town. She's new to the area and acts sweet. It's just…well…when I touched her on Friday, a shock ran through me, and I had a memory flash."

"What did you remember?"

Charles approached the table, flipping his dirty-blond hair from his eyes. "Are you ladies ready to order?" He faced Joy.

"I'll have the portobello mushroom ravioli and a Caesar salad," she said.

"And I'll have the fettuccini Alfredo, ditto on the salad," Suzi added.

"Very good, ladies." He left immediately.

"He's warming up to me. I can tell. See the way he snuck a glance?"

"The *glance* was toward the nearest exit." Joy chuckled. "Can we focus on my problems for a second and not your love life?"

With an exasperated gasp, Suzi proclaimed, "You are *so* needy sometimes. All right. I'll forego my burgeoning romance for the moment. Tell me what you remembered."

"Being on the back of a motorcycle with a man in

front. He brushed his hand up and down my leg. It gave me a hot flash."

"As in a sensuous sort of way?" Suzi arched her eyebrows.

Joy sat back in her chair. "I guess you could say that. The action did have a sexual connotation. I'm sure the man and I were more than friends."

"Do you believe he was the guy who died in the crash you were in all those years ago?"

"He's got to be the one. Why else would I be having those visions? Drake never rode a motorcycle. The thing is Harmony, that's the new girl's name, can't be older than twenty-five, if that. How could she possibly be connected to my past?"

Suzi bit her lip. "All very good questions. Tell me about the seeds. What happened with them?"

"Remember how they only had one instruction? Step One: Plant."

"Not really. I was too busy making my third lap around the shop to pay attention to you and the cashier. What was his name?"

"Pete."

"Right. Pete. Quite the hunk. Can't compare to my Charlie, though. Maybe we could double date."

Blushing, Charles set their salads in front of them. "Ground pepper, ladies?" His eyes focused on the plates.

Stifling a laugh, Suzi said, "Load it up, Charlie."

"It's *Charles*, madam."

"Right, sorry, Charlie. Oops, I mean…oh, never mind. You know who you are." She swatted the air.

He grabbed the pepper mill from the tray and ground a generous helping over Suzi's plate. Risking a look at his customer, he asked, "Enough?"

"Plenty." She winked.

With his face turning crimson, he turned to Joy. "And you, ma'am?"

"None for me, thank you."

"Very good." He hurried away.

"I guarantee, I'll have his phone number before we leave today." Suzi raised her hand in a high five.

Joy responded with a slap. "Stop harassing that young man. The only number he'll probably offer up is his lawyer's for sexual harassment on the job."

"Yes, mother." Suzi laughed. "Now, what about the seeds?"

"I bought three. The packets said, 'Five Steps to Celestia' on the front, and the back read, 'Step 1: Plant.' "

"Okay. Not the most explicit of instructions, but it's a start. You're good with plants anyway. What more direction do you need?"

"Apparently I required more."

Suzi crinkled her brow. "Meaning?"

"After planting each seed in a pot, I wanted to mark them with the packet taped to a stick. When I turned the package over, there was a second step listed that was not there before. It now had, 'Step 2: Nourish.' "

"You're kidding? You must've missed it."

"Nope. I am positive none of them ever had a second step." She trembled.

"I don't know what to say." Suzi reached over and touched Joy's shaking hand. "Calm down. Maybe it's some trick of the ink used on the packaging. Did it happen after you got them wet, maybe?"

Joy narrowed her eyes. "You don't believe that."

Suzi opened her mouth to answer, then closed it. She let out a deep breath. "No."

The women quietly ate their salads. Joy's thoughts kept circling back to the flashes of her being on a motorcycle and the man she rode behind. There was so much happening at once—the memories, Harmony, her daughter's marital problems. She doubted her ability to handle all these developments.

Joy asked, "Will you go with me to the accident site?"

"You think that'll help? Seeing it, I mean?"

"I don't know. It seems to be my next move as there aren't any other options in exploring my past. Will you go with me?" Her eyes pleaded.

Suzi slapped the table. "Like you even have to ask."

"I thought so but wanted to give you the chance to refuse."

Charles approached the table. "Finished with your salads, ladies?"

Both nodded.

"Your entrees will be out directly. Do either of you require another glass of wine?" He set his jaw and looked at Suzi.

"No thank you, *Charles*. I'm still working on this one." She gave him a crooked smile.

With a sigh, he nodded at Joy.

"I'm good, thanks."

He collected the salad plates and left.

"I see you're still wearing your new favorite jewelry. It really is unique. Maybe it's all this talk about 'mystical' plants, but I don't remember it being that bright of a purple. Did you polish the glass?"

Looking down at the vial, then back at Suzi, she said, "Thank you!"

"For what?"

"Confirming I'm not losing my mind. I noticed it too but thought it must be the lighting in different places. But if you see a difference also…" She lifted the pendant from her skin, holding it in the palm of her hand.

"What's *that*?" Suzi asked.

"What's what?"

"That pink area on your wrist. Did you scratch yourself on something?"

Joy's eyes widened when she took a good look. The spot she'd thought started as a rash looked worse. It had turned a darker pink and two raised, curvy parallel lines with a line crossing both could be seen. "I don't know." She released the necklace.

Suzi gently grasped her friend's wrist. "You said you planted those seeds. Did you rub up against them? For all you know they could be poison ivy or sumac."

"No, I saw the spot when I got out of the shower this morning. It didn't have those raised lines though. I must've scratched it on something. What else could it be?"

Shrugging, Suzi let go as their waiter approached with the pasta dishes.

"Careful, ladies, the plates are hot." He placed them on the table. Gritting his teeth, he muttered, "Parmesan?"

"I love cheese!" Suzi squealed. "Make it snow, Charlie."

Charles expelled air through his nose then grabbed

the grater and sprinkled a generous portion on Suzi's plate. "And for you, ma'am?" He aimed the device at Joy's plate.

"Just a smidge, please."

"Very good." He dusted her pasta then spun around, shoulders firmly set, and left.

"Why must you taunt him? He's a good kid," Joy chastised.

"I'm sure he's used to it." Suzi smirked. "Besides, at my age, he's gotta know I'm all bluster and no bite. Can't I enjoy a few cheap thrills?"

Instead of answering, Joy dove into her lunch. "Yum. This is delicious. Wanna try?" She held out a ravioli on a fork toward Suzi.

"No, I'm good." She shoveled her own pasta into her mouth. After swallowing, she picked up on the next subject. "Okay, we've talked about Harmony and the seeds. Now, what's going on with your daughter?" She waved her fork. "If that bastard is stepping out on her, I'll castrate him myself."

Continuing with his bad timing, Charles approached the table, turning a brighter shade of red than before. "Everything all right?"

"Perfect, Charlie. Couldn't be better, thanks," Suzi answered around a mouthful of fettuccini.

He stumbled as he retreated.

"He's gotta work on his timing," Suzi said.

"Maybe he wouldn't be turning different shades of purple if you would call him 'Charles' instead of 'Charlie.' Just a suggestion."

Suzi leaned in and whispered, "I think he secretly likes it." Sitting back straight, she said, "The blushing is for my benefit. Kind of like a male peacock showing off his colors, don't you think?"

Joy laughed. "No, I don't. Now, please stop harassing the poor boy before we get banned from this restaurant. They have excellent food and wine, and I'd like to come back again."

"All right. Sometimes you suck the fun out of razzing the help." Suzi winked. "You do have a point. Their fettuccini Alfredo is to die for, and I'd hate to get black-balled."

Charles returned as they finished their lunch. Stacking their plates, he asked, "Dessert?"

"You bet your sweet derrière, Charlie!"

Looking skyward, he asked, "What can I bring you?"

Suzi started. "I'll have the Napoleon."

"Very good. For you, ma'am?" He looked at Joy.

"Make that two, but pack them to-go." Joy handed him her credit card. "And run the bill, please."

He took it in his free hand and walked away.

Suzi sat back and sipped the last of her wine. "Where will we be enjoying our pastries?"

"My place. I'll dig out the police report, and we can locate exactly where my friend and I went over the edge. While this terrifies me, I need to stand in the exact spot. If touching a stranger inspires memories, imagine what a real connection could do?"

Suzi gulped. "I'll put 911 on speed dial."

Chapter 9

Suzi drove behind Joy's blue car with the dessert box snugged into the passenger seat. She thought about everything they'd discussed over lunch. While wanting to help resolve the situation, she wondered if this was really the right path to take. The past had been buried for so long, maybe digging it up wasn't the best of ideas.

After pulling up to the main house of Mystic Swirl, Suzi grabbed the pastries and followed Joy inside.

"Wine or coffee?" Joy asked.

"Let's have coffee. We need clear heads right now."

"I agree." Joy grabbed two single coffee containers and mugs. It had taken her a while to get used to the one-cup maker, but with Drake gone, it made sense.

Suzi plopped down on a stool by the counter. "Are you sure you're up for this?"

Joy leaned against the counter and took a deep breath. "Honestly? I'm not sure. All I know is if I don't figure out what's happening around me, I'll go crazy."

"Do you believe in mysticism? Fate? Destiny? Any of that?"

"What are you talking about?" She set the plates and forks on the counter, then came around and sat down.

Suzi dished a Napoleon onto each plate. "I know

you're a very grounded person. But everything you've talked about this afternoon hints of unnatural things. The vial. The shocks from Harmony. The memory flashes. Even the rash on your wrist. Somehow, they've got to be connected."

"Why?"

"What?"

"Why do they have to be connected?"

Shoveling a forkful of dessert into her mouth, Suzi chewed and swallowed. "Is the coffee done?"

"Oh, right." Joy jumped up and retrieved a full cup for Suzi then set her own up. "So, why do you think they're connected?"

"How could they not be? With all these things happening at once, that's more than coincidence." She sipped from her mug. "Maybe…maybe you're really from another planet?"

Joy chuckled. "Thanks for keeping it real."

"No problem." Suzi tried to put more food in her mouth but was laughing too hard. When under control again, she said, "Show me these mystical plant instructions."

Picking up a pot from the windowsill, Joy set it on the counter. "See for yourself. There's now a second step."

Suzi pulled the chopstick out of the dirt and read aloud, "Five Steps to Plan Celestia." Flipping it over she asked, "I thought you said there were two steps?

"There isn't?"

"No. There's three." Suzi held out the packet.

"What?" Joy grabbed the stick. Flipping it over she read, "Step 1: Plant. Step 2: Nourish. Step 3: Sunlight." Her legs almost buckled beneath her. She clutched the edge of the counter and propped herself up.

Suzi jumped to her feet. "Joy?" She grabbed the woman's arm and helped her to a stool.

Sweat formed on Joy's forehead. She stared at the back of the packet, then turned it over and read, "Five Steps to *Plan* Celestia. Suzi, it didn't say that before."

"Say what?"

"The front only said Five Steps to Celestia. The word *Plan* wasn't there!"

"Maybe we should go back to my original question?"

Eyes wide, Joy asked, "Which was?"

"Do you believe in mysticism?"

"I guess I better start."

Pushing her empty plate away, Suzi pointed with her fork. "You gonna eat that?"

Joy waved at her untouched pastry. "Help yourself."

"Great." She pulled the dessert closer and shoveled the custard delight into her mouth.

Joy drank her coffee while glancing at her wrist. The lines were more prominent, and the pink had faded to natural skin color. She ran her fingers over the ridges. *What did it mean?*

"Why don't you get that police report?" Suzi interrupted her thoughts.

"Good idea. I'll be right back." Going into the office at the far end of the living room, Joy pulled open the bottom drawer of the filing cabinet. At the rear was a tab labeled "Joy." When Drake was alive, he'd handled all the winery business. It wasn't until after the funeral she'd looked through the office cabinets. She never knew this file existed. Removing it from the drawer, Joy rifled through until she found the police report. Grasping it with both hands, her eyes shifted toward the shredder in the corner. It might be easier never knowing.

Suzi yelled from the other room, "Everything okay?"

Joy hugged the file to her chest. Five short steps, and this could be gone forever. *Would it really be forgotten?* "Yes," she called. "Be right there." She walked back to the kitchen.

Sitting at the counter and opening the file, she was disappointed at how little it contained. No name, address, or identifying information beyond the make of the motorcycle, a description of her and the other rider, and the location of the crash. Joy handed it to Suzi.

After flipping through the report while scarfing down the second Napoleon, Suzi said, "There's not much here, is there?"

"No, not really."

"The report states the rider went off a cliff on Bellington Mountain. I know where that is. When do you want to go?"

"Is tomorrow too soon?"

"Hmmmm…I'll have to check my social calendar, but I believe I'm available."

Joy sighed. "How did I get so lucky finding a friend like you?"

"Don't know, but you're welcome."

Suzi finished her second dessert, and they said good-bye, agreeing to venture to the crash site tomorrow.

Alone, Joy stared at the police report, hoping to extract more information than what it said. In the end, all the paperwork had was where the bike went over the cliff. She needed to stand on the exact spot and see what memories might stir. Shivers of fear crept through her body. *Did she really want to do this?*

Chapter 10

Suzi arrived at eight the next morning. Walking in without knocking, she went straight to the kitchen, lured by the aroma of a dark roasted brew. "Got a mug for me?"

"Right away." Joy bounced up and reloaded the machine.

"Are you ready for this?" Suzi perched on a stool.

"Honestly, I'm not sure." She squared her shoulders. "But we're going."

"Good answer."

Placing the steaming mug in front of her friend, she offered, "I've got fresh croissants. Want one?"

"Do you have to ask?"

Laughing, Joy put two on a plate.

Suzi slathered the bread with butter and marmalade. "We don't have to do this today if you don't want to. With so many weird things happening, maybe we should slow down."

Joy inhaled deeply. "I need to see the accident site. I need to stand there and...and see what it feels like. Putting this trip off won't change the outcome."

"Just making sure." Suzi quickly ate her breakfast and was on her feet, car keys in hand.

Joy grabbed her own key ring. "Let me drive. This was my hare-brained idea."

"Thanks, but what if you get a case of the lightning

bolts? I love you but have no desire to drive over a cliff with you. Got too much to do with the second half of my life!"

Joy chuckled. "You're planning to live to 118 years old?"

"Sure. Why deprive the world of my intellect and humor too soon?"

"Emphasis on the humor."

"You caught that, huh?" Suzi shrugged and walked toward the front.

An hour later the women cruised the Oregon highway in Daisy. Joy focused on her phone's GPS, trying to ignore the traffic blasting by them with blaring horns, sometimes giving the one-finger salute. "Hey, Suzi, why don't you leave the left lane clear for the lunatics traveling at light speed?"

"They can go around. Haven't you learned by now? I'm *not* moving over. It's the principle." She bobbed her head.

"See all those drivers flipping you off? I don't believe they have many principles right now. Or morals. Or...*underwear*! Oh. My. God." Joy's mouth gaped wide as she stared out the passenger window.

Laughing hysterically, Suzi shifted into the slow lane. They watched as a car full of guys shot down the highway with a young man's bare ass hanging out the rear driver's side window. "Now *that* I'll move over for. Finally, someone original."

Joy covered her face with her hands.

Her friend poked her from the driver's seat. "Come on. When was the last time you were mooned?"

The car sped off toward the horizon as she chuckled. "At least they got you to switch lanes."

Another hour of driving put the ladies at mile marker thirty-six on Bellington Mountain—the location noted in the police report. Towering pine trees stretched majestically toward the sky as the asphalt curved sharply around the hillside. Parking twenty feet down in a turn-off, they cautiously walked back, skirting the edge of the road.

Joy breathed in the piney fragrance as they pushed through the scrubby brush and tufts of grass. Dead leaves and twigs crunched beneath their shoes. She stopped a few yards in and wrapped her arms around her waist. Stiffening, she braced for a jolt. Despite standing where she *believed* her life changed forever— nothing happened. She jumped when Suzi touched her shoulder.

"Sorry, didn't mean to scare you."

"You didn't," Joy said quietly. "Okay, maybe a little. I was trying to see if…well…you know…if I sensed anything."

"And?"

Hesitating, she tried to look past the brush and trees to the drop-off. "Nothing."

Suzi hugged her from behind. "I'm sorry."

"For what? It was my idea to come here."

"I know. But with all my 'do you believe in mysticism' notions, maybe you expected too much."

She placed a hand on her friend's arm. "Suzi, I have no idea what's happening with me, but the one constant is your friendship."

"I love you too. Now let's figure out what's going on." Suzi released her and walked through the foliage to the edge.

Joy followed, then froze a couple of steps behind.

"I would guess the motorcycle veered off the road, for whatever reason, and went over the cliff here. What do you think?" Suzi turned.

Joy focused a few feet to the right. "I think he went off there." She pointed to a cross with the name "Michael" in black. Scabs of white paint peeled off the worn wood, but the name remained legible. Beside it lay a dried bouquet of roses tied with a faded green ribbon.

Suzi stood beside her. "His name *must* have been Michael. But those flowers are recent, maybe within the last month. Someone else knew he died here—and still visits."

"I don't know if I can do this anymore." Joy's legs gave out, and she dropped to the ground.

"Oh, honey. We can't give up now." Suzi eased down beside her. "Think about it. There's somebody out there who knows Michael—who knows *you*."

Joy stood. "If they wanted to find *me*, don't you think they would have by now?"

"How could they? Your name has changed. I doubt Drake was clairvoyant enough to pick your real name."

Wandering to the cliff's edge, Joy peered over the precipice. The drop sheered away, thousands of feet to the valley floor. She wondered how she'd managed to survive the accident. Suddenly, a jolt echoed through her body. With eyes closed, she felt the rumble of the motorcycle beneath her as she clung to the man driving. They tilted with the twisting road, almost scraping the foot pegs, then righted as they traversed the mountain. He peered over his shoulder, brown hair curling from beneath his helmet, a grin on his face. Desire coursed up her spine as Michael caressed her leg, his blue eyes twinkling behind ochre-tinted glasses. *She loved him.* Returning his hand onto the grip a moment too late, they went into a skid, and Joy screamed. The bike veered from the road, and they hit a log. She tried to hold on but bounced off the seat and flew backward into the forest, slamming hard onto the ground. Michael held onto the handlebars as the bike careened into space. Her vision blurred, then went dark.

"Joy!"

Her eyes flew open as Suzi pulled her backward, away from the empty space ahead. As she dragged Joy by the arm, Suzi backed into the cross, loosening it from the earth.

Joy gasped for breath. "I loved him."

"What? How could you know that?"

Hesitating, she reflected on the memory she'd just experienced. Looking Suzi in the eye, she described the vision. "He touched me. Rubbed my leg. Smiled—the kind of smile which held longing...desire...*passion.* We were soulmates. Love filled his eyes...his touch."

"You're that sure?"

"Yes. He meant something to me. He meant a lifetime. He meant eternity." Hot tears burned her face. "Then he was gone. I lost him forever."

Suzi opened her mouth to speak, but no words of comfort came out.

Joy looked up and envisioned Michael going over the cliff again. "No!" Her hands balled into fists.

"Stop it! It's over." Suzi placed her hands on the shaken woman's shoulders. "You can't keep reliving the scene. Look at me. You lost Michael and found Drake. Maybe not a fair trade, but you found happiness again. How can you question your life with a husband who cherished every moment together?"

"I'm not. But I need to know who I was. Who I…" Joy's voice faded when sunlight glinted off something jutting from the ground where the cross had been dislodged. Slowly, she bent down and retrieved a small, dirt-encrusted license plate. It was blue and white with a yellow mountain range across the top. By the size, it belonged on a motorcycle. The state read "Nevada."

Chapter 11

"Wanna have dinner at my place?" Suzi asked when they returned to the city limits. "I could drive you home afterward."

"Thanks, but I'm a little worn out." Joy clutched the license plate in her hand. "You understand, don't you?"

"Of course, I do. Just don't sit and brood until you drive yourself crazy. I'm the looney in this friendship, and you're the straight man...er...woman. Don't switch things up now." Suzi softened her voice. "You can't change the past."

Resting her head back against the seat, Joy sighed. "I know. All I'd like to do now is resurrect it for clarity. Whoever left those flowers probably erected the cross with the plate buried beneath. There was no mention in the police report about the motorcycle being registered in Nevada, but it must've come from there. All it stated was the bike had exploded on impact."

"Obviously, the authorities didn't find the plate when they investigated. It could have dropped anywhere between the road and the cliff."

"You would think whoever found Michael's departure site would have known how to find me. Why didn't they? If our mystery person came all the way from Nevada, he or she had to have known the whole story of how I survived and where I was taken."

Suzi pulled into the drive at the winery and stopped by the front door of the house. "Maybe finding you would have been too painful with the loss of Michael. We don't know what the relationship was to him—sister, parent, friend. Jilted lover maybe? My money is on the psycho ex."

"I never thought of that—*especially the jilted lover scenario.*" She lightly smacked her friend on the shoulder. "This person could be bitter about *my* surviving." She ran her finger over the smooth metal.

"Too much speculation can lead to wrong conclusions—especially if you keep listening to my hare-brained ideas." Suzi placed a hand on Joy's arm. "Let's focus on finding out *who* you are and *where* you came from. Nobody can fault you for wanting to know."

"You're right." Joy leaned over and gave her a hug. "Thanks for today."

"Any time." Suzi returned the squeeze. "Call me later if you want to talk. Or need a bottle of wine." She pulled back. "Scratch the wine. I think you have enough." She nodded toward the vineyard. "Maybe whiskey or tequila then. They're all worthy choices."

Joy got out and walked toward her house. She turned to watch Suzi's car pull away, and the horn tooted. She reached for the doorknob but stopped before turning it. Tucking the license plate into her purse, she went to the tasting room instead. It was just before closing time, and Grace would still be there—with Harmony.

Two cars remained in the parking lot. She held the door open for a couple exiting. The man carried a full box of mixed bottles. Once Joy was inside, Grace looked up and smiled at her, while Harmony engaged two young men in conversation as they twirled red liquid in their glasses.

"Where were you and Aunt Suzi today?" Grace asked, coming around the counter.

"Took a little day trip. You know how we like to ramble."

Grace crossed her arms and raised an eyebrow. "Don't even. With as strange as you've been acting lately, you're up to something."

"What?" Joy couldn't keep a straight face.

"Okay, Mom, spill. Where did the two of you *ramble*?"

Leaning on the counter, Joy purposely turned her back to Harmony. *Now why did she think to do that?* "We went to the accident site on Bellington Mountain."

Grace crinkled her forehead. "You mean where Dad…" Stiffening her back, she raised a hand to her mouth. Recovering, she asked in a hushed voice, "Is that where *your* accident happened before you met Dad?"

"Yes."

"Why'd you go there?" Her voice escalated.

Joy put a hand on Grace's arm. "Just want to know who I am. Understand?"

Grace scowled and looked at the ground, then back at her mother. "No. But…okay…yes, I understand. But you loved Daddy. Why go looking for something else? Or someone else?"

"Searching out my identity doesn't mean I love your father any less. He'll always be in my heart. But now that he's gone, I owe it to myself to find where I came from. What if I have loved ones looking for me?

People who've been looking for me for twenty-two years?"

"You have loved ones here." Grace stomped her foot like a petulant child.

"Oh, sweetie. Do you think if I find people from my past, you'll no longer be part of my life?" Joy's eyes widened.

Tears slipped down Grace's face. "Yes. With Daddy gone, I don't want to lose you too."

Wrapping her arms around her daughter, Joy pulled her close. "You'll always be part of my life. You're my daughter. Don't ever think differently." Squeezing harder, then releasing, she looked into Grace's eyes. "You're the most important person in my life."

Grace smiled, then turned and cleared the dirty glasses from her last customers, carrying them to the back room.

Joy clutched her purse, choosing not to mention what she'd found at the accident site—at least not yet. A hand on her shoulder caused her to jump. It was Harmony. The real shock came when no memory flashes surged through her body. *Maybe Harmony had nothing to do with them.*

"Everything okay?" Harmony's tasters left through the front door, each carrying two bottles. "I didn't mean to startle you." Looking toward the back room. "What's upsetting Grace?"

"She sometimes gets emotional when we talk about her father," Joy lied while taking a step back. "How were sales today?"

Harmony hesitated with her lips pursed. "Sales were good. I lost count but think we went through eighteen mixed cases."

"Not a bad take for a Wednesday." Joy forced a smile, still not comfortable around their new employee.

Grace returned and flipped the sign in the window to "Closed." She went to the counter and cleared the remaining glasses from Harmony's customers.

"I would've gotten those," her co-worker called.

"No worries. I'm on it. Why don't you head out? Mom and I can finish up."

Harmony hesitated. "Okay. If you're sure?"

Joy jumped in. "Of course. You run along."

"Thanks. I have a date, and this gives me just enough time to stop home and change." Walking out, Harmony called out, "See you tomorrow!"

"Why don't you head out too?" Joy said. "I'll finish up here. Do you and Owen have plans?"

"He does. Bowling with the boys." She blew a breath through her nose and fisted her hands.

"Stay for dinner?"

"Thanks, not tonight." She faced her mother. "I'm thinking bath and relaxation. You know the drill." She retrieved her purse and sweater. Hugging her mother, she said, "Love you, Mom."

Joy locked the door behind her daughter. Her mind returned to the day's expedition. She thought about the possibility of finding family left behind when she lost her memory, but would it be who she wanted to find? Would they be loving, kind, welcoming? Or would they be angry and accusing because she had lived, and Michael died?

Once she had the tasting room ready for the next day, Joy locked up and went to the house. She wasn't hungry for dinner but wandered into the kitchen anyway. The flowerpots on the windowsill each had a green sprig which sprouted tiny leaves growing up through the soil. She'd never seen a plant germinate so quickly. One more mystery to solve, she supposed. Filling a glass with water she *nurtured* them. On a whim she pulled out one of the sticks with the packets attached.

Flipping the instructions over to the front, she read the new title: *Five Steps to* Plane *Celestia.* Joy didn't bother checking the other two. She knew they'd say the same. The backside almost disappointed her. There remained only three steps. Maybe that's all there would be? No more magic beans for her.

Poking the stick back into its pot, Joy went upstairs to change into pajamas. With all the upheavals she'd experienced today, she knew it would be an early night. As she sat at the bathroom vanity brushing her hair, the purple vial on the necklace glistened in the mirror. *How could such phenomenal things become blasé to her?* Setting her brush on the counter, she held the necklace in the palm of her hand, wondering if it too had a connection to her past before the hospital. Maybe she should return to the gift shop where she'd met Pete. While she loved traveling with Suzi, this was something she needed to do alone. The town was a day and a half drive. With Harmony added to their small staff, her daughter could handle the tasting room for a couple days.

She returned to the bedroom. Grace's reaction to her explorations into the past distressed her. What if her daughter's emotions held more weight than just the fear of getting left behind? Tension between Grace and Owen had been obvious the other day. Were things more extreme than her daughter let on? From their argument, it sounded as if her husband might be having an affair. Could it be true? She relaxed her shoulders. Grace would discuss it when she felt ready.

Joy sat on the bed and traced the raised lines on her wrist. She followed the curve of the wavy lines and the straight one crossing them. *Could the vial have something to do with these too? Or the plants?* Tomorrow she'd plan a trip back to the gift shop. Hopefully Pete would be receptive to answering her questions.

Chapter 12

After driving the coast for a few hours, Joy veered inland a half mile to Toby's Treasures. Pulling into the parking lot, doubts assailed her. *What if he thinks I'm crazy?*

The bell jingled as she opened the door. Striding to the counter, she approached a young woman in her mid-twenties working the register.

"Can I help you?" the cashier asked with more enthusiasm than her face expressed.

"Yes," Joy said. "Is Pete here today?"

The girl cocked her head. "Who?"

"Pete. The owner's husband. Is he here?"

"Are you sure you're in the right shop? The owner's name is Harry, and, to the best of my knowledge, he's got a wife, not a husband."

Joy stepped back and looked around. She was certain this was the store she and Suzi had visited on their trip. Flustered by the girl's news, she stuttered, "I-I'm sorry. I must be mistaken."

"No problem," the girl said. "Let me know if you need help." She returned to her cell phone, her fingers flying over the screen.

Joy wandered the aisles and spied the etched glasses Suzi had been so enamored with on their last visit. Going farther toward the back of the store, she found the rack of seeds. Every spot was filled with run-of-the-mill herbs—nothing exotic or out of the ordinary like Celestia. It didn't make sense.

Returning to the front, she asked the girl again. "Are you *sure* no one named Pete works here?"

"Nope." She snapped her gum, punctuating the statement.

"Is the owner around?"

"Nope." Another pop.

The clerk didn't grasp Joy's urgency to talk to Pete or anyone in authority. "Is there *anyone* in charge that could possibly help me?" She had driven a long way and was desperate for information.

"Are you complaining about the service?"

"What? No. I was here about a week and a half ago and wanted to continue a conversation I had with the man working the counter—Pete."

"I'm sorry, ma'am, but like I told you, nobody named Pete works here. There are quite a few shops in this area. Perhaps you've mistaken this one for another?"

Sighing, Joy answered, "That must be it. Sorry to bother you." She went toward the door. Stopping short, she turned and asked, "Have you ever heard of a plant called Celestia?"

"Ahhh, no?" The girl's face screwed into a pout. "Should I have?"

"Never mind." Joy shook her head and left.

Sitting in the car, her hands gripped the steering wheel, tears flowing down her cheeks. She hadn't come to the wrong shop. How was it possible the cashier didn't know Pete?

Shifting the car into gear, she pulled out of the parking lot and drove slowly down the highway.

Turning off at the first beach access, Joy parked and strolled toward the surf. Her tears flowed as she sat on a log and watched the waves slam onto the shore. The water's cadence of hitting and receding grew louder the longer she stared. After driving all this way, she never expected to run into a dead end. She wanted to scream and pound her hands on the ground.

Not sure how long she'd been staring at the horizon, Joy caught a whiff of apple tobacco drifting in the air. A lone fisherman stood a short way down the beach casting his line. She wasn't sure if he'd only just arrived or had gone unnoticed by her.

She removed her shoes making it easier to walk across the sand. The cool grains caressed her feet with each step. When she approached the man, he turned and smiled. The leathery texture of his face spoke of hours in the sun, possibly near the ocean.

"Hello," she said. "Do you live locally?"

The fisherman pulled a pipe from his mouth. "Aye," he said in a gravelly voice as weathered as his skin. "Are you lost?"

Joy immediately recognized the irony of his question. Yes, she was lost. "Well, I think I might have gotten turned around. I came here looking for a gift shop that a friend and I found a little over a week ago. It's owned by a man named Pete and his wife. Do you happen to know of it?"

He bit down on the stem of his pipe and remained silent for a full minute. She thought he wasn't going to answer. Slowly he reeled in the line he'd cast when Joy first approached. Once it was in, he freed his mouth to speak. "Sorry, love, but I don't believe I've met the couple you're referring to."

"I thought the shop was Toby's Treasures, about a mile up the road. There was a young lady working the counter who said the owner's name was Harry. Do you know if it's changed hands recently?"

"No, the young lady was correct. I believe Harry has owned that shop at least twenty years. Maybe you did get a bit turned around and were in a different place." Setting his pipe on an upside-down bucket, the man re-baited his hook and cast it out again. His rough hands worked the rod with ease.

Shoulders sagging, Joy thanked him and went back to her car.

****

The fisherman watched as Joy drove away. Moving the extinguished pipe, he eased down onto the overturned bucket and set his pole on the ground. With a heavy sigh, he reached inside his denim shirt and grasped the purple vial hanging around his neck. *Pete was right. Not an ounce of recognition.* He'd spied the same necklace peeking from her blouse as well—the same one he'd placed around her neck in the hospital all those years ago. The memory loss should have only lasted one year. By then, things would have resolved themselves, and she could have returned home. Obviously, he overestimated the dosage. Maybe it was a blessing seeing how things turned out.

Chapter 13

Joy drove until she reached the hotel she'd booked for the night. Too drained from the day's disappointment, she skipped dinner and went straight to her room. A little after nine Grace called to see how her *buying* trip was going.

Joy had told Grace the purpose of this trip was to check out a new artist for their labels. They would be offering a new Tempranillo and Syrah blend this year and wanted a different design for its debut. She did have plans to visit the studio of someone she'd contacted.

"What did you think of the artist, Mom?"

"I didn't make it there yet. Got caught up in trolling through a couple of gift shops." Joy grimaced at the half-truth.

"You? In a gift shop? What's really going on? Now you have me worried." Her voice escalated an octave.

"Without Suzi along, someone has to support the local economy." Joy laughed, hoping her daughter bought the lighthearted banter.

Silence ensued before she eased into the conversation. "I guess you're right. Not taking Aunt Suzi along could really damage their sales margin. I'm glad you're carrying the torch."

The lines in Joy's face eased as they spoke for another twenty minutes. Grace filled her in on sales in the tasting room and how the internet business had been going extremely well. The warehouse would be busy getting shipments out over the next week.

Fatigue overtook Joy as she wrapped up the call. "I'm really beat, sweetie. Let me call you tomorrow after I've viewed the gallery."

"Sounds good, but don't make it too late. Since Monday is usually slow, Harmony suggested we close at four and head out for a girls' camp-out on Derringer Beach. You know how spotty cell service is there."

"Camping? Isn't it a little early in the season?" Joy gripped the phone at the thought of Grace going somewhere remote with Harmony. *How much did they really know about her?*

A sigh could be heard over the phone before Grace spoke. "Mom, don't worry, we'll be fine. Besides, I think I need some girl time. You know how things have been with Owen lately."

Joy let the words hang in the air a moment. "Do you want to talk about it?"

"Not now. When you get back, maybe. And don't worry about us. We'll bundle up in warm jammies."

Joy's heart broke at the signs of her daughter's marriage being in trouble. She had to admit she'd be happy if Owen disappeared, but the pain Grace would endure at the break-up wasn't something she'd wish on anyone. Leaning into the backrest of the bed, Joy gave in to the lure of her pillow. "All right. We'll talk when you get back on Tuesday from your *camping adventure.*"

"You make it sound like we're going on safari." Grace laughed. "Talk to you soon. Love you!"

"I love you too, sweetie. Be safe."

Pajamas sounded like an excellent idea. Joy changed into hers and snuggled under the covers. Like on her trip with Suzi, nightmares and tattered memories of the motorcycle accident tortured her. Waking up several times with sweat dripping from her body and the sheets twisted, she gave up about five but lay in bed until six. After making coffee in the brewer on the bathroom counter, she took it outside to the patio. Every room in the hotel faced the ocean, and she was glad to have gotten a reservation.

Wrapped in a blanket against the morning chill, Joy watched the surf explode in color. Clouds drifting over the ocean reflected the red, yellow, and orange hues of the sun rising behind the building. Seagulls floated on the breeze searching for their next meal.

Despite the caffeine kick, she must've set her mug on the table and drifted off to sleep. She awoke with the cold chill of a shadow over her. A man in a yellow rainslicker stood at the edge of her patio. Stifling a scream, she sat up and looked around to see if there were other people around.

"Sorry to startle you, love."

Joy recognized the harsh voice of the fisherman from the beach. "What are you doing here?" She instinctively pulled the blanket tighter.

"I fish up and down the beaches in this area. Seeing you here, I wanted to check and see if you'd found the shop you were looking for yesterday. You seemed so…anxious to find the right place. It bothered me not to be of help."

"Oh…well…I didn't find it."

"Maybe next trip then. I hope you enjoyed your journey anyway."

"Yes, thank you." Joy glanced sideways hoping to find anybody else out and about. While she didn't fear this man, his appearance at her hotel was unsettling. She unconsciously reached for her coffee cup. It felt icy cold against her trembling fingers. *How long had she slept?*

He set his bucket down, while holding his pole in the other hand. Pointing at her neckline, he commented, "That's an interesting piece of jewelry you're wearin'."

Grasping the purple vial, she said, "It was a gift. Someone gave it to me years ago. A stranger actually." She wondered why she felt compelled to share its history with a man she didn't know.

"The person must have become very special to you. Are you with him now, assuming it was a man?"

"No. I…I was in an accident many years ago. A stranger in the hospital put it around my neck. He said it would help me remember things."

The fisherman shifted back onto one leg. "That's a mighty full promise. Did you get to know this stranger?"

What an odd question. "I never saw him again. Honestly," she confessed, "the only thing I remember about him is his hands. They were rough, like someone who worked outside, but gentle."

He pulled his pipe and lighter from a pocket. In an afterthought, he asked, "You don't mind, do you?"

"No," she said a little too quickly. Breathing deeply, she forced herself to relax.

The man ignited his tobacco and took a couple puffs, the scent of apple swirling about him. "So, you don't remember his face?"

Standing, Joy tugged the blanket closer. "No."

"Hmmm…what about the memories? Did the necklace help with those?"

"I'm sorry." She walked toward the sliding glass door. "It's a bit nippy for me."

"Oh, aye, there is a bit of a chill out here. You get inside where it's warm. Nice chatting with you."

"You too." Slipping inside, Joy locked the door behind her. The man stared after her through the glass a moment before he picked up his bucket, nodded, and headed for the shoreline. As soon as he'd turned around, Joy swished the curtain closed.

Backing away from the drapes, she felt the bed behind her legs and plopped down. Joy grasped the comforter in her hands, letting the blanket fall from her shoulders. Sweat dripped down the back of her neck. While the fisherman's visit was disturbing, it almost had a familiar sense to it. Joy realized she'd never asked for his name, though she'd never offered hers either.

She got up and made another cup of coffee. Without bothering to shower, Joy dressed, packed her overnight bag, and checked out of the hotel. The man's visit flustered her more than she wanted to admit. Who was he? Was his turning up at her hotel truly a coincidence?

Chapter 14

Joy loaded her luggage into the back of the car then checked the GPS for directions to the artist's studio. It only took forty-five minutes to get there. The place didn't open for another hour. She should have thought of that before leaving so early. She scoped out a cafe down the street, and her stomach rumbled.

Once she sated her appetite with eggs and toast, she walked back to the Lost Memories studio. Part of the reason she picked this artist was the company name. The odd title beckoned her. Stepping inside the glass doors, Joy immediately felt she'd made the right choice. An older woman with long gray hair hurried to greet her.

"You must be Joy. I'm Candice."

"How did you know?"

"I have a sense of things. It's part of what inspires my painting. Please, come see my work." Taking Joy by the hand, she led her farther into the shop. "This is the tourist stuff." She waved a hand at the paintings on the wall. "You've come to see the back room."

Joy strolled beside the exuberant woman. As they went through the door at the rear, she found herself in a cavernous studio. Several easels held paintings in various stages.

"This is the one I think would be perfect for your label." Candice gestured toward a small canvas. It portrayed a gold necklace, the chain in a swirl, with a glistening purple vial.

Joy put a hand over the necklace resting beneath her shirt. Gasping for breath, she tried not to hyperventilate. Next thing she knew, she lay prone on the floor with Candice kneeling beside her.

"Breathe, honey. You'll be okay." The artist pressed a cool, wet rag to Joy's forehead.

Fluttering her eyes, she tried to sit up, but delicate fingers pressed against her chest.

"Rest a few moments. You took a bad spill."

As she pulled her arm away, the woman's wrist caught Joy's attention. Candice sported a raised symbol of a circle with a line through it. Slowly sitting up, she asked, "What happened?"

"You fainted. Has there been a lot of stress in your life lately?"

A smile spread across her lips. "You could say that. I'll be okay." Joy pushed off the floor and stood.

Candice supported her. "You sure?"

She nodded. "I'm fine."

"You know, I've always hoped my artwork would move people but not that drastically." She giggled. "So, what do you think of my design for your new label?"

"Honestly, I have to admit, I'm a little frightened."

"Frightened? Why?"

Joy reached inside her shirt and retrieved the necklace.

Now it was Candice's turn to be flustered. "I had no idea. Really. Are you from…"

"From where?" Joy almost shouted, clutching the woman's arm.

"You're one of the lost ones, aren't you?" Candice

pulled free and went to a sofa by the wall. "You don't know what that necklace really is, do you?"

Slowly, Joy walked over and sat beside her. "I got the necklace in the hospital twenty-two years ago when I'd lost my memory. The man who put it around my neck was a stranger to me. At least I believed him to be. Please help me. Do you know who I am?"

Candice stared, confusion in her wide eyes. "Twenty-two years? You've been wandering that long?"

"You know who I am, don't you?" Joy's desperation consumed her.

Covering Joy's hands with both of hers, Candice said, "I do not—and that's the truth! All I know is occasionally there are those who are…lost…or banished. It's only supposed to last a year though. Return is permitted, but the circumstances are different for each. But you say it's been twenty-two years? That's not possible."

"What are you talking about? Lost? Banished? Are you from an Amish community?"

Candice burst into laughter. "Amish? No. You really don't know, do you?"

"Know what?" Joy balled her hands. "And how did you get that symbol?" She pointed to the raised circle.

Candice's expression became a stone mask. "It's not my place." Standing, she gestured toward the front door. "I'm sorry, but you need to leave. I can't help you."

"Please, Candice. I can't remember anything. Give me something to go on."

"It's forbidden. I'm sorry. I like my life here, and they allow me to come back and forth. If I help you, I'll be forbidden to return to this world. You understand, don't you?"

Joy rounded on her. "No. I don't. If you know something, why won't you tell me? I'm just looking for my family. Aren't they looking for me?"

It was as if a switch had been turned off. The artist's eyes became cold and distant. "I'm not brave. My creativity will be stifled if I go back to that world full-time. This place opens possibilities for me. I'm sorry. You must leave." She propelled Joy toward the front door.

Stunned, Joy allowed herself to be escorted. Once outside, the door slammed behind her. She turned and looked through the glass, but the shade had already dropped. Knocking, she yelled through the door, "Candice, please, talk to me! What do you mean by *this world*?" Jiggling the handle, she found it wouldn't budge.

No response. These strange encounters continued to plague her. How was it her memories were trickling in, and she kept running into people who could give her answers, but wouldn't? First Pete, now Candice— maybe even the fisherman?

Shuffling to her car, Joy looked at the gallery one more time, then got into the driver's seat. The name, Lost Memories, fit more than she'd originally thought. Having reached another dead end, she drove toward home.

As much as her thoughts tormented her about this recent encounter, she couldn't stop worrying about Grace being alone with Harmony. She didn't have anything concrete against the girl, but the electric shocks weren't a dream. A physical sensation coursed through Joy's body when she touched her new assistant.

After a few hours' drive, Joy approached the city limits. Instead of going home to the Mystic Swirl, she found herself pulling into Suzi's driveway. If anybody could help sort this out, it would be her.

She rang the doorbell and was greeted by her friend sporting a full head of curlers with a green facial mask. "Only *you* would be allowed into my home with me in this state!" Suzi laughed. "What's going on?"

Joy hesitated. "Got wine?"

"Are you kidding? Get in here." She pulled her visitor inside.

They sat on the living room couch laughing and drinking for a couple of hours as Joy detailed her visit. At some point, Suzi excused herself to rake the green goo off her face.

"So, you're not mad I went without you?" Joy asked.

"Of course not. Some things need to be done alone. It doesn't sound like you got much accomplished."

"No. If anything, I have more questions."

Refilling Joy's glass, Suzi asked, "The artist truly asked if you were one of the 'lost ones' or 'banished?' Are you Amish?"

Joy roared. "That's exactly what I asked."

"You remember anything else from this little jaunt?"

She thought a moment. "Not a thing. Can I stay here tonight?"

"Do you even have to ask?" Indignation shone in Suzi's voice. "You know where the guest room is. More vino?"

Joy held out her glass.

"Did you tell Grace where you went?"

Joy bit her upper lip. "Sort of."

"Meaning?"

She twirled the stem. "Meaning I told her I was going to view the studio of an artist I was considering as a designer for our new red blend label."

"And she bought it?"

"Seemed to. She let me go." Joy shrugged.

Suzi sipped her beverage. "Did you call her yet to say the artist didn't work out?"

Slumping her shoulders, Joy admitted, "No. She's out of cell service anyway. Grace and Harmony went camping on Derringer Beach."

"What! You let her go to a remote beach alone with a woman who sends jolts through you? What were you thinking?"

Joy slammed her glass onto the coffee table. "I know! But what could I say? Grace has no idea the effect Harmony has on me. What if I'm wrong?"

"What if you're wrong about Harmony sending electric shocks through your body when she touches you? Do you really think you imagined those?"

"Okay, you're right. It was real. How do I explain it to my daughter? She's been through so much in the last two years with the loss of Drake. I can't tell her there are bizarre things going on with me."

Suzi leaned back into the couch cushion. "Yes. It's so much better to continue lying to her."

"Wow, don't sugarcoat it, Suzi, give it to me straight." She smirked.

"All I'm saying is at some point, you need to come clean with her."

She stared at the red liquid as it swirled about the

glass. "I know. I know. Just not tonight." She looked at her friend. "Okay?"

"Agreed. Besides, a drunken explanation isn't always best."

They giggled, and for a moment, Joy stopped her preoccupation over her daughter's camping trip. But only for a moment.

Chapter 15

On her way home the next morning, Joy's thoughts were consumed with her daughter and the camping trip. Hopefully the night away was nothing more than a bit of female bonding. Sometimes Grace needed to talk with someone closer to her own age.

Dropping her overnight bag in the house, she proceeded straight to the tasting room in preparation for the day.

At nine sharp, Harmony strolled in. "Hi, Joy. How was your trip?"

"Okay. How was camping?"

Harmony set her purse in the back room and returned. "Fun. Is Grace here?"

"No. Didn't you drive in together from the beach?" The lines in her face tightened.

"Um...didn't she call you?"

"No." Joy stopped setting out glasses. "Why would she?"

The young woman looked at the floor then back at Joy. "Well...um...she and I had a bit of a tiff. Grace took off down the beach about three a.m. I thought she'd be here."

Joy's pulse quickened. "She's not."

"Oh." Harmony shuffled her feet. "I feel really bad. I thought she would've called you since she didn't have a car. We drove mine to the beach. Maybe she contacted Owen?"

"I haven't heard from her." Joy grabbed her phone from a pocket. There weren't any missed calls. Immediately hitting speed-dial, she tapped her foot waiting for Grace to answer. It went to voicemail. She looked at her assistant. "What was the fight about?"

Harmony shrugged. "It's silly."

"Couldn't have been too silly. Grace doesn't anger easily." Joy looked her in the eye.

"She probably wouldn't want me to tell you. It's kinda personal."

"Harmony, my daughter is missing. Nothing can be too personal right now." Joy reached out to the young woman and risked touching her arm. A warm tingle pulsed through her.

Harmony touched Joy's hand and the warmth grew stronger. "I guess, under the circumstances..." She hesitated. "Did you know she accused her husband of cheating?"

Joy shuddered. "Yes."

"Well...it sounds ridiculous saying it out loud."

Harmony's chuckle sounded forced to Joy's ear. She tightened her hold on the young woman. "Tell me!"

Her head snapped up. "She thinks I'm the one fooling around with Owen."

"What?" Joy's eyes bugged wide, and she stepped back. "But you only arrived in town recently. Her problems with Owen began a while ago."

"That's what I said." She tapped the top of her head, as if everything was obvious.

"I'm sure she got a ride from her husband," Joy said, only half convinced. "Can you fill the water pitchers?"

Harmony set to work.

Ten o'clock came and went, yet Grace didn't show. Joy assumed if the girls had a fight, her daughter wanted to allow some space and not discuss it right now. Still, she feared another explanation.

She left her assistant to handle the floor and walked to the warehouse. Finding Owen, she asked, "Is Grace at home?"

"What are you talking about? She and Harmony went camping. Grace should be at the tasting room."

"She's not."

Owen dragged his hand through his hair. "Whadda you mean? They were supposed to come here for work, and then she'd ride home with me afterward."

"She isn't at work. Didn't she call you for a ride? Harmony said they had an argument in the wee hours of the morning. Grace took off down the beach."

"Uh-uh." Owen grabbed his cell. Doing the same thing Joy had done, he dialed his wife then looked up. "It went to voicemail."

"She didn't answer my call either. Where could she be?"

"I don't know." His face paled. "Is there some place she would go if she were upset?"

"My house. And she's not there." Owen appeared genuinely distressed.

Maybe he does care for her.

"Harmony said she left the campsite?"

Joy wrung her hands. "Yes."

"You know how Grace finds the beach soothing. Maybe she went farther down to…you know…collect her thoughts."

"For several hours? You know how spotty service

is out there. Maybe she tried calling and is out of range."

"I'll go to Derringer Beach and look around. She might still be there." Owen reached into his pocket and grabbed his car keys.

"Call me as soon as you find her."

He threw an arm around her shoulder in an awkward hug. "I will. Try not to worry." He bolted for the door.

Joy stood looking around the warehouse as if it might offer up answers. She knew it wouldn't but was at a loss of what else to do. Her daughter was missing.

She sat at the desk and called Suzi. Her friend wouldn't have answers, but right now she needed the support.

After hearing about the situation, Suzi said, "I'll be right over."

Joy waited in the warehouse as her imagination spun out of control. This couldn't be happening, she thought. She'd already lost Drake. She couldn't lose Grace too.

Finding the strength to get up, Joy went to her house. She left the front door unlocked, so Suzi could let herself in. After making coffee, she sat at the kitchen counter and waited.

Twenty minutes later, she heard the front door open. Suzi walked into the kitchen. "The cavalry has arrived."

Without hesitating, Joy threw herself into her friend's embrace. "I can't lose her."

"You won't. Coffee?" Suzi asked.

Pulling away she smiled. "Of course." Joy fixed a mug and handed it to Suzi.

"Thanks. Have you heard from Owen?"

"Not yet. Maybe he tried, but cell service at the beach isn't good. You think we should drive over there too?" Her hands trembled as she sat on a stool at the counter.

Suzi shook her head. "No. Let's wait here. He said he'd call, right?"

"Yes, but—"

"He'll let you know. Our rushing out there won't help. Let's wait here."

Her shoulders slumped. "Okay."

After a couple of hours, Joy's nerves were frayed. "Don't you think we should join him at Derringer Beach?"

"Just chill. Owen will call." Suzi placed a hand on Joy's arm. "Grace could've wandered pretty far along the beach by this time. He's got a lot of real estate to cover."

Finally, Joy's cell rang. She snatched it up. "Did you find her?"

"Meet me at the hospital." The lack of expression in Owen's voice scared Joy more than the words. He ended the call before she could ask more.

Suzi grabbed her car keys. "Where're we going?"

"County General."

****

Forty minutes later they arrived at the emergency room. Joy bolted through the automatic doors before they fully opened. "My daughter's here. Her name is Grace Colby."

Suzi huffed and puffed at Joy's side.

The nurse checked her computer. "She's been admitted. Fifth floor." She pointed to a bank of elevators down the hall.

The women wasted no time running to the elevator. After hitting the button, they waited for the next car. Only a few seconds later, Joy poked the button again. And then again.

"I think you've got it." Suzi elbowed her gently. "Now stop holding your breath before you pass out."

"What could be wrong? Why didn't Owen tell me over the phone? It must be bad!" She raked her hands through her hair.

The doors swished open, and they rushed inside. Joy pressed the button for the fifth floor then stood back balling her hands open and closed.

Suzi gasped and pointed at the label next to the fifth floor. "Did you notice what department is on that floor?"

"What are you talking about?"

Their destination was labeled "Obstetrics."

Joy couldn't utter any words.

The elevator dinged then opened. After being so anxious to get to the hospital, they hesitated. As the doors started to close, Suzi thrust out her hand, forcing them to re-open. They found Owen slumped in a blue plastic chair in the waiting room.

"How is she?" Joy's voice cracked.

Owen stood. "Joy." He placed his hands on her shoulders. "I won't lie. She's in bad shape."

"What happened? Where did you find her?" Her questions came rapid fire.

Owen shuddered and sat back down instead of answering. He buried his face in his hands and sobbed.

Suzi stepped in. "Look, son, if you don't start talking, there will be *two* of you in a hospital bed. Tell us what's going on!"

He looked up. "Grace was attacked."

Now it was Joy's turn to slip off her wobbly legs onto a seat. "By whom?"

The muscles in his jaw tensed. "She was unconscious when I found her on the shoreline. The tide was coming in. Another hour and she might have been pulled out to sea."

Tears leaked from Joy's eyes.

Suzi slipped an arm around her friend, pulling her close as she sat beside her. Looking at Owen she asked, "Why is Grace on the obstetrics floor?"

Tears streamed down his face as well. "The attack caused her to have a miscarriage."

"What!" Joy could barely contain her anger. "How long have you known?"

He shook his head. "I didn't know. The doctor said she couldn't have been more than a few weeks along. The trauma of the attack…" Owen stopped. "Joy, I'm so sorry."

"For what? It wasn't your fault." Glaring directly into his eyes. "Or was it? Were you at the beach with them?"

He sprang up, as if punched. "What do you mean? This happened while she and Harmony were camping alone. How could you accuse me of hurting my wife?"

Joy cringed. "I didn't mean…I'm sorry…I'm just…distraught."

Owen stormed down the hall. "I need coffee."

Suzi stroked Joy's hand. "Don't worry about him. Remember, he's the one who was stepping out on his wife. It's probably guilt more than anger."

"Right now, it doesn't matter. I need to see my

daughter."

"Let's go to the nurses' station and see if we can get a status."

Approaching the attendant behind the desk, the women didn't wait to be noticed. "Excuse me," Suzi said, tapping the back of the computer screen.

The man's purple scrubs looked as rumpled as the bags beneath his eyes. He jumped at Suzi's request, and his head shot up. "Can I help you?"

Joy stepped closer. "I'm looking for my daughter, Grace Colby. Can you tell me how she's doing?"

After tapping the computer keys, the nurse, whose name tag read "Cal," muttered, "You'll have to ask the doctor. She's allowed visitors. Room five-oh-two." With a little more force, he looked at Suzi. "Family only."

Joy hooked her elbow through Suzi's. "She's my sister."

Sighing, the attendant quietly said, "Keep it brief. Your daughter needs rest."

"Thank you," Joy called over her shoulder as she dragged her friend down the hall. The door to five-oh-two stood open, and they slowed their approach.

Suzi unhooked her arm from Joy's. "Do you want to go in alone?"

She shook her head. "You may not be related by blood, but you are *Aunt* Suzi. Let's go."

Grace lay in bed with her back to them. Her black hair splayed across the pillow and the sheets.

"Sweetie? It's Mom." Joy eased onto the edge of the bed.

The young woman didn't stir.

She placed a hand on her daughter's shoulder.

"Grace, honey, are you awake?"

In barely a croak, she responded, "No."

With a catch in her voice, Joy lay down next to her daughter and gathered her close. "Honey, I'm so sorry." Her daughter shuddered beneath her arms.

Quiet sobs became wracking convulsions as Grace cried hysterically. It was a pain a mother could never soothe for her child.

Joy was full of questions about what happened on the beach, but now wasn't the time to ask. She needed to act supportive and nothing else.

Suzi walked around the bed and pulled up a chair. She winced at the bruises on Grace's neck. Gently, she reached out and wiped the tears with her thumb. "Shhhhh, sweetie. You'll get through this. We're both here."

Opening her eyes, Grace looked at her aunt and rasped, "Why did this happen?" More tears poured down her mottled cheeks.

Joy held tight until her daughter's breathing became even. Not wanting to wake her, Joy slid away and sat up. Motioning to Suzi, the women left the room.

Throwing an arm around Joy, Suzi hugged her close. "Should we talk to the doctor on duty? Maybe he or she can give us a better picture of Grace's condition and how long she'll need to stay."

Joy nodded and they walked back to the desk. Cal still worked the station. "Is the doctor on duty available?"

"She's on break and will be back in about thirty minutes."

"Thank you. We'll be waiting over there." Joy pointed toward the plastic seats in the waiting room.

"Please have her talk to us when she's back."

"Yes, ma'am."

They waited forty-five minutes before a tall woman with fine cheekbones and coffee-colored skin approached them. She wore a white coat with a metal name tag pinned to it. "I'm Dr. Tory. You're Grace Colby's mother?"

Joy stood. "Yes. How is she?" Her voice quivered.

"She's stable. You know she lost the baby?" Her voice had a slight French accent.

"Yes. What happened?"

"I don't know, exactly. Your daughter remembers having an argument with her campmate and storming off down the beach. She was found unconscious. Those marks are puzzling though."

"The bruises on her neck?" Suzi asked.

"No. It's obvious someone attempted to strangle her. I'm referring to the scorch marks on her wrist. Your daughter doesn't remember how she got them."

Joy's jaw tightened, and her eyes grew wide. With the sheet covering her from the neck down, Grace's wrists hadn't been visible. Could Harmony be capable of such a thing?

The doctor continued. "Those wounds will heal, so there's no need for worry. Maybe she leaned too close to the fire or burned herself on the fire ring."

Finding her voice, Joy asked, "But the baby didn't survive? You're sure?"

"I'm sorry. Whatever trauma your daughter experienced, the child couldn't endure it."

Joy slumped in the seat and leaned into her friend. "This is all my fault. I should have said something."

"Pardon?" Dr. Tory asked. "How is this your fault?

Do you think the other young woman did this to her?"

Suzi jumped in. "She's distraught. You know how mothers get, thinking they can circumvent every mishap for their kids. Do you have children, Dr. Tory?"

"A boy and a girl, seven and ten."

"Then you know the feeling."

"Yes. We want to safeguard our children from every possible harm. It just isn't possible," the doctor sympathized.

Joy sat up. "Stop talking about me like I'm not here!"

"Sorry, honey," Suzi said. "We're not. And none of this is your fault."

"But—"

"Hush." Suzi kissed her cheek. "She'll be fine. Won't she, doctor?"

"Right now, she needs rest. Her throat will be sore, and it will be difficult to talk at first. We'll keep her overnight for observation, but she can probably go home tomorrow. The police will need a statement from her about the attack. Is her husband here?"

"Yes." Owen rushed over, a covered cup in his hand. "So, I can take her home tomorrow?" He squared his shoulders and glanced sidewise at his mother-in-law.

"Most likely. She'll need a few days of bed rest. I'll leave instructions for a follow-up visit at my office." Without saying anything further, she walked to the elevators and waited for the next car.

Joy reached out to her son-in-law and grasped his hand. "I'm sorry, Owen. I didn't mean to accuse you. I was upset."

"It's okay, Joy. It's a stressful time for all of us,

and we're all concerned about Grace." He returned the squeeze. "I'm going to sit with her tonight. I'll call you tomorrow."

Leaning back against the chair, Joy said, "All right. You know how to reach me. Let me know when she's home."

Suzi sat up straight. "That's it? We're leaving?"

"We can't do anything more right now," Joy said. "Suzi, will you drive me home?"

"Of course. Owen—" Suzi gave him a stern look "—take care of our girl." Her gaze never wavered.

He nodded. "Point taken. Just get Joy home, please."

Joy turned to look at her son-in-law as Suzi led her out.

He waved, then turned and walked into his wife's room.

Maybe he does still love her, Joy thought for the second time today.

Chapter 16

By the time they reached the house, it was nearly seven. Suzi dragged an overnight bag from the trunk of her car.

"You came prepared." Joy nodded at the suitcase.

"Well, duh." Her face twisted into a half smile. "Did you think I'd just slow down and have you tuck and roll as I passed your front door?"

For the first time that day, Joy gave a genuine smile. "No, I didn't suppose you'd leave me to my own imagination. What about Jester?"

"My neighbor will let him out and feed him. He's done it plenty of times when I'm only gone for a day."

Walking into the living room, the women sank down opposite each other on the leather couches. Neither spoke for several minutes. The stress of the day had finally taken its toll.

Joy bolted up. "Oh, my gosh! I forgot all about the tasting room. I left Harmony by herself. I'd better make sure everything is locked up."

"Well, you aren't going by yourself, in case she hasn't left yet." Suzi pushed to her feet and followed.

As they neared the building, Joy's shoulders relaxed at seeing no cars in the lot. Harmony had gone for the day. She wasn't sure she could face the young woman tonight. While Joy wasn't sure who would've tried to strangle Grace, she had no doubt where the burn marks came from…at least she thought she knew, as fantastical as it sounded.

The front door was bolted, which made Joy wonder how her new assistant had done so without a key. She unlocked the door and found the place tidy and ready for the next morning. As much as she hated to admit it, everything appeared to be in order. The register had been counted out and all the receipts left in an envelope on her desk in the back room.

Suzi checked the rear entrance and found it unlocked.

Harmony probably thought it best to lock the front and exit through the back. If nothing else, the girl was thorough, thought Joy.

Strolling back to the house, Joy asked, "Are you hungry?"

"Always!" Suzi brightened. "Can I help you make something?"

"Actually, I could use a few moments alone."

Suzi picked up her bag as they went through the entryway. "I can go home if you want me to. I just thought—"

"No!"

The blonde chuckled. "Okay, I'll stay."

"I want company tonight. How about I throw together a cheese and meat board with some crackers and condiments? I have some Jarlsberg, fresh mozzarella, and summer sausage."

"Sounds yummy. Mind if I open a bottle of your finest?"

"I think we both could use some. You know where the wine cellar is. Shall we reconvene in the kitchen?"

Suzi walked down the hall to a small room holding

a large wine refrigerator. "Meet you there. Any preference?"

"Nope. You pick." Joy walked toward the kitchen, then turned back. "And, Suzi?"

"Yeah?"

"Have I told you how much I love you?"

"Not necessary. I know."

****

With dinner prepared and the wine poured, the two sat at the counter. Suzi dove in and loaded up her plate, while Joy mostly picked at the food.

"So, are we going to talk about it? Or do you plan to brood while your imagination runs wild?" Suzi popped an olive into her mouth.

Joy sighed and put the cheese she was about to eat back on her plate. "This is so unreal. It's one thing for me to feel a jolt coursing through my body at Harmony's touch, but how could she actually burn someone?"

"At the risk of this getting too bizarre, maybe she isn't human?"

"You've got to be kidding me? There has to be another explanation."

Suzi crossed her arms and waited. Getting no answer, she walked to the plants on the windowsill, each having a solid green stalk with clusters of leaves at the tip. She plucked the sign out of one. Flipping it over, she gasped and dropped the packet to the floor.

Joy hurried over and picked up the stick. The front still read *Five Steps to Plane Celestia*, but the back listed a fourth step. Step 4: Melody.

Finding her voice, Suzi whispered, "What do you think that means?"

Joy shook her head, her eyes bugged wide.

"Maybe it wants you to sing to them. I've heard some plants thrive if the right music is played."

"Forget what the step means. How are these instructions appearing? And what happens when whatever those things are produce a flower or spore?" The pitch of her voice escalated. "Maybe we should quit looking for answers. It's obvious everything going on is related, and it all stems from *my* search for the past. All these happenings tell me I should stop before anyone else gets hurt or killed."

Sitting on a stool, Suzi patted the seat next to her. "Sit down."

With the seed label still in hand, Joy did as she was told. She gently placed it on the counter between them and stared as if in a daze.

Suzi gently took both her friend's hands in her own. "Look at me."

No response.

"Honey, look at me."

Bringing her vision into focus, Joy stared at the woman beside her.

"You can't stop now. *We* can't stop now. It's…it's like…it's like being in the middle of a roller coaster ride and deciding, 'Okay, I'm done now, I want off.' Yet, there's no way to stop and let you off in the middle. Whatever is going on, we need to ride it to the end."

"Suzi, I don't know what frightens me more— everything that's been happening or you beginning to make sense." Joy smiled. "I'll call Harmony and let her know I'm closing the tasting room for the rest of the week. There's no way I can be around her."

"And tip off the bolt-wielding witch you're on to her? She can't suspect you know she's involved."

Resting her elbow on the counter with her chin on her palm, she sighed. "But what do I really know? Maybe she doesn't have a clue about the reaction she causes in me. You saw the marks on Grace's neck. How could Harmony have done that?"

"She could have an accomplice."

"For what purpose? Despite arriving right when these weird things began, it could have no connection to her. We're probably overreacting. Let's focus on the other clues for now."

Suzi reached for her glass. "As long as you allow Detective Suzi to do a little Q and A with your new associate. Deal?"

"And how do you propose to do that without arousing her suspicion?"

Motioning with her arms toward the wine bottle like a game show hostess, she straightened her shoulders and said, "As your newest tasting room associate."

Joy crinkled her forehead. "Do you even *know* anything about wine besides how to drink it?"

"I've lived in the Oregon wine country all my life. Believe it or not, I've acquired a vast knowledge about the grape and its different varietals. Besides, you'll need help with Grace home recovering. What do you say?"

Joy laughed. "You're hired."

"I'll toast to that!" Suzi raised her glass.

"You do know when you're on the pouring side of the table, you don't get to taste, right?"

"Not even on breaks?" She pouted. "I'm kidding! I

need to stay sharp anyway, since I'll be pulling double duty—hosting customers *and* sleuthing."

"Let's tackle the rest in the morning. I'm beat."

Suzi helped clear dinner. "We need to figure out one thing first."

"What's that?"

She motioned over her shoulder with a thumb toward the plants. "Do you think they like classical, country, or jazz?"

Shaking her head, Joy left the kitchen.

Chapter 17

Joy phoned the hospital first thing in the morning. The nurse on duty told her Grace had slept fitfully throughout the night. Not waiting for Owen to call her as promised, she dialed him next.

"Hi, Joy. She's still sleeping," he whispered.

She heard soft footsteps and the click of a door closing. "Sorry to disturb you."

"It's fine. I was awake."

"How's our girl?" Joy needed to give him some reassurance that she didn't blame him for the horrible episode.

"She woke up several times. The doc said it might happen the first few nights. Once she gets checked out, I should be able to take her home. The police came by and took a statement from her. She couldn't tell much beyond feeling someone grab her from behind then passing out when the person squeezed her airway. They said she was lucky the culprit didn't succeed."

Tears welled in Joy's eyes as she thought of the horror her daughter must've endured. Had she been stalked? Did he or she sneak up behind her on the sand? Was Harmony involved? Aloud, she asked, "Should I meet you at home and help get her settled?"

"Um, Joy…I think it's best if you don't come by for a couple of days."

"You don't want me to see her?" She bolted to her

feet and gripped the phone tighter. "How…how does Grace feel about that?"

"I told you she isn't awake yet. Please, give her time. Your being there would force her to relive the trauma of the attack and losing the baby. It was difficult enough when she had to answer the policeman's questions."

Easing onto a stool, Joy had to admit he might be right. "Okay. But *please* have her call me later if she's up to it."

"I gotta go." He ended the call without acknowledging her request.

She stared at the phone puzzled at his adverse reaction to her coming by the house. Later in the afternoon she'd call Grace. Something wasn't adding up, and she wanted to get to the bottom of it.

Hearing Suzi pad down the stairs, Joy prepped the single-serve basket on the coffee maker and turned it on.

Seeing the mug filling, Suzi said, "Damn, you're a great hostess! When do we go see Grace?"

"We don't."

"What?"

She waited until the cup filled, then handed it to her guest. "Owen thinks it would be best not to have visitors for the first day or two."

"Well, Owen can just kiss my lily-white as—"

"No, he's right. He's afraid she'll relive the attack all over again and that she needs nothing but bed rest."

Adding cream and sugar to her coffee, she stirred it harder than necessary making it dribble over the sides. "Does that feel right to you?" She tore off a paper towel and mopped up her mess. "It sounds like he's hiding something. Do you think he and Harmony are in cahoots? Grace might be right in thinking she's the little hussy he's fooling around with behind her back."

"I'll admit, he's acting strange, but I don't think he would physically hurt his wife. And what reason would Harmony have to hurt Grace?"

"Hope you're right." Suzi walked to the back of the kitchen and opened the French doors leading to a covered patio. "Shall we go out to the veranda?" She spoke in a snooty accent.

"Great idea." After settling into an Adirondack chair, Joy inhaled the fragrance of the rose bushes lining her garden.

"If she's the other woman, she'd have plenty of motive."

Joy crinkled her brow. "What are you talking about?"

"Harmony. If she's the woman Owen is having an affair with, she may want to eliminate the competition," Suzi speculated.

"Even if she is, and we don't know for sure he's cheating, what motive would she have for hurting Grace? Couples split up all the time without harming their partner."

Suzi slurped loudly. "I guess I'll just have to find out. It might be a good idea for you to leave me alone with the voltage queen. She might get chatty if you're not around."

"I can't risk you being hurt." Joy set her empty mug on the table between them.

"Nothing weird has been happening to me, so I'd imagine I'm safe.

Joy shook her head. "I don't know about this idea."

"Well, I do." Suzi shoved herself out of the chair. "Let's get dressed and ready for work. I'll spend the day, and tomorrow you go see your daughter. Tell Owen he needs to handle some things at the warehouse, so you can get time alone with her."

Standing and walking inside, she said, "Let's see how things go today first."

"Aye, aye, captain." Suzi did a fake salute.

****

They ate breakfast in the kitchen before heading to the winery.

Wrapping her mouth around a fork full of fried eggs, Suzi's eyes lit up. "I almost forgot—I had a great idea!"

Joy glanced sideways at her. "Another one? Should I brace for impact?"

"It's not that earth-shattering." Suzi chuckled. "I was thinking about the license plate we found by the cliff. Do you remember my second husband, Nicky?"

"He was before my time."

"I'm not that much older than you."

Laughing, she said, "You know what I mean. He came and went before I knew you. What does he have to do with the car tag?"

"When we were married, he was a local patrolman. The most handsome one on the force. He looked like a Greek god—dark hair, smoldering eyes, abs to die for. And stamina? That man was *in-sane*! I'd come out of the bedroom—"

"Is there a point to this joyride down memory lane?"

Letting out a deep sigh, Suzi said, "Sorry. I have very fond memories of him."

"Hadn't noticed. Would you like a moment to compose yourself? Perhaps a cold shower?"

Taking a bite of her toast, she chewed as she spoke. "Nah, I'm good. Anyway, since we parted ways, he's worked his way up to police detective in Seattle." The bread was followed by her last piece of bacon.

"And how would you know this? You've been divorced at least twenty years, since you were about to cut loose husband number three when I met you. Please tell me you haven't been stalking the man on social media."

"Would I do something so low?" She wiped the grease off her fingers with a napkin then threw it on her plate. "Never mind, don't answer. Anywho, Nicky and I text each other occasionally. We parted on good terms. I decided I didn't like being married to both him and his mother, especially since her favorite word was 'grandchildren.' She thought we should have at least half a dozen."

Joy scratched her head. "That seems excessive."

"He moved on and married a *nice Greek girl*." Suzi accented the phrase making air quotes with her fingers. "Probably handpicked by Mommy. At last count they'd come close to their quota. I think her uterus waved a white flag after number five and requested amnesty."

"How does wife number two feel about you keeping in touch?"

"She used to go ballistic. The woman got paranoid and checked his phone constantly, according to Nicky. You'd think I was still sending him provocative photos of me." Suzi laughed. "So, he changed my contact name to Detective Fong, and she never suspected."

Joy put down her fork and grimaced. "How did he

come up with that name?"

"On our first date, he took me to Fong's Chinese Restaurant."

"Do you think he'd help us find the owner of the motorcycle?"

"I'll send him a picture, and he can run it through the system. Since this is kinda an ongoing case, he can skate around the rules a smidge. Besides, it will be coming from Detective Fong, so it must be work-related." She grinned.

Getting the slim metal plate from her purse, Joy handed it to Suzi, who took a picture and sent it with a brief text.

A response came back immediately. —*Happy to oblige, Detective Fong.*— A happy face emoji accompanied the message.

Chapter 18

"Mom," Grace's raspy voice came over the phone. "Can you pick me up from the hospital?"

"Of course, honey, but I thought Owen would be taking you home." Joy had mixed emotions over this request. *What happened now?*

Suzi stood up from where she'd been stocking the chardonnay in the refrigerator behind the counter and screwed up her face at Joy.

"I told him to leave. It hurts to talk. Can you just come get me?"

"I'll be there in half an hour."

"Thanks," her daughter said weakly.

"Should I come with you?" Suzi walked over.

"I really need you to stay here and open the tasting room. Harmony will arrive in fifteen minutes to help finish up. Would you mind?"

She put a hand on Joy's arm. "Go take care of your daughter. I've got this. Besides, I have a bit of my own…ahem…work to do if you know what I mean." Suzi waggled her eyebrows.

"Thanks." She gave her a quick hug then hurried to the house. As Joy drove down the driveway to the road, she passed Harmony on her way in. The younger woman tooted the horn and waved. Joy responded with a weak smile as she shot past.

****

Suzi looked around, hands on her hips. Through the window she saw her interrogation target parking her little blue car at the rear of the lot.

Going back to work, she looked at the board listing yesterday's tasting options. Deciding to go with the same line-up, she went into the storeroom to retrieve the reds. Hearing the bell over the door, Suzi waited for Harmony. The bell over the door chimed again. *Did she walk back out?*

"Why didn't you answer my calls this morning? And what the hell did you do to Grace?" The masculine voice belonged to Owen.

"My phone died. What do you mean, what did *I* do to her?" Harmony sounded even angrier. "The little witch accused me of screwing you."

Feet stomped closer to the counter. "I told you camping with her was a bad idea. How did she put you and me together anyway? As far as she knows, you recently arrived in town. Unless you told her out of spite?"

Suzi froze where she stood in the back room. This was better than subtly questioning Harmony. She had a ringside seat to the main event.

Harmony spoke in a calmer voice. "Quiet down before someone hears you. She asked to use my phone to call you because hers didn't have service. When she dialed your number, your name came up as being in my contacts."

"How stupid can you be?"

"How dare you?" Her voice escalated. "I'm not the one still trying to get the deed to the winery. When I met you three months ago, you said you practically owned the Mystic Swirl. A little over-exaggeration, don't you think?"

"I'll get it." A hand slammed on the counter. "Killing Grace wasn't part of the deal."

"It would have solved a lot of problems, wouldn't it? With Grace out of the way, you're the only logical one who could take over. I'm beginning to think you're having second thoughts. You still love her, don't you?"

"The woman treats me like the hired help."

Slipping into a seductive tone, she cooed, "Look, baby. You know I get jealous. I want us to be together. Please don't be mad. Can I help it if there happened to be a lunatic running loose on the beach who attacked her?"

What an operator, Suzi thought. *What's next, a few choruses of "You Don't Love Me?"* She strained to hear, but the voices faded to a murmur. After a few moments, Owen spoke louder.

"Damn, you make me crazy. You realize it'll take time for me to strong-arm her into giving me control, but she'll cave. She always does. After Joy retires, I'll have everything secured when I serve Grace the divorce papers. So, what did you tell her about my number being in your phone?"

"The most logical explanation—we're co-workers. If we run low on something here, I might need to call the warehouse."

"Did she buy it?"

"She went storming down the beach, so, probably not. You'll have to do some damage control."

"Might be a little tough right now. At the hospital this morning she confronted me, then called me a liar, and threw me out."

"That's why Joy left. I saw her on my way in. Do

you think Grace asked her for a ride?"

"Who else would she call? I'm going to meet them at the house and try to reason with her. It'll be hard to keep her mother out of it now."

"Want a little incentive..." Harmony's voice trailed off.

Taking a step closer to the open door, Suzi bumped into a tray of glasses, and they clinked together. Now that she'd been found out, she yelled as she walked toward the front, "Harmony, are you here? I was up at the house when Joy asked me to come help...oh, Owen."

The couple quickly stepped apart. Suzi didn't flinch, but her voice grew icy. "I didn't know you were here. Joy went to pick up *your wife*. Have a bit of a tiff this morning with *our girl*?"

"Hello, Suzi. I suggest you stay out of *our* family business."

Not to be outdone, she countered, "Of course, I'll stay out of your marriage. Now, if you don't mind, Joy asked me to help with *her* business." Turning to the young woman. "Good morning, Harmony. Can you see what's left to do before we have customers? Joy began but had to hurry off and asked me to assist."

"Sure, Suzi. Glad she was able to get help on such short notice." Her brow furrowed in confusion. "We'll probably need more reds." Turning to Owen, she added, "Thanks for the update. I hope Grace will be up and about soon. I feel awful having left her, but thought she'd gotten a ride."

Owen nodded at Harmony, glared at Suzi, then left.

"Too-da-loo, Owen," Suzi called in a cheerful voice.

****

Joy arrived at the hospital in record time. Parking in the visitor's lot, she practically ran inside to where Grace waited in a wheelchair. She bent down, and her daughter wrapped her arms around her and cried softly.

"Shhhhh. Let's get you home," she cooed.

"Can I…" Grace's voice faded. As she wiped her eyes, she tried again. "I want to stay at your place."

"Whatever you want, honey. Should we stop by your house and pack a bag?"

She nodded, still hanging on to her mother's hand as a nurse wheeled her to the exit.

Driving along the twisty road, Joy reached over and squeezed her daughter's hand. "We'll pick up your stuff and get you settled in your old room. You don't have to talk about anything until you're ready."

Grace nodded, then leaned back into the seat and fell asleep.

When they pulled up to the house, Owen's car sat in the driveway. Joy gently shook her awake and pointed to the car. "Do you want to talk to him?"

She shook her head adamantly.

"I'll ask him to stay away until you get your things. Wait here." Joy got out and walked into the house.

Owen immediately met her in the entryway. "I need to talk to Grace."

"That is not going to happen. She's asked to stay with me, and we're here to get a few of her belongings. I don't know what happened at the hospital, but she does *not* want to see you right now. If you're at all concerned about her well-being, you'll honor this request."

"Joy, you have no idea what's going on. She has

some mistaken idea that Harmony and I—"

She held up a hand. "I don't want to talk about this now. Grace needs rest. Please don't interfere or turn this into something ugly. I have no problem calling the police and pressing harassment charges if you don't step back."

Setting his jaw, Owen conceded. "Fine. I'll wait in the kitchen until you've gone."

"Thank you." Joy went back to the car and helped Grace into the house and upstairs to her bedroom.

The young woman pulled clothes from the closet and drawers then gathered toiletries from the bathroom, placing everything on the bed. "Ask Owen for my large suitcase. It's in the garage," she whispered.

Joy found him in the kitchen. "She needs her large bag from the garage."

"I'll get it. Joy, you must let me speak with her," he pleaded.

"She doesn't want to see you right now. Please respect her wishes."

"You do realize we *both* lost a child. It wasn't only hers." He left to retrieve the suitcase.

For the first time, Joy thought about everyone who had lost something last night. Grace lost a child. Owen lost his namesake. She'd lost a grandchild. Steadying herself on the counter, she awaited her son-in-law's return. When he handed her the luggage, she thanked him with a nod.

Good to his word, Owen stayed away and allowed the women to leave without interaction. By the time Grace had been ensconced in her old room, it was nearly two o'clock. Her appetite eluded her. She needed sleep more than anything else and drifted off before Joy had left the room.

****

Assuming her daughter would be asleep for a while, she went to check on the winery. The parking lot didn't look too busy, but there were a couple of tour vans. As she entered, the crowd inside appeared to be having a grand time with lots of laughter. Crowded around Suzi at one end of the tasting venue was a group of older women, all looked to be in their late sixties. One of them wore a bright pink tiara in her white hair with a matching sash proclaiming "Bride." The other four wore silver tiaras and their sashes read "Bridesmaid." Her *new* associate appeared to be having as much fun as the ladies.

Harmony assisted six young Japanese tasters, probably from the other tour group. Their driver, wearing a black polo shirt with the company name on it, waited off to the side. Usually, once they'd introduced the group, they hung back until their passengers were ready to move on.

Harmony glanced her way, then immediately turned back to her customers. The young woman had a concerned look on her face. Two men leaned on the counter as they read the wine descriptions. An older couple stood near them holding wine glasses and an opener. The husband looked from Suzi to Harmony, trying to catch the attention of either one.

Stepping in, Joy asked, "May I help you?"

"Yes," the man said. "We want to buy these items and a bottle each of your cabernet and merlot."

"Of course. Are you interested in tasting today?"

"We were here yesterday and came back to purchase more wine. Your reds are fabulous, especially the merlot," the wife answered.

"I'm glad you enjoyed them. Let me ring those up for you." She walked behind the counter and gave Suzi's arm a light squeeze as she passed by. While wrapping the purchase, she asked the two men, "Are you gentlemen waiting to sample some wine?"

The shorter of the two had shaggy brown hair drifting into his eyes. "Yes, but no rush. We're still making our selections. You finish with these folks, and then we'll be ready."

A steady stream of patrons came and went, barely giving the three workers a chance to exchange more than pleasantries. Joy became anxious, wanting to go back to the house and check on Grace but couldn't leave her staff with such a busy afternoon. She checked her cell but found no messages or missed calls. When the final purchase had been made at almost five, she flipped the closed sign around.

Suzi didn't waste any time. "Hey, Harmony, why don't you run along. Joy and I can get the room cleaned up."

"I don't mind staying."

"Suzi's right, Harmony. We'll wrap things up here." She kept her distance from the young woman. "Thanks for holding down the fort yesterday."

"No problem. I can't help feeling this ordeal with Grace is my fault. How is she?" She stepped closer to Joy.

"She's…she's fine." Joy inched away and busied herself clearing dirty glasses.

"Maybe I'll swing by her house on my way home and see if Owen will let me talk with her. I want to apologize."

Joy said, "She's sleeping."

Harmony hesitated a moment before asking, "How would you know that?"

She stopped. "Grace will be staying here for a while. She and Owen have some things to work out, and she felt more comfortable staying with me. For right now, it's probably best if you'd leave her alone too." It took all her will to look Harmony in the eye, but she stood her ground as only a protective mother could.

"Oh." Harmony held a firm gaze. "If you think it's best. Please let her know I asked about her and will come see her when she's up to it." Walking into the back room, she returned with her purse.

Before the young woman reached the door, Joy added, "Since you're off the next couple days, I'll see you Saturday."

"If you need help—"

"We've got this covered," Suzi chimed in. "See you Saturday."

Harmony didn't turn around as she left. "Right, see you on the weekend." Her voice had a touch of annoyance.

The women watched her walk to her car. Before getting in, she glanced back and flashed a smug grin, eliciting a gasp from Joy. A shiver of fear sliced through her body, though she couldn't pinpoint exactly why. Did she have reason to fear Harmony? Shaking the ominous feeling away, she turned to Suzi. "How did today go?"

"I'd forgotten how much fun working a tasting room could be. Did I mention I worked a couple throughout high school and college?"

"I guess you forgot that little tidbit. Here I thought

you were diving in with your eyes closed. So, are you going to tell me why we hustled her out of here?"

As they cleared the glasses and loaded the dishwasher, Suzi recounted the conversation she'd overheard earlier.

"Are you sure they didn't know you were listening?"

"Positive. When my clumsy rear bumped the glasses, I acted like I'd just come in the back door. I'm sure they didn't suspect anything. Besides, they were too busy making kissy faces. Now, the real question is what are we going to do about this?"

"The first thing I'm doing is firing Harmony. It sounds like she's intentionally trying to break up Grace's marriage. How does Owen believe he'll get the deed to this place?"

Suzi leaned against the counter. "You know how Grace lets him walk all over her. He thinks he'll have no problem pushing her into letting him run the winery."

"He can run it all he wants. My daughter's name will be the only one on the ownership papers. I'm glad she wanted to stay with me. Knowing this makes me fear for her life. What if Harmony did try to kill her? The next time she might succeed. We should go to the police."

"With what? The police already took a statement. Whoever attacked her came from behind. We have no proof. Besides, they'll claim what I heard was only hearsay. Both Owen and Harmony could deny it."

Joy sat on the edge of her desk. "I have to do something to protect my daughter."

"What if Grace isn't really the target?"

"Huh?"

"Think about it." Suzi paced. "What if it's just a ruse, and you're the intended victim? Maybe someone from Michael's past blames you for his death and is out for vengeance."

"That's a bit farfetched, don't you think?" Changing the subject, Joy asked, "Did you get anything out of Harmony about her past?"

"No. After her award-winning performance with Owen, I didn't want to raise any red flags. She might've figured out I'd heard their conversation."

"All the same, she's not coming back to work here. Whoever she really is, I don't want her around." Locking the back entrance, she followed Suzi to the front and flipped the lights off. As they walked to the house, she asked, "Do you want to stay for dinner?"

"Thanks, but I'm gonna grab my bag and head home before Jester thinks I've abandoned him."

Chapter 19

The sounds of mellow jazz lured the women into the kitchen where they found Grace sipping cinnamon tea. The darkened bruises could be seen above the scoop neckline of her pajama top. Her long sleeves concealed the scorch marks the doctor mentioned.

"How's my favorite niece?" Suzi threw her arm around the young woman's shoulders.

Without answering, Grace leaned into her aunt.

"I didn't mean to abandon you for so long, but the tasting room got busy." Joy grabbed a cup to make herself tea and motioned with another toward Suzi.

She shook her head. "Thanks, but I've gotta get going. I'll come back tomorrow and help with customers. Take care, kiddo."

Grace smiled.

"I'd tell you not to, but I could really use the help. Thanks."

The front door clicked as Suzi left.

Joy dropped a tea bag in a cup and poured hot water over it. While the brew steeped, she walked to the entry and turned the lock. Securing the downstairs windows, she went to the back of the house and did the same.

Back in the kitchen, she asked, "Would you like something to eat? Maybe some soup?"

Grace smiled at the suggestion. "If you have some

of your creamy homemade chicken and vegetable soup, I wouldn't say no."

"I'll put the ingredients on the shopping list for tomorrow. Would you settle for a can of organic chicken with rice?"

"That'll work. It feels good being home." Her voice rasped, like it still hurt to talk.

Tears moistened her eyes at her daughter's words. Not wanting her to see, Joy got up and went about heating the soup. She set out two bowls and spoons. With her back still to Grace, she stirred the pot sending the soothing aroma of chicken broth wafting throughout the sitting area. "I'm going to tell Harmony she needs to find another job. I don't think it's a good idea for her to be here anymore."

No response came at first. After a moment, Grace said, "I think that's a good idea. Inviting her to work here was a mistake."

Sensing there was more than her daughter let on, Joy chose not to bring it up anymore this evening. Tomorrow would be soon enough.

They ate their dinner with little conversation, allowing the sorrowful notes of the saxophone from the radio to fill the void. Grace turned in early, and Joy decided it best to call Harmony immediately and get her termination out of the way. She'd never had to fire anyone before, and it didn't sit well with her. The decision left no room for doubt that she was doing the right thing.

Dialing the girl's number, it rang five times before going to voicemail. Feeling like a coward, she left a message anyway. "Harmony, it's Joy. While I appreciate all the work you've done, I think it would be best if you found another job. I'll mail your last paycheck to the address on file. Best of luck."

She hit the end button and relaxed her shoulders as if a huge weight had been lifted. Now, how would she handle relations with Owen? If what Suzi overheard was true, she needed to keep him as far from Grace as possible. This would take a little more finesse than a simple phone call. She decided to discuss it with her daughter first. His not working here would affect her life too.

****

"Why would my mother-in-law be calling you? Did you get caught with your fingers in the till?" Owen asked as he traced Harmony's breast beneath the sheet.

She held the phone in her hand. "Maybe she has a sixth sense and knows her precious daughter's husband is being naughty." Grabbing his finger, she stuck it in her mouth and sucked.

Running the tip over her teeth, he traced across her lips and down her chin, planting it back where he started. "Looks like she left a message."

"I'll listen to it later. Maybe Joy decided that weird friend of hers couldn't handle the tasting room tomorrow and wants me to work." Tossing the phone on the nightstand, she rolled onto her side and covered his mouth with hers. After a long kiss, she pulled back. "We'll have to thank her for leaving you free to have a houseguest."

"Then we'd better not waste a moment of our good fortune." Owen flipped her onto her back pinning her body with his own. "Now, where were we?"

****

Later in the kitchen over a post-coital snack,

124

Harmony and Owen discussed changes they wanted to make at the winery once he took control. The aroma from the reheated lasagna filled the room.

Harmony went back to the bedroom and grabbed her phone to check the voicemail her employer had left. Listening to the message, a smug grin spread across her face. She retrieved her clothes from where they lay scattered on the floor and got dressed.

"Leaving so soon?" Owen asked as he walked in and wrapped his arms around her waist. "I thought you would spend the night. No reason to scurry away when you've got tomorrow off."

Tracing his mouth with her finger, she said, "Actually, I'll be working. Joy's message asked if I could come in tomorrow."

"Why can't you spend the night and go to your place in the morning?" He pouted like a child, sticking out his lower lip.

"If I stay, I doubt either one of us will get much sleep. I'm sure Grace will be spending at least a few days at her mom's house. We'll have plenty of time to misbehave." She pulled away and grabbed her phone. "I think I left my purse in the kitchen. Hey, it probably isn't a bad idea for you to stay away from the tasting room. You need to mend fences with little wifey, or our whole plan goes to hell. Let's not add fuel to the fire by having her see you and me anywhere near each other."

Owen followed her down the stairs. "I hate it when you're right. Even if Grace doesn't see us, we can't afford her mother reporting back either. We'll have to behave ourselves for a while."

Tucking her cell into her purse, Harmony gave him a lingering farewell kiss.

"Come back tomorrow night. I'll pick up sushi from the local place in town on my way home."

"I'll let you know. Since I won't have tomorrow off, I have a few of my own errands to take care of."

"What could you possibly have to do, except me?" He waggled his eyebrows as his hand slid around her backside and cupped a butt cheek.

Giving one more smooch, she pulled away. "You'd be surprised." Harmony threw the strap of her bag over her shoulder and left through the side door.

****

The drive to her place took about twenty minutes. Harmony rented a small guest casita behind a large, four thousand square foot house. The couple who owned it mainly used the home in the summer, which allowed her to come and go unnoticed. They wouldn't be in residence for another month and a half.

She unlocked the front door. A pair of black biker boots with silver buckles on the sides sat by the entry. Harmony assumed he parked his motorcycle out back as requested. Not that anyone would take note, but she needed to play this smart.

In the bedroom, Cutter lounged across the comforter reading. The man was naked from the waist up except for a gold chain with a black vial hanging around his neck. His sun-kissed skin accentuated a muscle-bound torso. The only blemish a jagged scar above his left hip where he'd been knifed in a fight. A thin film of road dust covered his faded jeans with the hemline fraying in spots.

"I thought I had the place to myself tonight," Cutter said with a touch of sarcasm. He set the book upside down on the nightstand. "Did lover boy kick you

126

out?"

"No man dictates what I do." Her eyes flashed. "I'm the one calling the shots, even when he thinks it's him. I thought you'd be lying low for a while. It doesn't look good having a stranger show up after a woman got attacked on a nearby beach."

"Don't get paranoid. Nobody'll connect me to what happened. Strangers roll through here all the time. I must've passed a dozen bikes on the road in the last few days. Besides, I've been here two weeks. There's even a couple of loners staying at the same boarding house with me. Both arrived after I did."

Harmony glared at the dust patches left on her burgundy bedspread.

Placing his hands behind his head, he leaned into the pillows lining the headboard. "Since you're *calling the shots*, what's our next step?"

"I'm working on it. Joy threw a wrench in my plans, so I need to regroup and hit her again when she's not looking." Harmony walked into the bathroom, washed off her makeup, and put on an identical necklace. The black vial nestled between her breasts. She removed her blue-tinted contacts to reveal jet-black eyes with a gray pupil. After tossing her clothes in the hamper, she returned to the bedroom, and allowed him to drink her in. Then she turned, got a pair of pajama shorts and tank top from a drawer, and moved to put them on.

Cutter leapt to his feet and swept her up in his arms. "You won't be needing those."

"I've already done this tonight." Exasperation dripped from every syllable. "Put me down."

"No."

Her ebony eyes blazed darker. The onyx in his deepened as well.

"I'm not in the mood for this tonight. You can stay, but you're sleeping on the couch."

He laughed, still gripping her to him. "You're not in any position to give orders right now. Remember, *you're* the one who asked *me* for help. Some privileges I will take—not wait for them to be offered." He carried her to the bed and threw her down.

Instead of jumping off, she threw her hands behind her head and grinned, watching him remove his denims and black briefs. "Then come *take* what it is you want."

Sliding on top of her, he murmured in her ear, "Oh, I intend to." He devoured her lips with his, then added, "His stench is all over your body. Haven't you heard of showering after sex?" He nibbled her ear.

She feigned trying to push him off before countering, "It never bothered you before."

Chapter 20

When Joy came downstairs in the morning, Grace sat in the kitchen with a mug cradled in her hands. The same jazz station from yesterday played on the radio. She tucked a stray strand of hair behind her daughter's ear, a gesture she'd been doing since Grace had been a young child. "How're you feeling, sweetie?"

"Fine," Grace whispered. The bruises on her neck had turned a mottled yellow and light purple. Her pushed-up sleeves revealed ugly gray marks on her wrist making Joy gasp. There were four parallel lines on one side with a fifth opposite—finger marks. She'd been grabbed.

"Does that hurt?" Joy pointed to the scorch marks.

"It's a little sore but looks worse than it feels. The doctor said the burn was mild, as if I'd touched a hot pan or boiling water. Kind of weird they're gray and not red though. She said it would heal but might leave a scar. Honestly, I don't remember burning myself on anything."

Joy made herself coffee then joined Grace at the counter. "You hungry?"

"Not really. It's sore when I swallow. Maybe I'll have some yogurt later."

"We need to talk about a couple of things," Joy said.

Grace snorted out a laugh, then rasped, "You want

to talk when I can't?" She placed a hand to her throat.

"Timing is everything." She grinned. Her daughter mustering a sense of humor eased some of the tension in Joy's muscles.

"Okay, shoot."

"I fired Harmony. And I'm thinking about firing Owen."

Grace put her cup down. "I'm glad about Harmony. After our argument at the beach, I have to admit, she frightened me. I couldn't say why, but there was something about her. More than my thinking she and Owen fooled around."

Joy refrained from sharing the conversation Suzi overheard. "What about Owen?"

She leaned back and bit her lip. "You know when I went to Portland last week?"

"Yes. Your girl's trip."

Grace hung her head. "That's what I told you and my husband. I'm sorry, Mom. I didn't want to worry you."

Joy sat up straight. "Now you're scaring me. Where did you go?"

"To see a lawyer—a divorce lawyer."

"Oh, sweetie. I would have gone with you. Why didn't you tell me?" Joy patted her daughter's hand.

"I needed to go alone. You understand, don't you?"

"Of course. Did…did you know you were pregnant at the time?"

"Uh-uh. When the doctor told me I'd miscarried, I didn't believe her at first." Grace's voice caught, and tears welled in her eyes. She wiped them with the back of her hand. "Maybe someday it will happen with a man who loves me."

"I understand," Joy said. "You'll have a family with the right man. Now this all makes sense. You didn't want me to give you the winery, because if you owned it while married to Owen, he'd be entitled to half when you divorced."

Grace nodded. "And I'll be damned if I'm paying him alimony either. For now, if you can stand it, please keep him employed."

"Whatever you want, honey. I agree he needs to be kicked out on his backside, but I understand about not wanting to support him. He'll stay on the payroll until after it's final. When will you serve him?"

"The paperwork is supposed to be ready next week. Until then, can I stay here?"

"You can stay as long as you want; you know that. I just want you to be happy." Joy stood to refill her coffee. She pointed at Grace's cup. "More tea?"

She shook her head. "I'm a bit tired. Woke up too early. Think I'll go read in bed and maybe get more sleep." Grace got up and pulled her sleeves down.

"Let me know if you need anything," Joy called as her daughter left the kitchen. She took the dirty teacup to the sink where she almost dropped it. The Celestia plants had each grown a flower bud, tightly closed, but they hadn't been there yesterday. Out of curiosity, she flipped one of the markers over, but the instructions remained at four. *What would the fifth step be?*

****

Suzi rushed into the tasting room at nine-thirty.

"Ready to work?" Joy set a tray of wine glasses behind the counter.

"You betcha!" She put her purse in the back room and carried another tray of glasses to set behind the counter at the other end. "What's on the menu today?"

Joy looked at the whiteboard. "Same line-up as yesterday. The new batch of merlot needs another week, but we still have some of last year's to finish up."

Mid-morning Suzi stepped into the back room and squealed.

Both Joy and her customers froze and looked toward the doorway. Joy excused herself to investigate.

Suzi danced a little jig.

"What on earth—"

"He found a name and an address!" She flung her arms around Joy, continuing to jump up and down.

"What?"

"Nicky. My ex. The cop in Seattle? He found out who the license plate belonged to."

"Really? That was quick." Joy absorbed some of Suzi's enthusiasm bouncing around the room.

She waved her phone. "Modern technology. It's all the rage, you know."

"Guess it isn't that surprising. What did he find out?" Joy asked.

Suzi plopped down onto the desk chair. "Wow. That took a lot out of me." She read the phone screen. "He says the license plate belonged to a Casey Pearce, who lived in Pahrump, Nevada."

"Where's that?"

"No idea." Suzi tapped her screen then typed in the town. "Looks like it's about an hour outside of Las Vegas."

"Excuse me." A woman's voice called from the tasting room.

Joy slapped her forehead. "I forgot we had customers. We'll finish this later." Returning out front, she apologized. Despite the distraction of the first solid lead they'd gotten, Joy did her best to focus on the patrons.

When they had a breather between tasters, Suzi read the text messages from her ex-husband. "He says the guy still lives in Pahrump, and Nick sent a current address. He also wants assurance I won't stalk the man." She laughed. "He's always been a clown. I told him why you wanted the information, and he was glad to help."

"This is getting real." Joy leaned on the counter.

"There's a phone number here too. Why don't you call him?"

"And say what? I'm sending a picture in hopes he can identify me? I don't want to scare him off in thinking I'm some lunatic."

Suzi raised her arms. "Then what was the point in finding the owner if you're not going to do anything with the information?"

"Oh, but I *am* going to do something. I'm going to talk to him in person. Even if he denies knowing me, his body language might transmit otherwise. A phone call wouldn't give me that insight."

Her friend clapped her hands together. "Road trip! I've always wanted to go to Vegas. When do we leave?"

Joy pressed her lips together. "Sorry, Suzi, but I need to do this trip alone. Besides, you're the only one I can trust to stay with Grace. Will you take care of our girl while I'm gone?"

Her face fell along with her enthusiasm. "If that's what you really want. We could always get one of Grace's girlfriends to check in on her. Are you sure you'll be safe going alone?"

"Why wouldn't I be? All I'm going to do is go talk to the man. As far as my daughter, I'd feel better if you were here given the problems between her and Owen right now."

"You got it. Aunt Suzi will keep the lions at bay." She struck a prize fighter's pose.

"That's what I'm counting on." Joy chuckled. "I'll close the tasting room for a few days next week and fly to Nevada. Thanks for understanding."

"Of course. No need to close the winery. I can run it. This way I can be close to Grace without smothering her. She'll be up and around by then and can help if it gets busy."

Joy crossed her arms. "Let me talk to Grace first before we make definite plans. She may not be up for socializing with strangers. Besides, I still need to figure out what to tell her about my trip."

"The truth is always a good option." Suzi tapped the top of her head. "She'll resent it if you don't level with her up front."

"I suppose you're right. Grace will find out eventually, so it might as well be now. I'll talk to her tonight." Joy nodded toward the door, where a van full of customers approached.

"Looks like show time again." Suzi perked up and put on a huge smile.

Chapter 21

"What if I came with you?" Grace's fork clattered onto the plate next to her untouched dinner.

"Honey, this is something I need to do alone. Don't look at it as if I'm shutting you out. I don't know what I'll find, if anything, once I arrive in Pahrump. If this Casey Pearce is part of Michael's family, he may be bitter about my living and Michael's dying." Joy pushed the pasta around her plate. The heavenly aroma of melted cheddar and parmesan sauce failed to spur her appetite.

Grace's voice came out in a hoarse rasp but had a much stronger tone. "All the more reason you shouldn't do this alone. Is Aunt Suzi at least going with you?"

"No. She'll be running the tasting room while I'm away. Do you think you'd be up to helping her? Otherwise, we can close for a few days." Betrayal roiled throughout Joy's body. She'd told her daughter about finding the license plate and tracking down the owner. However, the odd happenings regarding the raised mark on her wrist, the changing seed packets, and the necklace went unmentioned. Grace had endured enough over the last week and needed to be sheltered until Joy had concrete answers.

"When will you leave?" Grace attempted to eat her favorite comfort food.

"Tuesday morning out of Portland. I've already

booked my trip to Las Vegas and will return Thursday afternoon. The flight is only a couple of hours, so I'll have a little over two days to contact this Casey."

Her daughter took a small bite and chewed slowly. She grimaced while swallowing. "I'll help Aunt Suzi hold down the fort if that's what you want me to do."

Joy's jaw slackened, and she no longer gritted her teeth. "Thank you. It's a relief knowing you'll be here safe and sound. Should I ask Suzi to stay here while I'm away?"

"I'm not a child." She crossed her arms and stuck out her tongue, which elicited a laugh from her mother.

"Okay. No full-time babysitter. Just be sure to lock up so you don't have any uninvited guests. I don't know what your husband might try if he gets wind you're alone. Plus…"

"Plus, we don't know who attacked me and if they're still in town." Grace finished her mother's concern. "Everything will be locked up tight. Don't worry about me. I just hope you'll be safe. Promise me you'll stay in constant contact with either me or Aunt Suzi."

"Promise." Joy's appetite returned, and she made a small dent in the macaroni and cheese sitting before her.

****

The next morning a motorcycle roared up the drive to the parking lot of the tasting room. Joy and Suzi wouldn't be open for another forty minutes, and they had too much to do before ten o'clock to allow customers in early today. Joy hoped they'd understand and either come back or enjoy a walk around the vineyard or picnic area off the side of the building.

When a knock on the door interrupted their set-up, Joy exchanged a puzzled look with her co-worker before walking to the front window. A woman stood with her back to Joy, and a tall man with shaggy, dark hair and the darkest eyes she'd ever seen faced her. He gestured with his head, and the woman spun around.

"Joy, please let me in," Harmony said, her voice a bit muffled through the glass. "I want to explain a few things."

Joy turned away, and her shoulders sagged. "It's Harmony."

"What's *she* doing here?" Suzi demanded. "Do you want me to get rid of her?"

"She's with a man."

"Who?" Suzi stormed over to the window and looked out. She spun back to Joy. "He's scary looking."

Joy had to admit the older woman was right. With his black leather boots and vest, the man could intimidate the bravest of men. *What if Harmony wanted to cause more trouble and brought him along to help?* Pushing her fears aside, she unbolted the door. "We should at least talk to her."

"No!" Suzi threw her body against the door. "Let's think about this a minute. An employee you just fired, who may have harmed your daughter, shows up with a thug to *talk*? What if she goes postal?" Her voice lowered. "He might be armed."

"Suzi, I can hear you," Harmony yelled. "We're not here to harm anybody. I need to talk to Joy. This whole thing is a huge misunderstanding. Please give me a chance."

Joy gently pulled Suzi out of the way. "Let's hear her out." She opened the door, and a wave of nausea coursed through her. Her legs wobbled, and she gripped the door frame to keep her balance.

Harmony reached for her. "Joy, are you okay?"

Suzi stepped in between them and stood toe to toe with the young woman. Despite the height difference, she held her ground, even if she couldn't look Harmony directly in the eye. "Don't you touch her."

Joy backed away. The nausea subsided leaving her mouth parched and dry. She walked to the water pitcher on the end of the counter and downed two cups. Taking a deep breath, she faced the entry. "Harmony, as I stated in my voicemail, I think it's best you find other employment."

Harmony attempted to step around Suzi, who bobbed and weaved to block the woman's every move past the doorway. The scene bordered on comical.

Cutter inched forward, and his gaze pierced through Joy. "Look, lady, either call off your—" he snorted "—fluffy guard dog, or I'll move her out of the way."

"Fluffy?" Suzi puffed out her chest. "I'll have you know I'm trained in *several* forms of martial arts as well as some minor arts."

Joy picked up her phone from the counter and punched in 911 but didn't hit send. "A touch of the screen, and the police will be called. Harmony, if your large companion so much as breathes on Suzi, I'm placing the call."

Harmony backed away and raised both arms in front of her. "Whoa. Everyone, calm down. Like I said, I just want to talk." Without turning, she said, "Cutter, back the fuck down. I didn't bring you along to make the situation worse."

"Suzi, it's all right. Let her say her piece," Joy said.

With two fingers forming a vee, Suzi made a motion pointing at her eyes, then to Cutter's, then back to her own. She retreated to stand beside Joy.

Cutter smirked and put up both hands in a surrender position.

Harmony took a step forward. Before she could get any closer, Joy said, "Far enough. You can talk from there."

Her blue eyes glared, but her lips formed a polite smile. "Fine. All I wanted to say is I didn't hurt Grace. The things she accused me of aren't true. To prove it, I wanted to introduce Cutter, my boyfriend." She gestured to the hulk, who stood behind her.

"How convenient." Suzi crossed her arms and leaned against the counter.

"I don't need to prove anything to you, Suzi. Stay out of it," Harmony snarled.

"That's where you're wrong." Joy stood up straight. "This woman is just as much a part of my family as my daughter. You will treat her with respect."

Harmony narrowed her eyes. "Fine. That's all I wanted to say. I have a boyfriend. We've been together for over five years. So whatever Grace or the two of you believe is going on between Owen and me, isn't true."

Suzi scowled and pointed. "How do we know you're not cheating on Cut—"

"Suzi, it's okay. Let Harmony finish. We have a tasting room to prepare before patrons arrive." Joy nodded for her former employee to continue.

"That's all I wanted to say, other than I'm sorry my job here didn't work out. I enjoyed spending time with both you and Grace." She side-eyed Suzi with pursed lips.

Suzi snorted and looked away but remained silent.

"Please tell Grace I hope she's better soon, and I'll miss her."

Joy nodded once.

Harmony followed Cutter out the door but stopped on the threshold. Turning her head, she added, "Both you and Grace should be more careful. Wandering alone in places you don't belong could have dire results." A menacing grin spread across her face.

Both older women stood motionless with their jaws dropping toward the floor. The door slammed. A moment later the motorcycle revved loudly then tore down the driveway, and the engine faded.

Suzi found her voice first. "Explain to me why you thought it a good idea to let her say her piece?"

Chapter 22

Wind jostled the aircraft as it descended toward the Las Vegas airport. Joy tightened her grip on the handrest as beads of sweat slid down the back of her neck.

Her seatmate put a hand on Joy's arm. "Don't worry, love," the woman spoke with a British accent. "I've lived here twelve years and landings are usually a bit bumpy. The pilots are used to it."

With a nervous smile, she nodded. The plane bounced one last time, then the wheels met the tarmac and they taxied to the gate.

Glad to be on the ground again, Joy retrieved her bag from the overhead bin and made her way to the door. From the concourse, she followed signs to the car rental area. One shuttle and another line later, she was on the road to Pahrump in her rented SUV. Construction hindered her progress as she approached Mountain Springs and descended back to the valley floor on the other side of the mountains.

Following the GPS, she arrived at her destination—a small, one-story home. The pink stucco walls and red tiled roof were typical of the surrounding desert construction. Keeping unrealistic hopes in check, she clutched her purse and approached the door. She pressed the bell and waited. Then waited some more. No answer. Ringing again, she shifted from one foot to the other. The eucalyptus trees on either side of the entryway emitted a soothing fragrance.

Reluctantly, Joy trudged back to the car. Maybe he was at work. She'd check into the hotel in town then come back this evening. As she opened the driver's side door, a motorcycle zipped past her into the driveway. The man jumped off the bike and punched a code into the garage door keypad. Looking up as he went back to the bike, he stopped.

She slammed the door closed and approached the rider.

When he removed his helmet, shaggy blond hair fell onto his forehead. The sun-worn crinkles around his eyes coupled with flabby jowls and a paunchy middle put him at about fifty years old. "Can I help you? Are you here to tell me I've won the lottery?" A grin spread across his face.

"Sorry…no." Joy's shoulders relaxed, realizing this might be more of an encounter than the confrontation she'd expected. "Are you Casey Pearce?"

"I am." His brown eyes were bright with curiosity as he removed his riding gloves.

Joy swallowed. "Did you know a man named Michael?" She bit her lip.

Casey narrowed his eyes and tilted his head. "Michael who? I know a couple."

Tension swarmed up her neck as she fingered the handle of her handbag. "I…I'm not sure of his last name. He would have lived in this area about twenty-two years ago." Her eyes wide, she hoped this man wouldn't turn her away without answers.

Almost a full minute passed as Casey rested his hand on the grip of his bike. With a sidewise glance, he asked, "Do you mean the bastard who stole my Harley?"

Thinking back to the police report, Joy remembered they had ridden on a Harley. There wasn't much left since it exploded on impact. "I believe so."

"Who are you, lady?"

"My name is Joy. I'm trying to find…well…Michael died twenty-two years ago. He went over a cliff. On your Harley." Her eyes welled with tears. She'd thought she could handle this trip, but maybe she was wrong.

"And how would you know this?" Casey remained calm, yet determination laced his voice.

He deserved the truth—or as much as she knew. "I know this…I know this because I rode on the back of the bike when he had the accident." Her legs shook, and she grabbed the backrest of the bike to steady herself. "Sorry. Maybe I shouldn't have come. I'm sorry to have disturbed you." She turned to leave and tripped on a weed sticking from a crack in the driveway.

"Wait!" Casey stepped forward and supported her arm. "Why don't you come inside? I don't bite." That contagious grin covered his face again. "Though I am a bit disappointed you're not here about my winning the lottery."

Joy attempted a weak smile, but it came out as a grimace.

Releasing her arm, he said, "Give me a minute to put my bike away." He set his helmet on a shelf just inside the door, then walked back to the bike and threw his leg over the seat. Starting the engine, Casey worked the clutch and eased the motorcycle into the garage. Hopping off, he motioned for her to follow.

As they went into the house, Casey hit the button to close the door behind them. "Would you like something to drink? Water, soda? Whiskey perhaps?" He smirked.

"Water would be great."

Gesturing toward the couch in the living room, he disappeared through the kitchen door, returning quickly with a bottle of water. He broke the seal on the lid and handed it to his guest.

"Thank you. You're very kind."

"I gotta admit, you've piqued my curiosity. You were Michael's girlfriend, huh?"

Taking a long drink, she felt the cold water slide down her throat. "I guess so. Do I look familiar at all?"

"Why would you? We've never met." He raised his hands in the air.

"How did you know Michael?"

"We worked at the local winery. I still do."

She did a double take. "Really?"

"Why is that surprising?"

Joy sighed. "I own a winery in Oregon. It seems like a coincidence. Anyway, you were friends?"

"I guess you could say that. We'd occasionally have drinks after work but not much else. We were both vintners mixing the red blends."

"How did he end up with your motorcycle?"

Doubt shadowed Casey's face. "If I can ask, why don't you know this if you were his girlfriend? And why don't you know his last name?"

Joy would have to come clean at some point if she wanted the answers she sought. She gulped more water. "My name is Joy. Not because I was born with that name, but because the doctor at the hospital, where they took us after the accident, gave it to me. I fell off the bike before it went over the cliff. Michael wasn't as lucky. I only lost my memory." She stopped and hung her shoulders. "He lost his life."

"Did you get your memory back?"

"No."

"Then how did you know to find me? Did you remember Michael mentioning my name?"

Joy explained to him about flashes of memories and dreams calling Michael's name. She also mentioned marrying Drake, and his loss a couple years prior.

"I see. Michael had asked to borrow my motorcycle for a trip because his girlfriend was visiting for a while. She said she wanted him to take her to see forests because she didn't like the desert. How did you find me without any recollection?"

"Using the police report, I got the location of the accident site and visited. Someone had erected a cross there. The friend who came with me accidentally knocked it over. We found this beneath it." Reaching inside her purse, Joy pulled out the license plate and handed it to Casey.

He studied it with recognition in his eyes as his fingers ran over the raised numbers and letters. "Wow. I always wondered what happened when he didn't come back. Michael was a bit wild, but it surprised me he'd not returned my bike. Guess I'll have to forgive him and take back all the cuss words I'd attached to his name." Looking up he asked, "So you survived, but don't remember anything?"

"Yes. There were flowers lying against the cross, where he...he went over the cliff. They couldn't have been there more than a month or two. Maybe his family found him and still honors his death. Do you know if he has any relatives in the area?"

Casey thought for a moment. "If I remember correctly, he lived with his parents."

"Do they still reside here?"

"They didn't live in town. Their place was in a remote area between here and a tiny burg called Tecopa. The house is actually in California. The border kinda wanders in this part of the state. I'd never been there, but he told me he had about a thirty-minute drive to work each day. Honestly, that's all I know."

Joy squeezed the bottle, and its plastic crackled. It sounded more like thunder as it echoed off the walls in the silence. "Would you know how to get there?"

"I could write down which roads to take. Couldn't give you the exact location, but he did say it was a big green house, and the nearest neighbor lived almost a mile away. Hopefully that'll be enough to locate the place if they still live there. Houses are pretty sparse around there, so it shouldn't be hard to spot."

"Can you remember anything else that might help me?"

Another moment passed as he sat with his face scrunched and biting his upper lip. "Sorry, no."

Setting the empty container on the coffee table, Joy rose and extended her hand, as Casey did the same. "Thank you for your help. Sorry about the motorcycle."

"I lost a bike. Seems to me you lost a lifetime." He went into the kitchen then returned a few minutes later with written directions. "Maybe if you find his folks, you can get some of those memories back."

Joy walked to the door then turned. "I hope so. Maybe they can help me find my parents or siblings if I have any. Do you remember his family name?"

"Tremont. Michael's last name was Tremont. Good luck, Joy."

"Thank you, Casey." Pulling a business card from the side pocket of her bag, she said, "If you remember anything else, I would appreciate you contacting me."

He took the card. "Will do." Closing the door behind her, he watched from the front window as she drove away.

****

Casey grabbed a bottle of beer from the fridge, took a gulp, then snapped his fingers. There had been a tasting room attendant whose last name was Tremont, but she'd quit a few months back. *What was that blonde's first name? Oh well, if she's related, Joy would find out from the family.*

Chapter 23

Following Casey's directions, Joy cruised the desolate highway through the desert. The road, which had no streetlights, wound past rock formations and around several tight turns. Definitely not somewhere she wanted to drive after dark. On the far side of a large set of boulders, she caught a glimpse of a green house. Making a quick right off the main road, she stopped at an old-fashioned, steel mailbox with a number but no name.

Joy pulled into the driveway of the dilapidated residence. Paint peeled from the sun-scorched siding, and the porch needed to be repaired in more than a few places. The front yard, if you could call it that, was dotted with scraggly palm trees and sagebrush poking out of the dust. Could Michael's parents live here? Would she be welcome? She got out of the car and approached the door, tentatively knocking.

A man with white hair and dark glasses answered. "Yes? Who is it?"

"My name is Joy. I'm looking for the family of Michael Tremont. Do you know them?"

The man remained silent several moments, before quietly saying, "Michael is my son." Squaring his shoulders, he asked more firmly, "Why are you looking for him?"

Joy shifted nervously, not sure if he was angry or

upset. "Do you know what happened to him?"

"He left years ago and never came back. Not a word since." His grip on the edge of the door tightened. "Do you know where my son is?"

Joy's eyes moistened. Trying hard to keep her voice from cracking, she asked, "May I come in and speak with you?"

Another hesitation, then his arm dropped to his side. "Of course, how rude of me. Please." He stepped back and allowed her entrance. "Have a seat on the couch."

Joy sat while he walked to a settee and felt for the handrest. Moving in front of it, he turned and eased down.

"How do you know Michael?" He looked in her direction, yet not directly at her.

Wringing her hands, Joy hesitated. She had prepared herself with the notion that his family knew about the accident and had left the cross and flowers. Apparently, she was mistaken. "I don't know how to say this, but your son died in a motorcycle accident twenty-two years ago."

The man slumped, squeezing the armrests. "I've always wondered." His chest heaved in and out with heavy breaths. Looking her way, he asked, "How did you know him?"

She avoided the question. "You never knew what happened?"

"He and his girlfriend rode off on a friend's motorcycle for a trip north. We never heard from them afterward. His mother and I thought the responsibility had grown too much for them."

Responsibility? While the sadness in the old man's

voice tore at Joy's heart, his reference filled her with confusion. Fearing he might shut down once he learned her identity, she avoided sharing too much. "I was a friend of his years ago. The police never notified you?"

"No. Were you with him?"

Chewing her bottom lip, Joy mustered her nerve. "Not exactly. Did you know his girlfriend?" Lying left a sour taste in her mouth.

"Not well. She'd only been here a week or so. The gal hated the desert and wanted to see the forest up north somewhere. Michael wouldn't tell us where they were going, just that they'd be back in a couple of days. Are you sure he's…he's dead?" The last words rasped from his lips.

"Yes." Her hands fidgeted in her lap.

Wiping his eyes beneath his glasses, the man murmured, "I'd always suspected. I knew he wouldn't intentionally leave us wondering all these years." He leaned into the backrest and took a deep breath.

Searching for a distraction from the awkward silence, Joy rose to examine the pictures sitting on the mantel. There was one of a young man—the man from her dreams. It had to be Michael, yet she felt no emotion at finally seeing his face for real. His brown hair curled on the ends, reaching partway down his neck. Piercing blue eyes stared back at her from the frame. He stood on a mountain with a sweeping green valley behind him. Her hands rested on the rough bricks as she struggled for some recognition to stir in her, but none came. At the next photograph, her face grew cold. Mustering her voice, she croaked, "Who…who is this…blonde woman in the picture next to Michael's?"

Despite the blow she'd delivered only moments

ago, his lips curved into a smile. "You must mean my granddaughter, Tru. She's a looker, isn't she?" His voice lifted as he spoke of the young woman.

"Yes...yes she is." Joy's hands trembled, as she touched the gold frame surrounding the angelic likeness of her former tasting room associate. "Is she Michael's niece?"

"What the hell are you doing here?" A plump woman with her hair raked into a tight bun stood in the front entryway. Grocery bags hung from each hand. A loose gray strand wavered across her cheek, having escaped the band holding it.

Joy's eyes widened. Maybe it was Michael's mother who left the flowers at the cross. "Do you know me?" Her hands balled into fists, the nails biting into her palms.

"You're older, but I'd know you anywhere. How could I forget the woman who lured my Michael away and abandoned her own child?"

Joy stumbled to the couch and fell onto the cushions.

The man rose on wobbly legs, his face turned toward Joy. "Justine, is that you?"

Looking from the old man to his wife and back to him, she asked, "My name is Justine?" She furrowed her brow. "I have a child? Michael and I left a child?"

"Get out of my house! You are *not* welcome here. Twenty-odd years later you think you can waltz back in and what? My son is gone because of you. And that wretched creature you bore has bolted."

Understanding settled into Joy's eyes. *She knew, but her husband didn't.* "Please, I didn't come here to upset you, but..."

"But what?" Michael's mother dropped the sacks onto the floor. "I told you to get out! Your child left. There isn't anything here for you. You can't go back. You've been banished, and because of your actions the portal has been sealed, which means we're trapped also. Not that they would have let us return with that creature anyway. Maybe had she not survived as expected, we might have had a chance."

"Banished? Not survive? I don't understand."

For the first time, the old woman hesitated. "What do you mean you don't understand? It's the law. The law you grew up with. You lured my son into a forbidden affair and produced a monster. I agreed to keep the child for the designated year until you recovered your memory. Guess once you did, you chose not to look back. Too much of a reminder of the man you got killed."

Her husband clasped his hands together. "Marla, what are you talking about? You knew our son was dead?"

"Yes, Benjamin." Her shoulders drooped. The tension in her face softened as she looked at her husband. "It seemed best if you thought he just left us. At least then you had hope he still existed somewhere happy and alive. When Justine didn't return after a year, I saw no point in hurting you."

Tears streamed down the man's cheeks. "You should have told me." He stomped his foot. "I had a right to know."

Finding her voice, Joy said, "I'm sorry. Maybe I shouldn't have come. I'd hoped to find answers as to who I am."

For the first time, Marla softened toward Joy.

"What do you mean who you are?'"

"After the motorcycle accident, I lost my memory."

Marla shook her head. "No...no you didn't. Silas, your father, caused that. It's the law. If he didn't enact it, someone else from the Council would have. But you got it back after a year, right?"

"Marla? That's your name? I've spent twenty-two years wondering who I am. What do you mean my father caused this? Do you know where he is? Does he live nearby?"

Wringing her hands, the old woman asked, "So you don't remember...anything?"

Joy moved toward the older woman. "No. Please help me. Where do I come from? And...and...why did my child leave you?"

"You've done too much harm to this family. Find your answers elsewhere!" Marla collected her groceries off the floor and carried them toward the kitchen.

Joy ran after her. "You have to tell me who I am! How do I find my father?"

Marla's face reddened as she set the bags on the floor once again. Turning to face Joy, she said, "Your father washed his hands of you. Just like you did with your own child."

"I...I couldn't have abandoned her. Tell me how I lost my memory if it wasn't in the accident. Tell me why you called my child a 'wretched creature.' "

With a calmness that frightened Joy more than her anger, Marla seethed, "I'll do better than tell you. I'll show you." She dragged Joy by the arm toward Benjamin and ripped the shaded glasses from his face. "This is why!"

Joy put a hand to her mouth. Her stomach churned,

and she wasn't sure she could hold back the bile rising in her throat. Benjamin stood cemented to the floor, his jaw tense. Where the color of his irises and pupils should have been, his eyes were coated in a milky white. "How...how did this happen?"

"Your *daughter* did this to him. Children like her, of mixed lineage, have a darkness about them. They don't normally live past the age of five. Somehow Tru beat the odds and survived to adulthood. Her evil grew, and her touch, when angered, can have dire consequences. Benjamin," Marla stuttered as she looked on the face of her husband, "is the kindest and gentlest man I've ever met." She put her hand on his cheek, then just as quickly turned back to Joy. "Your *child* got angry with him and sent tremors through him so powerful that it singed his eyeballs and left him blind. She should have been your burden to bear."

Joy backed away from Marla. "I...I didn't know. Please forgive me. I didn't know. How can I..."

"Get out of my house! Don't ever come back!"

"But...please...let me..."

"Get out." Marla shoved her so hard she almost fell over.

"Marla, stop. She's now the only connection we have to Michael," Benjamin pleaded as he stepped forward and reached for his wife.

"We don't need her." Marla leaned back into her husband as his hands wrapped around her waist.

With tears streaming down her face, Joy bolted out the front door, pounded down the steps of the porch, and didn't stop running until she reached her car. Once inside, she leaned her forehead against the steering wheel. The heat radiated off the metal into her skin.

Michael's family rejected her, and she left with more questions than answers. Who could help her now?

Chapter 24

Joy returned to her hotel in Pahrump and threw herself across the king-sized bed. Her body, wracking with sobs, melted into the organic cotton comforter. She lay there until she'd been drained of tears.

Her grumbling tummy reminded her she hadn't eaten all day. With incredible effort, she dragged herself into the bathroom and washed her face. After running a brush through her hair, she touched up her make-up, and spritzed on her favorite body spray. The fresh linen scent bolstered her spirits. She slipped on her shoes and went out to find dinner.

The desert heat sweltered around her the moment she stepped outside. The lengthening shadows offered no relief to the high temperatures. Despite being late April, the waning sun still baked everything it touched like mid-day in August.

Across the street she entered the Hot Tamale Mexican restaurant. The desk clerk at her hotel recommended it for good food and great margaritas. Rarely did she drink alcoholic beverages other than wine, but the traditional Mexican concoction enticed her. This trip had been nothing like she'd imagined, and she needed to reverse her downward spiral.

With the time almost six-thirty, the place bubbled with energy. Waitstaff rushed between the kitchen and the mostly full tables with sizzling trays of fajitas, enchiladas, and other dishes Joy couldn't identify. Her stomach did a double somersault reminding her it needed sustenance now. The seating hostess asked if she would mind sitting at the bar since she was dining alone. Joy agreed and found a stool at the end.

Before she had even a moment to peruse the menu, the bartender came to take her drink order. He rattled off the fruity flavors of their most popular margaritas, but Joy chose to go with the traditional style on the rocks. She waved off his suggestion to go large when she saw the fishbowl-sized glass.

"I know my limitations." Joy giggled. "Just bring me the regular one, thanks."

He shook his head and clucked his tongue causing her to laugh harder. "Okay. I bring kiddie-sized drink," he feigned in broken English. "But I think you make big mistake."

"I can live with my poor choices," she told him.

"You are a wise woman. They are a bit heavy-handed with the tequila here." Casey stood beside her holding a bottle of Mexican beer. "Mind if I join you?"

"Please." She gestured to the stool beside her. "Do you come here often?"

"Awww. Are you trying to pick me up?" He raised his shoulders and shot her a cherubic grin.

"I am so out of practice I wouldn't know if I were offending a man or sending off signals of seduction. But to answer your question, no, I am not hitting on you."

Casey sat down. "Well good. I'm glad we got that conversation out of the way. You find the Tremont house?"

Their talk halted when the bartender delivered her

margarita. "Let me know when you're ready to order or if you need recommendations," the young man said.

"Thank you. I need a few minutes." Joy picked up the menu.

"And let me know if this guy is bothering you." He jerked a thumb at Casey. "I also double as the bouncer."

"Come on, Roberto. Don't harsh my vibe," Casey told him with a big grin.

"Señor, your vibe got *harshed* two decades and fifteen pounds ago," Roberto shot back.

"Ouch. You really know how to hurt a guy. Are you going to have the shuttle take me back to the senior home when I'm done gumming my food?" Casey asked.

"Si, señor." Roberto's accent thickened, and he walked away to help another customer waving an empty glass.

Joy's earlier tension drained at the friendly banter between Casey and the bartender. "I guess you don't have to answer the question about coming here often."

"No." He chuckled.

"Good. Then what would you recommend? I'm starving."

Without hesitating, he said, "The fajitas, hands down. Best thing on the menu. If you like seafood, their shrimp is out of this world, but the beef is also very tender."

Joy looked over the menu. "Good enough. I'll order the fajitas for two with beef and shrimp. You will join me, won't you? My treat."

"I would love to. But I'll pick up the tab."

"Not an option. It's the least I can do since it sounds like I was an accomplice in stealing your motorcycle."

Casey raised his beer. "In that case, madam, I accept."

She clinked her glass to his bottle, and they drank.

He eyed her. "You didn't answer my question earlier. Did you find the answers you'd hoped for?"

Tension crept back into her jaw, and she pressed her lips together. "Michael's parents still live in the green house. They weren't very happy to see me. His mother knew about Michael's accident but never told her husband. He could've gone to his grave believing his son left and lived a happy life somewhere. I spoiled that illusion by showing up."

"If you have no memory of the accident and your life before, how could you have known any of that? Seems to me it's his wife who has some explaining to do for not being honest with him."

"Maybe." Joy ran a fingertip over the gritty salt on the rim of her glass. "His mom blames me for taking her son away. Maybe it was my fault."

"That boy was as wild as they come. I'm sure you weren't the only culprit in the scheme. By the way, I remembered something after you left earlier."

She quirked her eyebrows.

"Up until a few months ago, there'd been another Tremont working at the winery for the past two years. Her name was Tru. She worked in the tasting room, but swore she wasn't related to Michael. I asked once, and she shot me down in no uncertain terms. Her full name may have been Tru Harmony Tremont, but she reserved any pleasantries for the customers alone. She shared an apartment with one of the other gals who worked there. However, that didn't last long after Tru's boyfriend moved in with them. The roommate said he scared her, but Tru wouldn't kick him out, so the coworker found another living arrangement. I don't blame her. Even his name had a sketchy ring to it—Cutter."

Joy wrapped her hand around the glass and squeezed so hard her fingers whitened. While Harmony told the truth about Cutter being her boyfriend, she had lied to Casey about her family ties. The question remained whether Harmony discovered Joy on her own, or if Marla found her and gave the information to her granddaughter. Either way the young woman hadn't shown up in Huntsville by accident. She'd also given a last name of Gibbons not Tremont. Another lie.

"It usually takes a woman an hour of listening to my yammering before her eyes glaze over. I seemed to have achieved a new record with you, Joy."

She shook her head and pulled herself back to the present. "I'm sorry. Guess the traveling has caught up with me. You said Tru left the winery a few months ago. Do you know why?"

Casey signaled the bartender to bring him another beer. He pointed at her glass, but she shook her head. "Nope. All I know is she didn't give them any notice. Just up and quit one day. She'd called in at the beginning of her shift and said she wouldn't be coming in anymore. The owner got upset at being short-handed and asked if she could at least finish the week. From what I heard she wasn't very polite about turning down his request."

Joy had seen both sides of Harmony, and it didn't paint a pretty picture—especially the version who got angry. She excused herself and went to the restroom. Once there, she called Grace to make sure everything was okay at home. The stories about Harmony, a.k.a. Tru, frightened her, especially with Cutter in town as well. There wasn't any doubt in Joy's mind who had left the scorch marks on her daughter's wrist, but had it been Harmony or Cutter who tried to strangle her? What if Harmony had lured Owen into attacking his own wife?

Joy kept the call brief so as not to keep Casey waiting. Grace assured her everything was fine, and things went well at work. Owen kept his distance, but his absence was due more to Suzi blocking the doorway than his adhering to Grace's request to leave her be.

When Joy returned to the bar, their food had arrived, and Casey sipped his beer. "You should have started without me before it gets cold," she said as she climbed onto her seat.

"It's still sizzling. I think we've got time before we can even eat it, never mind it getting cold." Casey laughed. He offered her a plate and insisted she go first.

She filled a flour tortilla with shrimp, wrapped it up, and sank her teeth into one end. The explosion of flavors on her tongue sated her appetite and seared her mouth with a spicy bite all at the same time. "Mmmm. You were right about this being delicious. Thanks for the suggestion."

"Wait until you taste the beef. It's just as good with a little less kick." He shoveled toppings onto his own fajita.

With her next bite, the sauce dribbled out the other end of the rolled-up fajita, so Joy quickly leaned in over her plate. The purple vial on the chain around her neck snuck out through the open vee of her blouse.

Casey pointed at it. "Now that's an interesting

necklace. I've only seen one other like it."

She looked down and caressed the glass with her hand before tucking it back inside her top. "I've had it for years. It had been given to me by a volunteer at the hospital where Michael and I had been taken after..." Her cheeks drained of their warmth. *What a strange coincidence he'd found the same gift shop in Oregon where she'd met Pete.* "You said you've seen someone else wearing one?"

The man sat back and swiped an arm across his forehead. He'd finished two fajitas by this point and sweat formed at his temples. "Those jalapenos can be pretty powerful!" With two huge gulps, he drained half his beer, then tilted the bottle toward Joy's necklace. "Yeah, like I said, I've seen one like it, but it wasn't as pretty as yours. Hers was black."

Joy froze with her drink halfway to her lips. "Hers?"

"Yeah. Tru wore it all the time."

She set her margarita down and reached for her water glass.

Chapter 25

"Michael, stop," Joy screamed running after him as he rode toward the cliff with Harmony on the back of his motorcycle. She waved her arms in a futile effort to get his attention.

The scene before her slowed as if time were winding down for its final moment before the universe went dark. Just before they went over the edge, Harmony turned her head Joy's way. Her daughter's eyes glowed red, and a malicious grin spread across her face. The bike careened into the air with Harmony's long hair streaming behind her as they arced downward.

"No." Joy tried to scream but the word came out in a whisper.

She awoke in her hotel room with her arms stretched toward the ceiling. Moisture covered her blazing body as it heated and cooled at the same time. She shoved off the bed covers, pushed herself into a sitting position, and reached for the water bottle on the nightstand. After drinking half, she gulped in air as if she'd been choking.

When Joy's breathing normalized, she raised a hand to her mouth. Her nightmare hadn't been a memory this time. It couldn't be a prediction of the future either since Michael had died long before Harmony had reached adulthood.

The clock read three fifteen. Her flight back to

Portland wasn't until tomorrow. She'd planned to call the airline this morning and see if they had availability on something today, but now another plan formed in her mind. With her body calmed, she lay back down and tucked the covers beneath her chin. The prospect of falling back to sleep seemed unlikely, but a few hours later Joy awoke when her phone pinged with a text from Suzi.

—*Good morning, lady. Just wanted to check in and say everything is running smoothly. Grace is fine. How's the hunt for your pre-Joy identity?*—

Too much to tell via text, Joy thought. —*Filled in a couple of gaps. Will tell you about it when I get home tomorrow.*—

A sad face emoji came in answer. —*Not even one juicy tidbit?*—

Joy laughed out loud. Suzi deserved something to keep her active imagination at bay. Her friend had become just as invested in this mystery as she was.

—*My real name is Justine.*— Joy's finger hesitated over the send button. This might incite a slew of questions rather than satiating Suzi's curiosity. She got out of bed and walked to the window. The desert behind the hotel stretched for miles edged by a line of mountains as unsurmountable as this next task before her. *Did she really want to learn more?*

Tapping the back button on her phone, Joy deleted the message. Instead, she typed, —*Nice work on doubling as security. I heard you kept Owen away. Thanks for that.*—

In response she received a thumbs up, and the conversation ended. A great friend knows when to stop asking questions. Joy uttered, "Thank you, Suzi."

Once she'd gotten showered and dressed, she went downstairs. The hotel set out a self-serve breakfast bar. After a traumatic awakening in the wee hours of the morning, she didn't think she'd have much of an appetite until the aromas of corned beef hash and scrambled eggs lured her.

She sat alone at a table for two and enjoyed the ground-level view of what she'd seen from her room. Putting food and caffeine into her system gave her a new perspective on what lay outside the window. Instead of a hopeless expanse of dirt and rocks, she found beauty in the desert plants as well as the striations of red and brown in the surrounding landscape.

An hour later Joy tucked a fresh bottle of water into the cupholder of her car and drove the lonely road to Marla's and Benjamin's house. Convincing words and phrases ran through her head making a case for why they should trust her and share what they knew of her background. They had to acknowledge she was a different person now, not the irresponsible young woman who supposedly took their son away. She'd lost people too—a boyfriend, a father, a child.

Marla's car sat parked in the driveway. As Joy got out of her vehicle and into the stifling heat, her footsteps hesitated. She opened and closed her hands, something she'd always done when nerves made her doubt herself. *No, she wouldn't let this woman intimidate her.*

Striding to the front door, she knocked firmly. After a few moments, Marla opened the door and glared. Before the woman could speak a word, Joy held up a hand. "Just hear me out. Please. Then I'll leave you alone." Desperation echoed through her voice.

The old woman's stance softened, and her shoulders slumped. Stepping aside, she gestured for her to enter.

As Joy opened her mouth to offer a thank you, Marla put a finger to her own lips and pointed to the kitchen. Joy obeyed the signal.

"Benjamin is sitting in the study listening to an audiobook. I'd prefer he not know you're here. After you left yesterday, it took him hours to calm down."

"I'm so sorry to be the one who caused his distress." Joy sat at the table.

Without asking, Marla poured two cups of coffee and set one in front of her unwelcome guest. "Cream and sugar are over there." She nodded toward the end of the table.

"Black is fine. Thank you."

Marla sat across from Joy, added two packets of sugar to her mug and a healthy dose of cream. "You're not the only one who caused him stress. I should have told him about the accident years ago. His trust in me is shaken, but we'll heal. Our marriage is strong. It would have to be with everything we've been through." She blew on the hot liquid before taking a sip. "You ever marry?"

A sad smile came to Joy's lips. "Yes. His name was Drake."

"Was?"

"He died two years ago in a car accident. Hit a patch of black ice on a mountain road." Joy wrapped both hands around her coffee warming her hands, which had suddenly gone cold.

"Tragedy follows you everywhere, don't it?"

Marla couldn't have hurt her more if she'd slapped her across the cheek. Joy wiped a tear from the corner of her eye.

Marla's face pinched. "I'm sorry. I've felt so much anger toward you for so many years. The ugliness slips out sometimes."

"I understand." Joy's voice trembled.

"You have any more kids?"

"None of my own. Drake's first wife died, leaving him a young daughter to raise." She focused on the wall clock, not registering what it read. Her gaze returned to Marla. "I know about deception, like the kind you had with Benjamin. My stepdaughter, Grace is her name, didn't know about my missing past until recently. Her father had been the doctor at the hospital where…where we'd been brought after the accident. She'd always thought we'd met at his work but didn't know I'd been a patient with special circumstances."

Marla chuckled. "Special circumstances. That's an interesting choice of words, given where you really come from."

Joy leaned heavily into the back of her chair. The wood creaked at the pressure. "Yesterday you said odd things about my being banished and how mixed lineages were against the law. What does all that mean?"

The old woman placed a hand to her chin and drummed her fingers on the table with the other. Uncertainty crossed her face, and her eyes narrowed. "First, tell me how you found us if you don't remember anything before twenty-two years ago."

With a nod, Joy detailed the events beginning with her recent nightmares and concluding with tracing the origin of the license plate to Pahrump. She explained how Casey had remembered where they lived when he worked with Michael.

Throughout the explanation, Marla's expression remained stoic, except at the depiction of the motorcycle going over the cliff. She'd flinched and bit her lip.

Joy grimaced, regretting her graphic description of what she'd dreamt.

When the tale had finished, the old woman got up and refilled her coffee. Without turning from the counter, she asked, "Are you sure you want the truth?"

That one little question, asked not with curiosity but foreboding, caused Joy to stiffen. The moment had arrived. The moment she'd waited a lifetime to reach. Now, the urge to flee from the house and forget she'd ever met Marla and Benjamin Tremont overwhelmed her.

Chapter 26

Joy barely focused on the road ahead as she drove home from the Portland airport. Ever since she'd left Marla's house the day before, the shock of what she'd learned continued to shake her in relentless waves. As much as she didn't want to believe the extraordinary tale Michael's mother related about where they came from and who she really was, the events over the last few weeks made it hard to deny.

When she stepped inside her house, the aroma of lasagna embraced her like a warm blanket. The garlicky aromas whet her appetite. She dropped her suitcase in the entryway and went straight to the kitchen.

"We thought you could use some comfort food after your trip. How'd it go?" Grace tossed a bowl of salad with two wooden forks then sprinkled croutons on top.

Suzi set a goblet of wine on the counter and gestured toward the stool in front of it. "Take a load off."

The fatigue from the last couple of days eased slightly as Joy sat. She wrapped her fingers around the stem of the glass, and a smile found its way to her lips. On the flight home from Las Vegas, she'd deliberated about how much of Marla's story she should share with either of the two women before her. Would they hate her for the foolish choices she'd made in her youth?

Without warning, Joy blurted out, "My real name is Justine Arcana. Michael's last name was Tremont, and I met his parents, Marla and Benjamin."

"Oh, Mom, you found them! Did they know what had happened to you and Michael?" Grace perched beside her mother.

Joy drank before answering. "Marla knew, but she'd never told her husband, wanting to protect him from the heartache. She also knew I'd lost my memory but not for this long."

Suzi eased onto a seat across from them. "Then why in hell didn't she contact you?"

The complications of only doling out certain details of her past were already presenting themselves. If she dove into the rabbit hole of explaining about her father, she'd need to reveal everything.

Joy took a deep breath. Protecting Grace had to be her top priority. If she didn't reveal everything, her stepdaughter could be in danger from the one person who felt there was a score to settle—Joy's biological daughter.

"She had agreed not to get in touch with me until after a year. By then my memory should have returned."

"How could she know that? Do you come from a group of psychics?" Suzi's face brightened.

"Not exactly. Wait!" Joy bolted up and ran to the windowsill where the three pots each had a large yellow bloom. "When did those grow?"

Suzi walked up beside her. "Apparently, they like jazz. The buds first cracked open yesterday, and today they looked like this. Grace had left the radio on all day, and we discovered these flowers after closing the tasting room."

Joy pulled one of the packets from the dirt and flipped it over. A fifth step had appeared: HARVEST. The front of the packet had also changed to read: Five Steps to *Planet* Celestia. How could harvesting these blooms show her how to proceed? Marla hadn't said a word about the plants, and Joy didn't ask.

"Mom, forget the plants. Why did Marla believe you would remember in a year?" Grace leaned her elbows on the counter.

Joy and Suzi returned to their seats. "Actually, the plants tie into this mystery somehow. You see, the place I come from is called Celestia. When Marla mentioned the name, I meant to ask her about the seeds. As she continued with her story, I got so inundated with information I forgot about them."

"Don't keep us in suspense. Where is Celestia? Maybe we need to take another road trip." Suzi spread her arms wide with palms up.

"That's the thing. It isn't someplace we can just *go* to. The people who live there are…I can't believe I'm saying this out loud. They're on another planet. The planet Celestia. They travel through portals between our world and theirs."

Grace's mouth gaped. "You've got to be kidding! That Marla must've still been angry to tell you a load of crap like that. How could you believe her?"

Joy covered her daughter's hand with her own. "Honey, I know this sounds fantastical, but let me finish." She flipped her hand over to show the inside of her wrist. "See this raised marking?"

Her daughter did a double take. "Where'd that come from?"

"I was born with it. When I came to this world and removed my necklace"—she pulled the purple vial from inside her neckline—"it faded. After Aunt Suzi and I returned from our road trip where I'd seen a man wearing one just like it, I dug mine out from my jewelry box. Once I started wearing it, this appeared."

Grace traced the symbols with the tip of a finger. She touched both curvy lines and the straight one crossing them. "Did that man have this mark as well?"

She shook her head. "I don't know. He wore long sleeves, but I wouldn't have known to look for it anyway."

Gently picking up the vial from where it hung around her mother's neck, Grace held it between her fingers. "I thought you said an old man in the hospital gave you the necklace."

The vision of rough hands fastening the chain around her neck flashed into her mind. She wished she could remember his face. "Yes, but he came from Celestia and knew I would need it to remember. According to Marla, she'd given it to the old man. He was my father."

"Your father? If he knew you were there, why didn't he take you home?" Grace asked.

"That's a separate story." Joy sighed.

Suzi pointed at Joy's wrist. "The mark is a lot more defined than when you first showed it to me. So did Marla and Benjamin have them too?"

"They haven't worn their necklaces for years, so the symbols faded. I imagine if they put them on again, like mine, they would return. Marla told me their necklaces were blue, and the symbol would be a circle with a line through it. Michael had the same as his parents. While the people of Celestia are all from the same race, there are two distinct bloodlines. And they aren't permitted to mix."

Suzi leaned her head back and cackled. "So, what you're saying is you and Michael were the rebellious, star-crossed lovers? That's downright cliche! Did he have to duel your cousins to be allowed to whisk you away?" She made a jabbing movement with her arm.

Before Joy could answer, Grace asked the obvious question. "Does all this mean you aren't human? You're an alien?"

Joy bit her upper lip. "Not exactly, though that had been one of my questions too. The beings on Celestia are human with a few special qualities. Their technology is more advanced than here on Earth, especially when it comes to medicine." She looked at Suzi. "And yes, we weren't supposed to fall in love, but we did. Michael's parents lived near one of the portals and had been the caretakers until we came through without permission. They should have sent us back to Celestia, but I pleaded with them not to." She brought the glass to her lips and savored a bit of Merlot before continuing. "Because of their duplicity, the Council, which is the ruling body of the place, sealed the portal stranding them on Earth. That happened after Michael and I took off on our fateful motorcycle trip."

"If they'd been against you and Michael being together, why would they have risked trapping themselves here for your sake?" Grace asked.

Joy leaned against the seatback, the wood creaking from the sudden pressure. With her eyes cast down, she said, "They didn't do it for me. They did it for their granddaughter."

The other women gasped in unison.

Facing Grace, Joy said, "You have a stepsister."

Grace stuttered when attempting to speak. She gulped and tried again. "Did you meet her?"

"We all have." Joy laced and unlaced her fingers where they rested on the counter. The timer dinged signaling the lasagna had finished baking. No one moved to take it out of the oven. "Her name is Tru...Tru Harmony."

Suzi shot to her feet. "The lightning bolt-wielding vixen?"

"Harmony? Your daughter is Harmony?" Grace grasped her mother's arm.

"Welcome to the family, Sis!" Harmony leaned on the door jamb of the kitchen. A black vial hung from a chain around her neck, and her usual sparkling blue eyes blazed dark as coal. "Marla filled me in on your visit. I hope you don't mind that I let myself in, *Mommy*. Or would you prefer I call you Justine?"

Chapter 27

Joy slowly rose to her feet. A kaleidoscope of emotions battled within as she considered the young woman in a new light. This was her child, her own flesh and blood, and the reason the Tremonts lost their place in Celestia. Joy had willingly given up her life and her world for love, but in doing so, she'd destroyed the lives of others. Was it worth it? Had Harmony's anger festered from being abandoned by her parents, or did it come from an innate evil corroding her genetic make-up? Joy and Michael were responsible for everything that had led up to this moment—the moment Joy confronted her past sins.

"Get out!" Grace stood. "You don't belong here."

"On the contrary, Sis, I do. You call her 'Mom' because she married your daddy. Her blood runs through my veins, not yours!" Harmony inched closer. "You're only the leftover crumb of a life she built after she abandoned me."

Joy stepped between the two women with her hands held up. "Don't come any closer, Harmony. I'm sorry you got left behind. It's taken me twenty-two years to find anything about my past. Neither your father nor I meant to desert you."

"Do you want me to call the police?" Suzi glared at Harmony. "You could have her arrested for trespassing. Maybe even breaking and entering."

Jester chose this moment to tear into the room through the partially open patio door. He barked as he ran at Harmony then stopped at her feet emitting a low growl.

Harmony let out a hysterical laugh. "This your idea of security?" Cutting her amusement short, she shot out a foot, and launched the poor animal across the floor. "Keep that little mongrel away from me."

"Jester," Suzi cried running to his side. She scooped up the whimpering animal and cradled him in her arms.

"What's wrong with you? There was no need for that," Joy said. "Harmony, I think it best if you leave now. We'll talk at some point but not with tempers flaring. Please respect my request and stay away."

"Oh, aren't we civilized and refined. Will the butler be escorting me out?" Harmony crossed her arms and looked directly at Suzi.

Stomping over to Grace, Suzi thrust Jester into her arms. "The *butler* would be happy to show you to the door." She approached Harmony and grabbed her by the forearm.

"Suzi, no," shouted Joy.

Everyone in the room froze. Silence descended, as if they'd reached a stalemate.

Harmony glared at the short blonde, who now attempted to shove her toward the front of the house. She ripped her arm from Suzi's grasp. "Get your damn hands off me, witch. One of these days you and I are going to have it out." With a chuckle, she added, "And your little dog too!"

Suzi stood her ground unfazed with hands on hips.

Harmony's eyes flashed daggers at Joy. "This isn't

over. You *will* regret the day you tossed me aside like garbage."

"You know that isn't true." Joy wore a pained expression.

"Don't give in to her, Joy," Suzi said. "She's a master at manipulation and is only trying to get under your skin. You don't owe her anything."

With one last glare, Harmony spun on her heel and blasted out of the room like a gale-force wind. A moment later the front door slammed, and all went silent.

"Maybe I do," Joy whispered.

Holding Jester under one arm, Grace placed the other around her mother's shoulders. "Mom, let it go. Aunt Suzi's right. She's only trying to con you into feeling guilty for things beyond your control. If Harmony can't see the truth, it's not up to you to convince her."

Suzi retrieved Jester and set him on the counter beside the sink. She filled a small bowl with water and placed it in front of him. "Here you go, my little cupcake. Did the mean lady hurt you? Don't worry, next time Mommy will knock her block off for you." Her hand smoothed the fur along his back. With a scritch behind his ears, she left him to finish drinking.

"He okay, Aunt Suzi?"

"He'll be fine. Oh no, the lasagna!" Suzi ran to the oven, put on a pair of mitts, and rescued their dinner. "This might be a little crispy around the edges, but it smells delicious." The lasagna bubbled with cheese and tomato sauce as she lifted it off the rack and placed it on the stove top.

Joy collapsed onto a stool. "I'm not sure I could eat

right now."

"Sure you can. We'll let this set a few minutes. More wine?" Suzi asked.

"I'll take more." Grace held up her empty glass.

"Mine is still mostly"—Joy dove up—"Jester, no!"

The puggle tore apart one of the yellow blooms and shredded the stem. When Joy called his name, he gave a final yank, and the pot fell off the windowsill crashing into the sink. Dirt, flower petals, and chewed stem parts spilled over the stainless-steel basin and drain.

"Oh, Joy, I'm so sorry." Suzi picked up her naughty puppy and set him onto the floor. "Bad doggy." She shook a finger at him then pointed. "Go lie down."

With tail tucked between his legs, he slunk to the corner of the room. Once there, he circled twice then plopped onto the tiles. His head now resting on his paws, he looked like a petulant child sent to time out.

"Don't worry about the plant, Suzi. I feared it might be poisonous and make him sick." Joy pulled the trash can over to the sink. Carefully, she removed the broken pieces of pottery and tossed them into the bin. With a paper towel, she gathered the shreds of decimated plant and threw them away as well.

"Maybe you can replant it, Mom." Grace reached inside after the paper-wrapped remains.

Joy stopped her. "Don't worry about it, honey. We've still got two more to experiment with. Besides, they may have run their course now that the five steps are complete."

"We haven't figured out what to do with the fifth step. Maybe we can find more seeds," Suzi said.

"It's only a silly plant. We've got other things to

worry about." Joy pushed the trash back where it belonged and sat down again.

"You betcha. Like how much lasagna do you want?" Suzi poised a spatula over the pan of cheesy goodness.

Joy smiled. "I guess I could have a small piece with salad."

"Now you're talking." Suzi sliced into the dish cutting neat squares then slapping them onto plates. None of the pieces could be considered small.

The women toasted and dug into the meal.

After inhaling several large bites, Suzi said, "I guess the ball is in your court, Joy. So what's our next step?"

"Honestly, I'm not sure." Joy poked lettuce and a crouton with her fork. "I do need to talk to Harmony."

"That's if she's willing to have a conversation and not just hurl accusations at you," Grace said.

"I understand why she would be hurting. With all Marla told me about my younger self, I'm ashamed to think some of her accusations might be true. Maybe I couldn't handle being a parent and wanted to escape. Or the thought of raising a child, only to lose her at the tender age of five, became too much of a burden. Marla explained the majority of the mixed breed children didn't live past that age."

"Mom, you had no way of knowing things would turn out the way they did." Grace put down her fork. "Do you regret meeting Daddy and…and me?"

Joy's eyes widened. "Why would you ever think that?"

Grace played with the stem of her glass. "Well, it's kind of like you chose us over your past life."

"Your mother didn't *choose* one over the other. Circumstances beyond her control chose for her." Suzi placed the spatula over one of the pasta squares about to cut it in half. With a shrug, she slid the server under the whole piece and slipped it onto her plate. "Anyone else for seconds?" She held the spatula in the air. Strings of mozzarella hung from the edge and sauce dripped onto the stove.

"I'm good," Grace said.

Joy shook her head.

Tucking into her food, Suzi said, "You told us your father was a separate story. Let's hear it."

This time Joy put her utensil down and pushed the plate of mostly uneaten food away.

Chapter 28

Harmony sped up the drive to her guest house apartment and slammed on the brakes. The car screeched on the pavement. She'd wanted to confront Joy and Grace alone. Having that pain-in-the-ass Suzi there sucked the wind from her sails. The damn woman's car must've been parked at the tasting room since Harmony hadn't seen it near the house. As sidekicks go, Suzi came across as a puffy annoyance but turned into a mama bear protecting her cubs when it came to Joy and her stepdaughter.

Cutter lounged on the bed, his boots dirtying the comforter. "How'd the family reunion go?" He barely glanced up from the book he read.

"Get your boots off my bed. Wait!" Harmony stopped in the doorway.

"What?" He gave her his full attention.

"When did you learn to read?" She smirked.

He threw the book on the floor. The cover depicted a classic drama by Shakespeare. "I just look at the pictures." With one leap, he sprang off the bed and pulled her close. "Maybe you can give me a few lessons."

She pushed him away, and he released his hold. "Get off me. That meddling Suzi was still there and had her claws out. I got their attention though. The battle lines have been drawn. None of them is up to the challenge."

"Why bother playing with them at all? Honestly, your mom appeared genuinely sorry she fired you. It must've really hurt discovering you're her daughter."

"Don't go all soft on me now. Are you growing a conscience?"

"Nah! Not even sure I know what that is. I just don't know what you hope to gain." He took a drink from the whiskey glass on the nightstand. "C'mon. Let's blow this joint and head for LA. There's lots more trouble to stir up there than we could ever hope for here."

Harmony went to the kitchen and poured herself a drink. "If you want to go then go! I can handle this on my own. That woman and her *daughter* took my life from me. Justine owes me something in return."

Cutter followed her to the kitchen. "And you owe me." He snatched the glass from her hand and downed the whiskey. With an angry grunt, he threw the empty glass into the sink where it shattered. One arm swung around her neck and pulled her in. His lips devoured hers, and he held her tightly as she fought to get away. Easing his grip, he whispered, "I love it when you struggle." In one swift motion he threw her over his shoulder, carried her to the bedroom, and flung her onto the mattress.

"You bastard! I'm not in the mood." She tried to get up.

He pressed her down with his body. "Well, I am." He caught hold of her wrists and held them in one hand while fumbling with the zipper on her jeans. "And I'm leaving my boots on."

****

Joy leaned back in her chair. "As Marla explained, because Michael and I had basically gone rogue and traveled without permission, we were banished for a year. The council had wanted me to abort the child, but I refused. She was born on Celestia."

"They wanted you to kill your baby?" Grace asked.

"Yes. Half-breeds either die by five years of age or grow up evil. Either way, our society wanted it gone. We chose to take her to Earth and raise her without their permission." Joy got up and topped off her wine glass.

Suzi held her empty one up to be refilled. "Thanks. So, what happened once you'd arrived here?"

"Against their better judgment, Marla and Benjamin took us in. I'd tried to cope with everything, but I hated the desert. After begging Michael to take me somewhere green, his parents agreed to watch Tru Harmony for a few days.

"Right after we took off, my father showed up furious at our behavior. After the accident, he'd managed to find me. He gave me the memory loss serum. Somehow it went wrong, and I never recovered. I'd already had amnesia from the accident, which might have affected the dosage. Silas, my father, gave me the necklace to help me remember, except the serum never wore off." Joy held the pendant in her hand, and the purple substance inside glowed brightly.

"What kind of parent intentionally causes his daughter to lose her memory?" Grace asked.

Joy sighed. "He followed the directives of the Council. If he hadn't administered it, someone else would have. Silas felt responsible for me, even though I'd made my own choices. Michael was dead. There wasn't anything my father could do to help him. He gave me the serum and necklace then returned to Celestia."

"That's pretty cold," Suzi said. "One toe out of line, and they cut you off. Doesn't sound like a very caring community. You're better off having landed here."

Joy walked to the sink and admired the yellow blooms. Turning back to the other women, she said, "Maybe. The people of Celestia had to protect their way of life. I broke the rules and needed to pay."

"Still seems harsh, especially after what happened to Michael." Suzi leaned back in her chair. "What happened next?"

"Next? Marla and Benjamin paid the price for our transgressions. When Silas returned to Celestia, the Council sealed the portal the Tremonts had been assigned to monitor. Each person guarding a portal had no knowledge of where the others were, so they had no way to return. They raised my daughter and grew more bitter with every passing year I didn't come back to claim her."

"Obviously, she outlived her five-year expiration date," Suzi snorted.

"Yes. Harmony maintained stability, until the day she grew angry at her grandfather. She'd grabbed his hands and lightening pulsed through his body causing him to go blind."

"She has that much power?" Grace's eyes widened.

Joy shrugged. "There's still much I don't understand. She should only be able to affect beings from Celestia yet look at your wrist."

Grace pushed up her sleeve. While the scorch

marks were faded, she still remembered the dark smudges when she awoke in the hospital.

"Who left the cross at the accident site?" Suzi asked.

"I didn't ask." Joy laced her fingers. "I assumed Harmony did. A couple years after Benjamin had been blinded, Harmony came knocking on their door. She demanded to know where her parents were, and Marla told her our story and where to find me."

Grace twirled the stem of her glass. "If you had the chance to go back to Celestia, would you?"

The question hung in the air, pregnant with trepidation. *Would I?* With answers flooding in, Joy had decisions to make. How would she know which choices were right? "I don't know."

"Oh." Grace looked down.

Joy placed her hand beneath Grace's chin and lifted it. "Regardless of what I decide, *you* are my first consideration. That is a given."

The young woman smiled.

"There's another possibility about Grace's injuries." Suzi walked to the corner and gave Jester a pet. The dog stood and wagged his tail.

"You don't think Owen hurt her, do you?" Joy asked.

Suzi shook her head. "Did you see Harmony's eyes? They were black as night."

"Maybe they change color when she's angry, though I suppose it would have been easy enough to hide them with colored contact lenses." Joy fingered her vial. "When I spoke with Casey, he'd mentioned Harmony wore a necklace like mine, except it held a black substance instead of purple."

"Well, your eyes could be considered violet. Do you think the necklaces are meant to match your eyes, kind of a way of delineating the genetic differences amongst your race?" Grace asked.

"That's an interesting theory." Suzi walked back and sat at the counter. "We do know one other person whose eyes match that evil vixen's peepers. Someone who could have also been at the beach the day you two went camping."

Joy gasped. "Cutter."

"Who's Cutter?" Grace asked.

The women had never told Grace about Harmony's appearance with Cutter the day after she'd been fired. Joy placed her wine down.

"Her demonic lover, that's who," Suzi spat before her friend could answer. "What if they've started their own satanic gang of evil half-breeds who've survived past their fifth birthday? The countryside could be infested with them!"

Grace shook her head. "Aunt Suzi, you really need to cut back on the vampire movies. Evil creatures? Demonic lover?"

"Let's not blow this out of proportion," Joy reasoned. "Cutter showed up with Harmony the day after I fired her. She wanted to prove she had a boyfriend and no interest in Owen. This man had black eyes. I guess it's possible he's also an outcast from Celestia, and they found each other."

"Boyfriend or not, it doesn't prove she and my husband weren't having an affair. If she'd mess with a married man, I wouldn't put it past her to cheat on her so-called boyfriend."

Joy yawned. The fatigue of the trip and the night's

events tugged at every muscle in her body. "There isn't anything more we can do tonight. Suzi, you're welcome to stay the night, but I need sleep."

Grace went to the sink and started rinsing dishes before placing them in the dishwasher. "You go upstairs, Mom. The stress of everything is taking its toll on you."

She gave her daughter a weak smile. "Thanks. We'll talk more in the morning."

Suzi gave Joy a hug. "Jester and I are gonna head home."

"You sure you'll be all right? It makes me nervous the way Harmony taunts you. She's as angry at you as she is with me." Joy furrowed her brows.

"Not to worry. I can handle that punk. She's too busy storming around making threats to you and Grace. I'm sure she's forgotten all about me by now. You get some sleep, and I'll see you tomorrow."

Joy kissed her daughter good night, then locked the front door before trudging up the stairs with her suitcase. They needed help, and she knew of only one man who could provide it. She had to find her father.

Chapter 29

Suzi jolted awake at Jester's barking and tugging on her sleeve. She opened her mouth to speak, but it filled with smoke, causing her to cough and sputter. After rolling off the bed onto the floor, she tucked the dog under an arm and crawled to the dresser. Remaining on her knees, she groped the top until her hand landed on the satchel she used for a purse. Yanking it to the floor, Suzi slung the bag across the shoulder opposite her pooch and crept across the carpet to the door.

As she placed her hand on the knob, her arm jerked back from the heat radiating off the metal surface. Crackling from the fire on the other side of the door raged in her ears. "Plan B, Jester." Another fit of coughing overtook her.

The dog whimpered and shook. His snout nuzzled into her chest.

The long flannel robe impeded her progress across the floor to the window opposite. Without losing her precious cargo or bag, she pulled herself up until she could unhinge the lock. With her free hand, she pushed the window upward. The wooden frame creaked as she forced it higher until it stuck only inches above the sill. Cool air touched her face but not enough to banish the acrid smoke filling her nostrils and throat. She exerted more effort on the window, but the frame held fast. As she gasped for breath, her vision blurred. Suzi shoved Jester through the narrow opening before darkness descended over her, and she slipped to the floor with her back against the wall.

A faraway voice pierced through the fog, and something banged on the window. The wooden frame above her head groaned and splintered as a rush of air forced its way in. Large hands grabbed Suzi beneath the arms and pulled her up and over the sill. When her feet landed on the ground, she slumped back into her savior. He dragged more than carried her several feet from the burning house before laying her against the trunk of a large oak.

"Miss Suzi, are you all right?" The man shook her shoulder and shouted louder than necessary.

Suzi sucked in air. With one hand, she rubbed her eyes, still stinging from the smoke. Panicked voices drifted across the yard, and blaring sirens drew closer. Glass shattered accompanied by a crash as part of the roof caved in. Flames engulfed the little cottage. Black smoke billowed from holes in the roof as well as the open window from which she'd been rescued moments earlier. With her head leaning back against the rough bark, she closed her eyes.

"What is on her face?" a woman with a Slavic accent asked. "Is she wearing shower cap? Why she shower with nightgown on?"

"Suzi!" Jeb Russell's voice boomed over the din of the farm hands who'd come running from their nearby houses. "Was there anyone else in the house with you?"

She pried her eyes open and focused on the owner of the vineyard where she lived. Unable to talk between gasping and the burning in her throat, she shook her head.

"Okay, everyone, stay back," Jeb shouted. "The fire department will be here any minute. Suzi and Jester are out of danger. That's the important thing."

The dog rested his front paws on Suzi's arm. He alternated between licking her hand and yipping.

Veronica, the person who questioned the gasping woman's appearance, knelt beside her on the ground. She put an arm around Suzi and scratched Jester's head, who promptly growled, then tucked his head down. "Miss Suzi, you be okay now. The ambulance come. My Boris pull you out before you burn. Good thing he come home late tonight. But is that from the fire?" She touched Suzi's cheek.

Suzi squinted her eyes and brought her fingertips to her rough, taut skin. "Oh, no," she whispered. Pain flashed through her as she tried to clear her scratchy throat. She rasped, "I fell asleep with my face mask on."

"You wear mask to bed? Like costume?" Veronica leaned back on her haunches and patted the top of the plastic cap covering the other woman's hair. "And a hat?"

Suzi sighed. Veronica and her husband came from a small town in Romania and probably didn't know much about American beauty rituals. Before Suzi could educate her about facials and hair curlers, two male paramedics pushing a gurney rushed to her side.

The young men, who couldn't have been over thirty-five, hesitated a moment. One stifled a smirk.

Suzi ignored their surprised looks. When they asked if she was hurt anywhere, she told them only her pride. One placed an oxygen mask on her face while the other checked her vitals.

"We'll need to take you to the hospital. They'll probably want to keep you overnight for observation from smoke inhalation. Your talking isn't too bad, so you may have escaped without damaging your lungs. Is there someone who can keep the dog?" He reached out to scruff Jester behind the ears, and the dog snapped at him. The young man withdrew before losing fingers.

She pushed the oxygen mask from her face. "Can't I take him with me? He's traumatized." Suzi scooped him into her arms and hugged him close.

"Sorry, ma'am, only service animals are allowed," the other paramedic chimed in.

A pout formed on her face. "But he's my snuggle-monster. Doesn't that make him one?" She scratched Jester beneath the chin.

"I'll keep him for you, Miss Suzi." Veronica stepped forward and reached for the dog.

Reluctantly, Suzi handed over her pet, who struggled in Veronica's arms trying to get away. Suzi replaced the oxygen mask and allowed the paramedics to help her onto the stretcher. She didn't fuss when they covered her with a blanket and strapped her in but refused to release her bag, still slung over her shoulder. This she clutched even closer.

The ride to the hospital had her more upset at leaving Jester behind than worrying about her own condition. She felt fine, except for a scratchy throat, and didn't understand why she had to go at all.

****

Shortly before five in the morning, Joy hopped into her car and drove herself and Grace to the hospital. She'd received a call from one of the emergency room staff explaining what happened. Suzi had listed Joy as her emergency contact stating she was her sister.

Once there, the two women raced across the parking lot and through the doors of the ER. The nurse on duty explained Suzi was in with the attending doctor, who was signing off on her release. She'd escaped with minor injuries and could be taken home. Joy breathed a sigh of relief.

They took seats in the waiting room. A male nurse finally brought Suzi out in a wheelchair. The shower cap atop her head sat askew with strands of hair poking out from under the edge. Her pink flannel robe was spotted with soot stains, and the skin on her face appeared blotchy and red.

Joy stared.

"What?" Suzi raised her arms. "You never seen anybody in a wheelchair before? Or is it the hunky nurse I scored to escort me out?" She jerked a thumb at the blushing young man behind her.

"Don't you think Charlie will be jealous?" Joy eased the tension in her jaw.

"Nah. We can keep this between us. Right, Cecil?" She cocked her head toward the nurse.

His complexion matched the red fluff of hair atop his head while his knuckles whitened where he gripped the handles.

Joy bent down and threw her arms around Suzi's neck. "I'm so glad you're okay. What happened? Are the red spots on your face from the fire?"

"I woke up, and the place was filled with smoke. If it hadn't been for Jester's barking and pulling on my sleeve, I might not have gotten out in time." She put a hand to her cheek. "The spots are probably from the mud mask a nurse scrubbed off me. I'd smeared it on when I got home but fell asleep before removing it. I guess I made quite the sight when I got pulled from the house." She chuckled.

The nurse cleared his throat.

"Guess that's my cue to disembark," Suzi said in a stage whisper with her hand beside her mouth. She leaned on the arms of the chair and attempted to get up.

He put a hand on her shoulder. "Sorry, madam, but hospital policy requires me to see you out the door."

Suzi pointed toward the exit. "Then let's roll, Cecil."

Once outside, the young man helped her out of the chair and onto a bench. "Looks like you're in good hands now, madam. I'll leave you here." He spun the wheelchair around and hurried through the automatic doors before she could comment.

"Why is it when I'm giving off my best flirtatious vibe, they call me madam?"

"Could it be the slight age difference which makes them uncomfortable?" Joy asked.

Suzi pursed her lips and shook her head. "Nah. That can't be it."

"Do you think someone set the fire?" Grace pursed her lips.

"Don't know. Guess the fire inspector will determine that, but I know where you're going with this." Suzi crossed her arms. "I wouldn't put it past her."

"That settles it," Joy said. "You're staying with us."

"I'd appreciate the accommodations, considering everything I own went up in smoke. At least I grabbed my essentials." She patted her satchel.

"Aunt Suzi, what on earth made you take your handbag while escaping a fire?" Grace asked.

"Oh, I never leave the house without it. My momma raised me right." Suzi bobbed her head once.

"Let's get you home. I'll bring the car around." Joy took one step toward the lot then stopped. "Suzi, what happened to Jester?" She hated to ask but hoped for the best. That dog meant the world to her friend.

She put a hand to her chest. "I almost forgot! He's at Veronica's. Boris pulled me out through the window. Can we pick Jester up on the way?"

Joy checked her phone. "It's a bit early. Why don't we get you settled at home, then we'll pick him up after breakfast?"

Suzi huffed like a toddler. "Okay. I guess he can wait. I just hope Veronica doesn't fill him up with cabbage rolls and sweet bread. He'll be farting all over the house."

Joy chirped the lock on her car and got in. Choking back a sob, she rested her forehead on the steering wheel. How many more people would be hurt from her stirring up the past?

Chapter 30

After Suzi settled into the guest room and Grace headed off to her old bedroom, Joy crawled under the covers. She tossed and turned for two hours before giving up when her phone read eight o'clock.

Not wanting to wake the other women, she carried her coffee mug to the back patio and reclined in one of the loungers. The delicate scent of roses drifted on the breeze. Her garden, lining the pavers, boasted varying shades of pink and yellow petals above their thorny stems.

With shaky hands, Joy typed a message on her phone to Harmony. Her finger hovered over the screen. She doubted her wisdom in doing this but saw no other way but to forge ahead. Expelling a breath, she hit send. The whoosh from her phone put her on edge. Joy's quest for knowledge had come back to bite her and those she loved. Why was it wrong? She'd led a good life and had a loving husband and daughter. How could wanting to know her past have such tragic results?

Her phone pinged with a response. —*Huntsville Diner 11:00.*—

At least Harmony had picked a public place. Joy wanted a chance to understand her daughter's motives for being here and ask her forgiveness. She needed Harmony to believe they hadn't intentionally abandoned her as a child. Would it be possible to make peace with this young woman and blend her old family with new?

By nine-fifteen Grace and Suzi hadn't stirred. Joy drove to Veronica's and retrieved Jester, so he would be there when Suzi woke up. She assured both Veronica and Boris their neighbor had escaped the fire without major injury and would be staying with her.

Before leaving the vineyard where the couple lived, Joy stopped in front of the charred remains of Suzi's cottage. Blackened wood beams from the roof lay askew where they had smashed the walls of her tiny home. The odor of wet, burnt kindling mingled with the stench of whatever else had been incinerated by the blaze and doused by fire hoses. A shiver ran through her body seeing the decimated remains of the back bedroom where Suzi had slept. What if Jester hadn't woken her in time?

Joy reached over and scratched the little dog's head where he stood on the passenger seat wagging his tail. "You're a real hero, buddy. Thank God you were there."

Jester gave out a woof and wagged his tail.

Suzi's SUV, speckled with black and white ashes, sat in the driveway. She hadn't parked it against the house, which had allowed the vehicle to escape harm. Joy would drive her friend over later to pick it up.

When she arrived home, she heard both women in the kitchen. Joy set Jester down to find his owner, which he immediately took off to do.

His little nails tapped along the tiles as he ran.

"Jester!" Suzi squealed. "You're my hero."

Joy walked into the kitchen where Suzi hugged her wriggling dog as he licked her face. Grace sat at the counter laughing at her aunt.

"Thank you for getting him," Suzi said. "You could have woken me to go with you."

"Not a chance. You needed rest," Joy said. "Besides, I knew you would want him as soon as possible. He doesn't look a pound heavier, so he must've escaped Veronica's cooking."

"Let's hope so, or we'll all need gas masks." Suzi kissed Jester's nose.

"We have a regular hen party here," Grace said. "You sure you can handle all of us under one roof, Mom?"

Suzi stepped closer. "I promise I'll be out of here as soon as I find another place."

"Me too," Grace chimed in.

"You'll do no such thing, either of you," Joy said. "This house is huge, and I'm happy so many of the rooms are now full. Both of you may stay however long you want. Honestly, I like the company."

Suzi and Grace clinked mugs in a toast.

"To roommates," Suzi said.

"To roommates," Joy joined in. "I'd toast but haven't got a cup."

"I'm on it!" Grace set a mug beneath the coffee maker, dropped in a pod, and hit the button.

The women enjoyed a leisurely breakfast. Even Jester lapped up pancakes as if he'd not eaten in days. When ten-thirty rolled around, Joy had Suzi make a list of dog food and clothing sizes so she could pick up a few necessities.

"Let me go too, so you only need to make one trip into town," Suzi said.

"Suzi, are you forgetting the only clothing you own

is that robe and pajamas you're wearing?" Joy pointed at her friend.

She pulled at the neckline of her robe, looked down the inside, then back at Joy. "Nope, just the robe."

"Where are your pajamas?" Joy asked.

"Up in smoke I'd imagine. I normally sleep in the buff. So much freer. Good thing I fell asleep with this on, or Boris might not've pulled me out that window."

Grace covered her mouth stifling a laugh.

"People wander around in their bedclothes all the time. Nobody will bat an eye at this outfit." Suzi held up her hands.

"Aunt Suzi, you don't even have shoes to wear besides those flimsy hospital slippers." Grace pointed. "And the only place I've ever seen people wearing pj's to go shopping is in those big superstores."

"Oh, come on. I'll just look fashionably challenged is all." Suzi swatted the air with her hand. "Lend me a belt, and I'll fit right in."

If Joy didn't go alone, she'd have to cancel her meeting with Harmony. Until the authorities determined whether the young woman had a hand in setting the fire, she didn't want Suzi or Grace anywhere near her. "Suzi, you sit and relax. Besides, you don't want to leave your little savior alone just yet, do you?"

"True. My little snuggle monster deserves some attention." She scooped him up into her arms.

Grace offered to accompany her mother, but Joy asked her to open the tasting room. Business wasn't the worry, but if she didn't leave soon, she'd be late, and Harmony might not wait around.

When Joy drove up to the café, only a few vehicles were parked in the lot. None of them belonged to

Harmony. Joy took a booth by the front window, so Harmony could easily spot her. She also wanted to be in a visible location in case Cutter decided to come as well. His appearance in town around the same time Grace had been attacked on the beach convinced Joy of Owen's innocence. Either way, Joy's instincts pegged Harmony as being the root of everything.

She ordered a glass of iced tea when the waitress came by. Joy waved off the menu saying she would wait for her friend to arrive. A half an hour and two refills later, Joy paid for her drink and left a generous tip, apologizing to the server. "I must have gotten the time mixed up."

"No worries, hon." The woman in the uniform waved her arm at the mostly empty room. "It isn't like we've got a line waiting for your table."

Joy gave a weak smile and dug her keys out of her purse as she left. Something white sat pinned under a windshield wiper. *Don't tell me I've gotten a ticket?*

Approaching her car, she slipped the folded paper from where it lay. It wasn't a citation. Scrawled across the page in black marker, it read, "You are way too trusting." The note wasn't signed, but it didn't need to be. Panic overtook Joy as she fumbled for her phone and hit Grace's cell number.

Her daughter picked up on the fifth ring. "Hey, Mom. You home?"

The tightness in her shoulders eased. "No. My shopping took longer than planned. Everything okay at the winery?"

"I've been busy, but it's fine. I could use some help when you get back."

"Sure. I'd send your aunt over, but she's still in an

unclothed state." Joy forced a chuckle. "I'll be home in about half an hour."

"Okay. See you shortly. Gotta go." Grace ended the call.

A loud engine revved on the street in front of her. Joy almost dropped her phone as her head shot up.

Stopped by the curb, a woman on a blue motorcycle revved the engine again. The face shield obscured her identity, but a long, blonde braid hung down her back. She slowly shook her head at Joy, tapped one hand on the top of her helmet, then hit the clutch and tore off down the street. Brakes screeched and a horn blasted when she ran a red light and cut off a car about to enter the intersection.

Joy leaned against her car and took a deep breath. She hadn't noticed her purse fall to the ground until an old man picked it up.

"Are you all right, miss?" He extended an arm toward her, offering the bag.

Without looking up, Joy took hold of the strap. "Yes. Thank you. I'm fine. The sound of the motorcycle startled me."

"They can get pretty loud, especially in a quiet burg such as this."

Glancing into his face, she gasped. The man Joy ran into after her failed attempt to find Pete at the giftshop stood before her. "You're the fisherman. From the coast. What are you doing here?" Instead of yellow waders, he wore jeans and a checked flannel shirt with a pipe sticking out of the pocket. A lingering scent of apple tobacco hung in the air.

"Ah-ya. My daughter lives in Huntsville." The man tilted his head.

Joy stared. Her knuckles whitened as she gripped her phone and purse. "You're Silas," she whispered.

Chapter 31

Joy's face paled, and her palms dampened with sweat. A mix of anger and fear swept through her fueled by Marla's description of this man's past actions. Regret joined the party as she conceded to a sense of loss and abandonment.

Silas was to blame for her not returning to Harmony after the accident. If deceit and betrayal were commonplace in Celestia's culture, maybe it was best she walked away. She had a family with Grace and Suzi. Did she need to explore further, simply to find those who'd turned their backs on her?

"You're angry," Silas said.

"Why didn't you admit who you were the first time we met on the beach? You knew I searched for where I'd come from and my real identity. Why all the lies?"

Silas sighed. "I never lied to you, Justine. When you didn't return after a year, I came back to Huntsville and found you'd moved on to a happy life. Nobody believed Harmony would survive beyond the age of five, and I thought it best to leave you in peace."

Joy leaned against her car. "You might have talked to me about it. Deserting my child was not your decision to make. I would have gone back for her."

"I did speak with you."

She narrowed her eyes. "Yes, in the hospital when you gave me the necklace. It was you, wasn't it?"

"That's not what I meant." Silas shifted his stance. "Eighteen months after you'd left, I came into the tasting room of your winery. We spoke, you and me. Had a twenty-minute conversation while you poured me wine samples. You didn't know me."

She brought a hand to her mouth.

"I chose—"

"You chose. You chose!" Joy stepped closer. "You had no right. It was my choice to make!" Her face reddened.

"Maybe in hindsight, I could have handled it better. But you were so angry as a young woman with nothing but hard times ahead. You allowed your heart to lead you down a dark path." His voice cracked. "All I wanted was for you to be happy."

Joy's eyes brimmed with tears. "Why are you here now?"

Silas released a breath. "To give you the chance I took away all those years ago. You need to move forward with your life as you see fit, but you can't do that without knowing where you came from. Look, is there some place we can talk away from listening ears?"

She remained silent.

"Please, Justine. Allow me the opportunity to explain." He reached out to touch her shoulder, but she backed away. His hand dropped to his side.

"I have errands to run. Meet me at my home in an hour. My friend, Suzi, is staying with me, but I'll send her to help my daughter at the winery. We'll have privacy."

He nodded and left.

Joy forced herself to focus on the shopping.

Whatever Silas had to say didn't frighten her, but the choices to move forward did. How could this ever come out right?

****

Back at the house, Joy gave Suzi the velour track suit she'd requested and asked her to help in the tasting room for a short while.

When Suzi emerged from her room in the bright pink outfit and matching sneakers, she struck a pose. "How do I look? Pretty snazzy, huh?"

Joy stifled a smirk. She'd tried to convince Suzi muted colors would look better on her, but her new housemate wouldn't hear of it. The only choices she wanted were fuchsia, royal blue, or Kelly green. The store only had pink in the right size. She struggled for an appropriate response. "Um, it complements your eyes?"

"Darn tootin' it does!" With a scratch of Jester's head and a promise to return soon, Suzi left to help Grace.

Ten minutes later the doorbell rang. Hesitantly, Joy checked the peephole and found Silas. An old green pick-up truck sat in the driveway behind him.

As they walked through the kitchen, he stopped at the sink. "I see you have a green thumb." Silas gestured toward the yellow flowers on the windowsill. "Some have difficulty growing these to full bloom the first time and need to start over. Yours are starting to peak and should be ready to harvest in about a week."

"Harvest?" Joy asked.

Her father pointed to the center of one flower where a hint of thin wood protruded from the plant.

"That's odd. I could swear that wasn't there when I

watered them this morning. Since I know Celestia is a place and not a plant, what am I supposed to do when they're ready to *harvest*?"

"Follow the instructions. They're very specific." Silas withdrew a pipe from his shirt pocket. "There someplace I can light this while we speak? It calms me."

She eyed the new development on her plants as she led the way to the back patio. A table with four chairs sat beneath an open umbrella, where she'd already set out a pitcher of iced tea and two glasses.

Silas settled onto one of the cushioned seats. When offered tea, he declined and filled his pipe from a bag in his pants pocket before lighting it. The strong aroma of apple tobacco immediately permeated the air.

Joy had to admit, the scent did have a soothing effect. She filled her own glass and sat across from him waiting for the man to begin.

After puffing a few times to get the pipe going, he leaned back. "Your mother didn't know what happened to you or if you were even alive. At least until you showed up in Pete's gift shop."

With only two sentences, Silas had already rocked her off balance. "My mother?" Joy hadn't considered her mother all this time. When Marla filled her in about her father's involvement with no mention of the other parent, Joy assumed she wasn't alive.

"Tessa and I had a bit of a falling out twenty-two years ago."

"When I left." Moisture formed on the outside of the glass where her fingers wrapped around it.

"Yes. It broke her heart when you took up with Michael. Along with his parents, we tried to keep the two of you apart, but you both had a defiant streak. We all knew it would end in disaster."

"Marla explained the danger of mixing bloodlines. I guess I can understand you wanting to keep us from staying together. You would think with all the medical advances she'd mentioned, your people could have found a way to fix the genetic incompatibility."

Smoke puffed from his mouth. "Our people."

Joy scrunched her brows. "What?"

"You said 'your people,' Justine. Like it or not, you're one of us."

Leaning her head back, she massaged her shoulders, but it failed to relieve the gnawing tension. He wasn't wrong, but did she belong on Celestia anymore? They'd kicked her out.

"Our healers have tried for centuries to successfully mix the blood lines. They've yet to achieve a cure. The only way couples of different races can remain together is if they agree to sterilization."

"That sounds barbaric." Joy sat up straight.

Her father chuckled. "You said the same thing when your mother and I told you it would be your only option if you remained with Michael. We didn't know by then it had been too late."

She jerked her head up. "What do you mean? The only thing Marla would tell me is I came through the portal without permission and carrying my infant daughter. She told me I'd have to ask you what had occurred before that time."

"Like I said, we got to you too late. You were already two months pregnant. Meanwhile, to slow your relationship, Marla and Benjamin had taken a post here on Earth as guardians of the portal in the desert region near Pahrump, Nevada. They'd forced Michael to join them before any of us knew you were expecting."

Joy gave a mirthless laugh. "After meeting Marla, I bet she claimed the baby couldn't possibly be her son's."

Silas nodded. "You aren't far from the truth. She refused to believe it, until the day you showed up with your black-eyed child. The evidence couldn't be refuted."

Joy drank her tea and struggled to absorb everything he said. "Tell me what you and my mother disagreed about."

"You, of course. As a member of the ruling Council, I had an obligation to uphold our ways. When you refused to terminate the pregnancy, the remaining option had been for you to give birth and surrender the child. Mixed breeds are raised in a separate facility because they're prone to anger and violence so can't be around other children. Your mother supported your decision to have the child but wanted me to allow you to raise her in our home. When the Council denied the request and you left, she never forgave me for driving you away."

She removed her damp hand from the glass and wiped it on her jeans. "How did Harmony survive? And Cutter too for that matter?"

"Cutter?" The pipe nearly slipped from his lips.

"You don't know about Cutter?" Concern seared through Joy's words. Silas no longer held all the cards like she'd originally thought.

His eyes widened as he shook his head.

"He's the guy Harmony calls her boyfriend. His eyes are black like hers. I'd assumed he came from the same place once I learned about Celestia."

"Hmmmm." Silas rubbed his chin. "To answer your question, Harmony survived because she'd been raised here on Earth. There must be some properties in the atmosphere we haven't been able to discover which allow a few of the children to thrive and grow. Unfortunately, the darkness of their soul remains. In fact, it gives them certain powers that don't become evident until they reach adulthood."

She laced her fingers together in her lap. "Powers like the scorching she inflicts on people when touched?"

"Yes. As for her boyfriend, there have been others who've gone through the portals without permission and disappeared. His parents must have raised him on Earth."

Unable to sit still any longer, Joy paced the length of the patio. She stopped and asked, "Is my mother back in Celestia?'

He slumped his shoulders. "She is now. Shortly after you left, she couldn't bear to remain and chose to be a guardian of one of the portals with her brother. They ran a gift shop on the Oregon coast. It was there your memories began to spark."

Nothing surprised her anymore. "So it was actually *Uncle* Pete who sold me the seeds, wasn't it?"

Again, he nodded. "Your mother watched from the back room. When you didn't recognize Pete, he made her stay out of sight so as not to cause a scene. He contacted me, and they were recalled to Celestia."

"That's why I couldn't find him when I returned to the shop. Why would you pull them back when I'd begun to remember?"

"We couldn't allow Tessa to start searching for you until you recalled more on your own. When you bought the seeds, we knew your recovery had begun, but you needed to work through it alone. If one of us simply told you, you'd never know the difference between true memories and ones you'd learned. The temptation would be too great for your mother if she remained here on Earth."

"Did Tessa take you back when she discovered I wasn't dead?"

He snorted. "Nope. She grew furious at my not telling her what had happened to you. I tried to spare her the pain of losing you all over again when your memory didn't return."

"You've made many decisions that weren't yours to make. What happens now that…" Joy turned as the sliding glass door slammed open. "Suzi, what's wrong?"

The heaving woman leaned on the door frame. "I've been calling your cell for the last ten minutes." She huffed, struggling for air. "It's Owen. He's…"

Suzi straightened as she pointed at Silas. "Who's the fossil?"

Chapter 32

Joy rushed over to Suzi. "What about Owen? Is Grace okay?" Without waiting for an answer, she ran through the house and out the front.

At the tasting room parking lot, she found Owen and Cutter embroiled in a fistfight. Both were bloodied, but Owen had borne the worst of it. Blood gushed from his nose and a gash above his eye. The other man had a good six inches and fifty pounds on him. Grace jumped up and down screaming for them to stop, while Harmony leaned against her car with arms folded and a smug grin across her face.

Cutter knocked the other man backward. Owen grabbed the biker's shirt as he fell, pulling Cutter on top of him. Before he lost momentum, Owen rolled them over, only to be thrown off. Loose dirt from the parking lot covered their clothing mixed with the blood from their hands and faces. Both jumped back to their feet and leaped in, continuing to throw punches.

Suzi ambled along the path at a slower pace, holding her side and wincing.

Joy ran to her daughter and pulled her into a hug. "Thank goodness, you're okay."

"Mom, we need to stop them. Cutter will kill him," Grace cried.

Stepping closer to Harmony, Joy asked, "Can't you make him stop? Please."

The young blonde shrugged. "What am I supposed to do? They're only blowing off a little steam." She nodded toward Owen. "Besides, one of them will tucker out soon."

Joy grasped the woman by the arms. "You need to do something." A jolt seared through her, as if struck by lightning. Her body flew backward and slammed into the ground. White spots danced before her eyes and a ringing in her ears crescendoed louder and louder.

"Mom!" Grace rushed to her side.

The men continued swinging at each other. Cutter nailed Owen with several blows to the gut. He might have done worse, but a cascade of water crashed over them. Each staggered backward and looked toward the source. The dirt turned to mud, and Cutter almost slipped as he backed up.

Suzi stood a few feet away blasting them with a garden hose she'd dragged from the side of the building. In her pink neon sweat suit, she resembled a cherub standing in the middle of a fountain. "Now, you boys cool off!" She turned the nozzle, shutting off the flow. "I don't know why I didn't think of this before." A chuckle escaped her lips.

Grace helped her mother stand. "Mom, are you okay?"

Joy shook her head to clear the fuzz. "I'm fine. Help Owen."

After a brief hesitation, she squeezed her mother's shoulder and rushed to her husband's side. Throwing her arms around his neck, she said, "I'm so sorry. I had no idea he would attack you." She pulled back. Tears streamed down her face, her shirt stained with a mix of his blood and water from the hose.

Through ragged breaths, he placed a hand to her face, and whispered, "Shhhh. It's not your fault. I'm glad you called me."

"What's this all about?" Joy asked Cutter.

The big man jerked a thumb in Harmony's direction. "Ask her. I'm just the hired hand." He spit a mouthful of blood onto the ground and stomped to the car.

"I wanted to spend a little quality time with my *sister*," Harmony said. "Instead, that psycho friend of yours slammed the door in my face. When your soon-to-be ex-son-in-law showed up, he took the first swing."

"Don't make me turn this on you too, you little hussy!" Suzi took aim with the hose, ready to release the nozzle once more.

The young blonde narrowed her eyes at Suzi, then snapped her fingers, as if the action would banish the older woman.

"That's not true," Grace stepped closer. "If your asshole boyfriend hadn't shoved him, none of this would've happened. Take a hint and get out of here. Can't you see you're not wanted?"

Harmony turned her gaze on Grace, and her tone became sultry. "That's not what your hubby said the other night."

"That's enough." Joy held up her hands. "Suzi, put the hose down. Harmony, we need to talk, but now isn't the time. Take your man and leave. Please."

"Well, you did say please." She jingled her keys and got into the car.

The biker walked to the passenger door, but not before glaring at Owen. "This ain't over, little man."

Not budging an inch, Suzi held her weapon at the ready.

The engine started, and the car backed out of the parking space. After shifting into drive, the tires spun in the mud before catching and propelling the vehicle forward. As it sped down the driveway, Harmony's cackling carried from the open window.

"Grace, I can explain..." Owen began.

She put a finger to his lips. "Enough. Let's get you cleaned up. There should be a first aid kit in the back room." With an arm around his waist, she led him into the tasting room.

Joy's shoulders sagged. She needed to find a solution to this volatile situation before anybody else got hurt. From the description Silas had given of the half-breed children, she feared there wouldn't be a way to reason with Harmony. If she possessed that destructive nature, the only way to end this was to cut ties with her biological daughter. She would have to turn her back on her child again, except this time it would be intentional. Could she do it a second time? Would Harmony allow her?

Joy turned to her champion, who still held the hose. "I think you can put that away now."

"Just making sure they don't return." The woman held it a moment longer before hauling the thing back where she'd found it.

In the back room, Joy found her daughter doctoring Owen's wounds. "The cut above his eye looks bad. Maybe we should take him to the ER and have it looked at."

"Ouch," he said. "It'll be fine, if little Miss Nightingale here takes it easy on me."

"Don't be such a baby. I barely touched you." Grace dabbed at the gash with an antiseptic swab. "I'll put a butterfly strip across it, which is probably all they'll do at the hospital. Did Cutter damage any ribs? You took a few nasty blows."

He placed a hand over his left side. "They're sore, but I don't think he pounded hard enough to break anything."

"Owen, I'm so sorry about all this," Joy said.

"How could you know they would show up and start a fight?" He scrunched the bottom portion of his shirt and squeezed out the excess water. "I'm just glad Grace called me before they got inside. Suzi is one tough cookie. I'll give her that."

Joy chuckled. "That, she is. I need to get back to the house. Honey, can you and Suzi close up shop? I know it's early, but I want to take your aunt into town to pick up her car and shop for more clothes."

"Sure, Mom." She continued to clean the cuts on his face. "Besides, Owen and I have some things to talk about."

Joy caught the gaze exchanged between her daughter and husband. Despite Joy's own mixed feelings about her son-in-law, Grace did love the man. Maybe they could work things out.

Suzi walked into the tasting room as Joy returned to the front room. "The coast is clear. I made sure they didn't circle back."

"I didn't think they would," Joy said. "Look, I need to wrap up something at the house. You want to rescue Daisy and buy a few additional things for your wardrobe when I'm done?"

She rested an elbow on the counter. "Who was that

man?"

Joy sighed. "Silas—my father."

She brought her hands to her face. "No! He just showed up on your doorstep?"

"Not exactly. I ran into him in town. Or should I say, he turned up by my parked car. We'll talk later. I asked Grace to close, so come to the house when you finish."

"Aye, aye, Captain!" Suzi mock saluted.

As Joy walked across the parking lot, her pace slowed. Silas had left. They'd have to finish their conversation whenever he chose to show up again, except this time she had different questions.

The jolt she'd received from Harmony had shaken loose the rest of her hidden memories. Joy hadn't snuck out of Celestia. Silas helped her leave.

Chapter 33

Suzi hurried after Joy. "Wait up," she called.

Joy stood by the front door. "Are you done closing already?"

"Grace kicked me out. It seemed she and Owen had things to discuss. I know neither one of us wants to hear it, but I think those two are headed for marriage counseling and reconciliation."

"I'm not sure that's the best of plans, but it's her life. I need to support my daughter, whatever she decides." Joy walked into the entry and Suzi followed.

"So what's going on with your father? Kinda strange how he showed up after all these years."

"Not exactly. It turns out the gift shop we stopped in on our trip up the coast belonged to my uncle—Pete. He and my mother, who'd been in the back room, recognized me. When I didn't remember Pete and introduced myself as Joy, they knew something had gone wrong. Rather than trying to convince me of who I was, they stayed quiet and contacted Silas. Apparently, my mother, Tessa, never knew what happened to me. She and my father have been separated ever since I left."

"Wow. No drama there." Suzi shook her head. "What else did he tell you?"

Joy picked up her purse and car keys. "I'll tell you on the way. Sure you're ready to see what's left of your place?"

"Gotta face it sometime. Besides, Daisy survived."

****

When Joy drove up to the remains of the cottage, Suzi sucked in a quick breath. "I didn't realize how bad the fire had been. The place is totaled. Thank goodness, my little Jester and I got out when we did." Her voice hoarsened as she wiped tears from the corners of her eyes.

"There's nothing left. The fire inspector should be able to determine if the blaze got set intentionally or accidentally," Joy said.

Suzi's hands balled in her lap. "Either way, my money's on Harmony. She's had it in for me from the moment we met like a bouncer evicting a party-crasher."

Ignoring Suzi's theatrics, Joy got out of the car. The damp ash smell hit immediately, though not as ripe as it had been earlier this morning.

"Whew!" Suzi held her nose as she walked to her car. "Smells like somebody hosed down a giant ash tray."

"Do you need me to come shopping with you?" Joy asked.

"Nah, I got this. I'll see you back at the casa later. Need me to pick anything up from the grocery store?"

She shook her head. "I got everything this morning. Let's aim for dinner at six. Sound good?"

"Works for me," Suzi said as she got into the driver's seat of Daisy. The vehicle started without hesitation, and Suzi took off down the road.

Joy waved. Before getting into her own car, she walked around the charred husk of the dwelling. She peered inside between blackened wooden beams and smashed window frames. Nothing appeared salvageable from where she stood. Remnants of furniture lay crushed inside among metal curtain rods and shards of glass. As she rounded the kitchen entry, the cement steps remained intact and speckled with scorch marks.

She backed away from the devastation and offered up another prayer of thanks that her friend got out alive. Her foot landed on a rock and twisted to the side. When she looked down, a small gasp escaped her lips, and a chill ran down her spine. Joy picked up a necklace similar to the one she wore—except the substance inside the vial glistened with inky darkness.

Only one of two people could have dropped it. Could she go to the police with this evidence? They won't need to know the significance of the item, and maybe they could remove fingerprints from the glass. Even if Harmony's or Cutter's prints weren't on file with the authorities, surely this would be reason enough for them to check into the couple. Did people from Celestia have fingerprints unique to each individual? Joy studied the swirling grooves at the tips of her own fingers.

With too many "what ifs" to figure into the equation, she decided the police wouldn't be a good option yet. Joy tucked the necklace inside her purse. As she drove away, fear consumed her thoughts. One or both had set the fire. There couldn't be any other explanation for why the black vial would be outside of Suzi's home. Would they try again? What if they tried to burn her home down with the three of them inside?

Joy drove home faster than the law allowed. Owen may have left by now, and Grace would be alone. When she reached the house, Owen's car sat parked in her driveway.

Grace stood at the counter chopping vegetables on a cutting board while Owen watched from a nearby stool looking the worse for wear. One side of his face sported mottled patches of bruises from the beating he'd received. The cut over his eye had crusted.

"Hi, Mom. I invited Owen to join us for dinner. Hope you don't mind." Grace continued her prep work.

"Not at all. How are you feeling?" Joy asked her son-in-law.

"A bit sore, but I'll live. Grace filled me in on the fire at Suzi's. If you suspect Harmony was involved in starting it, you should go to the police. I wouldn't doubt Cutter helped. The sooner he's off the streets the better for everyone."

"Without proof, what could I tell them?" Joy remained quiet about finding the necklace. For now, they needed to keep Owen out of the loop on her true identity and bearing. The last thing they needed was more violence if Owen decided to take things further in protecting his wife.

After dinner Grace walked Owen to his car. He had wanted her to go home with him, but she said she needed more time alone, but they would talk tomorrow.

"Having second thoughts about those divorce papers?" Joy asked her daughter when she returned inside.

Grace slumped onto one of the stools at the kitchen counter. "Do you think I should?"

Joy sat beside her daughter and rubbed her shoulder. "It's not my decision to make. Do I have an opinion? Yes. At the end of the day, you need to do what you feel in your heart. All I ask, is you take your time in deciding what your true feelings are."

Her eyes glistened. "I know, Mom. Owen cheated on me. There's no denying that fact. Doesn't everyone deserve a second chance?"

Unconsciously, Joy held the vial hanging from her necklace. It's not my decision to decide who does, she thought. "I'll support you in whatever your decision. Make sure it is what's best for *you*."

Her daughter hugged her, then pulled away. "What's going on with your weird plants?" She pointed at the pots on the windowsill.

Joy strolled across the kitchen with forehead scrunched. The slim board sticking out from the center of each plant had doubled in size since Silas pointed it out earlier. She brushed the edges with her fingertip. The rough substance reminded her of veneer, but the thinness stumped her. Letters were carved into the wood, but she couldn't make out what they said.

She turned back to Grace. "I'm not sure, but Silas, my father, was here earlier and told me I would need to harvest them. He said the instructions would be implicit. Whatever that means."

Grace bolted up. "Your father came here? When? Why didn't you tell me?"

"I ran into him in town, or I should say he found me. He met me back here, and we talked about my past, until Suzi ran in telling of the fight."

"Why didn't you say anything earlier?"

"Owen knows nothing of my past, and I'd prefer to keep it that way," Joy said.

Her daughter eased back onto the stool. "I get it. I know he still cares for me, and maybe…just maybe…we can work our way back to a loving relationship again. While I know he cheated, I feel there were outside forces working against us to get to you."

"Harmony."

"Yes." Grace nodded. "He participated, but I don't know how much coercion got thrown at him, coupled with my indifference over the last year. We're both at fault for our relationship deteriorating. With a little work, maybe we can find our way back."

"I'm done for the night. Suzi already turned in, tuckered out from today's excitement. I wouldn't doubt the trauma of the fire is still wearing on her. She really had luck on her side getting out when she did." A shudder ran through Joy's body.

Grace grabbed the kettle and filled it with water. "I'm making tea. Would you like a cup?"

"No, I'm good. Good night, sweetie. I'll lock up before going upstairs."

"See you in the morning." Grace dropped a teabag into a mug.

Joy scooped her purse off the counter and carried it upstairs, where she removed the necklace with the black vial. It dangled from the chain with the light reflecting off it. *Who did it belong to?* Either way, Harmony had been involved. Cutter wouldn't have set the fire without direction. He had nothing to gain from harming Joy's loved ones.

Chapter 34

Joy awoke to the chirping of her cell phone. A text from Harmony.

—*Noon. Accident site. Come alone.*—

How could Harmony possibly believe she would go along with such a meeting? Joy carried her mug to the back patio, where she found Silas puffing on his pipe. A few weeks ago, she would've been shocked to find an uninvited guest. Now, such occurrences no longer fazed her.

"Coffee?" Joy asked.

"I wouldn't be opposed to a cup, thanks." Silas pulled on his pipe and blew out a stream of apple-scented smoke.

"How do you take it?"

"Cream and sugar, if you don't mind."

When Joy returned with a steaming mug, she set it before him. "I had another encounter with my daughter. Her *powers* shocked my body, restoring my full memory. If you were so against my union and bearing a child with Michael, why did you help me get through the portal?"

Silas's poker face gave away no emotion. "What do you remember?"

"Everything. You pushed to keep us apart. You pushed for me to abort the baby. You refused to let me raise her in your home. But then you went against the

Council's ruling and helped me leave with her. Why?"

"Your mother told you I'd given you the passes, huh? She never said as much." He leaned back and crossed his legs.

Joy expelled a breath. "Well, she said as much to me. Care to explain?"

Silas stood and tamped out his pipe. "Nope."

"What?" Joy jumped to her feet.

"It's complicated. Maybe we should leave things as they are."

"Don't you think it's a bit late to put the genie back in the bottle? You're here for a reason. You wanted me to remember." She came around the table and stood toe to toe with him. "Now I do. What's next?" Receiving nothing but silence, Joy's tone sharpened. "Were you hoping I'd never recover, and you could give me a watered-down version of what you *think* I should know?"

"Mom, what's going on?" The sliding door rattled in its frame as Grace came outside. "Is this your father?"

Joy and Silas looked to her then back at each other.

"I should go." Silas walked toward the corner of the house.

"Wait!" Grace ran after him. "You may not be my biological grandfather, but we're still family." She stuck out her hand. "Grace. Nice to meet you."

Silas looked down at her hand then back at his daughter. With a sigh, he grasped the hand. "My pleasure. Silas, though I suppose you should call me Grandpa."

She nodded. "Nice to meet you, *Grandpa.*"

"I need to be going." He turned.

"Please stay," both Joy and her daughter said at the same time.

He hesitated, then returned to his chair. "Would breakfast be included if I linger?"

Joy smirked. "How do you like your eggs?"

While they ate, Silas refrained from talking about much more than the weather and fishing on the Oregon coast. He spoke of enjoying the shores of the Pacific in this area of the country.

Grace asked questions about Celestia and its similarities to Earth. In response, she received little information from her grandfather. Most answers came in the form of a nod or tilt of the head.

Joy chalked it up to their privacy being interrupted and his unwillingness to divulge any past secrets to anyone but her.

Suzi didn't make an appearance until breakfast had been eaten and Silas left.

Joy held her discouragement in check. Another missed opportunity to learn about her father's actions nagged at her, but she couldn't force him to divulge things in front of a virtual stranger. *How well did he even know her anymore?*

She reread Harmony's text. Joy feared the young woman had a hidden agenda and might not arrive alone herself. Meeting at the spot Michael died wouldn't resolve anything.

"Mom?"

Joy broke from her reverie. "Sorry, Grace, what?"

"Can you spare me from the tasting room today? And your warehouse guy? Owen and I want to talk, and it's best if we're on neutral territory."

Joy studied her daughter's face for a moment.

"You do what you need to. Aunt Suzi and I can handle things. Right, Suzi?"

"Absofuckinglutely!" Suzi said. "You take care of business and let us know what color smoke comes out of the chimney."

Joy and Grace gaped at her.

"It's the new me. Unencumbered of worldly possessions and free speaking with no regrets!" Suzi raised her arms in the air while sporting a huge grin. "What do you think?"

"Um…well…" Joy said. "Perhaps our tasters aren't quite ready for the new Suzi."

The older woman dropped her arms. "Too much?"

Grace held her pointer finger and thumb an inch apart. "Just a tad."

"Okay, I'll reel it in. Some. Can't lose all my enthusiasm. Life would be too dull."

"Believe me, Aunt Suzi, life with you around is *never* dull." Grace kissed both her mom and aunt on the cheek and left.

"So, what did I miss this morning besides breakfast?" Suzi plunked down onto a stool at the counter. "I saw a green pick-up driving away when I got up." She snagged a piece of buttered toast left on a plate and slathered it with jam. "Was the cranky old man back?"

Joy chuckled. "If you mean my father, yes. I found him on the patio when I got up. He didn't tell me anything new because Grace interrupted us."

"What aren't you telling me?" Suzi munched a bite of toast.

Joy smiled. "You don't miss a beat, do you?"

"Nope. Spill." She slapped the counter.

"You know when I touched Harmony asking her to stop the fight between the boys?"

Suzi nodded her head. "Yeah."

"Well, she sent another jolt through me. This time, I remembered everything." Joy involuntarily shivered.

"By everything, you mean…"

Joy took a deep breath. "Everything. My life before the accident, my parents, Michael—"

Suzi inhaled. "Michael. What about Michael?"

"Michael. My love. My hope of a life together. The life we lost. Everything. And the memory of Silas helping me escape with Tru—a.k.a. Harmony." A tear slipped down Joy's cheek. She wiped it away with the back of her hand.

"What? The man who wanted your reproductive parts neutralized? He helped you escape?" Suzi's eyes bugged wide.

"Yeah." Joy sank onto one of the stools by the kitchen bar.

Suzi sat up straight. "I'm confused. He was totally against you being with Michael and any offspring you might have produced. He didn't want you to raise your own kid. And then he turns around and helps you leave Celestia? Hello, Mr. Hypocrite."

"I know. It doesn't make sense, yet he helped me. He helped us. My mother told me when she'd led me to the portal with my baby."

"What happens now?" Suzi raised a finger into the air. "Wait, if you know how and where you got to Earth, can't you go back through?"

Joy shook her head. "It's not that simple. Remember, as a punishment to Michael's parents for giving me shelter, the Council had the portal sealed.

We'd also need passes."

"Kind of like a key card? Maybe we could figure out a way to hack it!" Suzi rubbed her hands together.

Joy laughed. "It's not a safe to be cracked. There's an attendant who takes your passes and sends you through."

"Okay. I could distract this attendant." Suzi swayed her hips as she sauntered across the kitchen. Dressed in a bright green velour sweat suit, she didn't exactly telegraph seduction. "While I have the guy mesmerized with my womanly figure, you could sneak through the portal."

"Remember the part about the entry being sealed?" Joy asked.

Suzi placed her hands on her hips. "Drat! It was a good plan."

"Look, it's time for us to open the tasting room." Joy picked up her cell phone. "You ready?"

Suzi cupped a hand over her nose and mouth, expelled a breath, then wrinkled her nose. "I'll be right behind you. Gotta brush my pearly whites, so I don't melt any customers with my morning breath."

With her housemate out of sight, Joy replied to Harmony's text. —*Sorry. Working the tasting room today. How about meeting someplace in town?*— She hesitated before sending it. They'd arranged to meet at the café once before, and Harmony didn't show until afterward. With a shrug, she hit send, and tucked the phone into her pocket.

Her cell chirped before she reached the front door. Joy gasped. Harmony's response contained no words—just an emoji of a flame.

Chapter 35

As the hour approached noon, Joy checked her phone—no additional messages. She went to the house to make lunch since they had a lull in customers.

Grace loaded a suitcase into her car where it sat in the driveway.

"I take it things went well with Owen?" Joy asked.

"We have a lot to work through, but yes, we've decided to try again." She closed the rear hatch.

Joy gestured toward the house. "You can stay here if you'd rather move slowly."

"I thought about it, but I miss him, Mom. There's no denying I love him."

"Your love for him isn't in question. It's everything else. But you already know that. If you feel good about this, then it's the right thing to do."

Grace hugged her mother. "Thanks for understanding and not trying to talk me out of it."

Joy pulled back and placed a hand on her daughter's cheek. "I love you."

"Love you too, Mom." She released her hold. "We also talked about the winery."

"This sounds like a longer conversation. Come inside while I make lunch for Suzi and me."

Grace followed. "There isn't much to discuss." She sat at the breakfast bar while her mother pulled items from the refrigerator.

"Are you staying for lunch?"

She shook her head. "I'm meeting Owen at the café in town."

"Okay, tell me what you're thinking." Joy made sandwiches for herself and Suzi.

"I'm accepting your offer to take over the winery. And I will be the sole owner."

The sense of relief she'd hoped for didn't happen. "This decision feels fast in light of what's gone on between you and your husband lately. While my offer to you still stands, maybe we should table this action until the two of you are back on even ground."

Grace bolted to her feet. "Are you saying you don't trust me anymore?"

Her daughter's reaction felt like a slap in the face. "Of course, I trust you. The timing of this doesn't sit right with me. Please answer me honestly. Was it you or Owen who brought this up today?"

She waved her arms in the air as if warding off an attacker. "You still don't trust Owen's intentions."

Joy held up her hands. "All I'm saying, honey, is maybe you should tackle one obstacle at a time. Get your marriage healthy, then we'll revisit my retirement."

"I can't talk about this right now. It's obvious your opinion of Owen hasn't changed." She stormed toward the front door with her mother in pursuit.

"That's not what I meant. Come, let's talk about it."

Grace turned, let out a breath, and gave her mother a brief hug. "I don't want to fight. I'll see you at work tomorrow morning."

"Grace, wait—"

"Mom. Not now." She walked to her car and got in without a backward glance.

Joy watched from the doorway as her daughter drove away. As settled as Grace claimed to be, talk of handing over the winery came up too abruptly. She wanted to trust her son-in-law, but his sudden reform rang a bit hollow.

She wrapped up the lunch and brought it to the back room.

Suzi reclined in a chair with her feet propped atop the desk. "Did I see Grace's car driving away?"

Joy nodded. "She's moving back into the house with Owen."

"Guess we're down a roommate. I still don't trust that weasel she's married to. He may be all apologetic now, but who's got the most to gain from their getting back together?"

"I suggested she stay here a little longer and got turned down. Stranger still, she accepted my offer to run the winery." She took a seat on the other side of the desk.

Suzi swung her legs to the floor and sat up straight. "Why bring up ownership now? Unless that husband of hers angled to gain control again."

"The timing is puzzling." Joy bit her lip. "When I suggested we re-visit the conversation after their marriage got on track, she became angry and accused me of not trusting Owen. Something isn't right here."

Almost on cue, Joy's phone pinged with a text. A picture of Grace and Owen eating in the town café—except it had been sent by Harmony. Another text came through. —*Ain't love grand?*—

The phone slipped from her hand and landed on the

desk.

Suzi grabbed it and looked at the screen. "What's this?"

"I'm not sure what to make of it. This morning I'd gotten a text from Harmony wanting me to meet her at the accident site today at noon." She took the phone back.

"Of course, you told her to go to hell, right? Now you remember everything, is there any reason to even talk to the little vixen again?"

Joy pressed a button, and the screen went dark. "She's still my daughter. Maybe she could forgive me for leaving her, and we might find common ground which could lead to a friendly relationship."

Suzi's mouth gaped open. "Forgive? I doubt the word has ever been part of that woman's vocabulary. Now *revenge* and *arson* are probably at the top of her list."

Pushing away her half-eaten sandwich, Joy reached into her pants pocket and retrieved the necklace she found by the burnt house. "Speaking of arson, I found this on the ground after you drove away." She held the necklace at arm's length; the murky substance inside glistened as it reflected the light.

The blonde slipped the chain from her friend's fingers. "We need to go to the police. After what you told me about the vials matching the eyes of the wearer, there're only two suspects who could've dropped this."

"I thought about taking it to the authorities. How could I possibly explain what we suspect to be true without revealing anything about Celestia? Even I have trouble comprehending everything I've learned over the last couple weeks. Without proof—" Joy startled at the opening of the front door and walked to the tasting counter.

Suzi wrapped both hands around the chain. "You're right," she called. "Unless this thing can talk, we need more to connect Harmony and Cutter to the crime."

Joy poked her head around the door jamb. "We've got a van load. Done eating?"

The woman nodded as she slipped their contraband into a drawer, stuffed the last bite of sandwich into her mouth, and washed it down with a gulp of iced tea. "On my way."

Chapter 36

The women closed shop and strolled to the house after what turned into a busy afternoon. A steady stream of tasters kept them hopping.

"I think we deserve a night on the town. What do you say to dinner at The Wandering Vine, my treat?" Suzi asked.

Joy sighed. "Sounds like a great idea. We could both use a fun outing after the drama of the last couple days." She unlocked the front door and stepped aside, allowing her friend to greet the stampeding furball storming across the tiles.

"Jester! Mommy missed you too." Suzi scooped the dog into her arms and kissed his nose.

"Why don't we meet back here in an hour. I need a shower and change of clothes before going anywhere," Joy said as she mounted the stairs.

Suzi nodded as she set Jester on the floor.

"By the way, where did you put the black necklace?" Joy called from the top of the stairs.

Suzi smacked the side of her head with her hand. "I'm such a dummy sometimes. When all those customers interrupted our lunch, I stuck it in a drawer in the desk. I'll run back and get it."

"Thanks. I don't want to risk losing it until we decide if the police can use it to catch the arsonist. See you in an hour." Joy went to her room.

Sixty minutes later, her body refreshed from a shower and make-up, she looked forward to a relaxing meal away from the winery. Not finding Suzi waiting in the entry, Joy went to the kitchen to water the plants. The thin wooden slat in the center of each bloom had grown larger and more letters formed. Full words hadn't emerged yet, so they still left her speculating as to what kind of message the plants would convey.

Jester's toenails clicked on the ceramic floor as he entered the kitchen. He walked to his food bowl, nudged it, then gazed up at Joy.

"Didn't your mama feed you yet, little guy?" Joy bent down and scratched him behind the ear.

His tail wagged.

She walked back to the stairs and yelled. "Suzi, did you want me to feed Jester?"

After a minute with no response, Joy went up the stairs and knocked on the guest room door. "Hey, sleepy head. Did you lie down for a nap?"

No answer. She cracked open the door. "Suzi, you in there?" Stepping inside, she found the bed made and the room empty. The light in the bathroom remained off. She searched the downstairs floor and checked the back patio. When she peeked out the front window, Daisy sat parked in the driveway beside her own vehicle.

Joy hurried along the path leading from the house to the winery. The front door gaped open with the key sticking out of the lock. *She must've gotten busy with something.* Everything had been cleaned and prepped for tomorrow, so what did they miss?

"Suzi, what are you doing…" Joy froze. Broken wine bottles lay scattered across the floor with pools of red liquid seeping into the floorboards. Sunlight from the window reflected off the shards. She prayed the splotches were wine and not blood.

Rushing into the back room, she shouted Suzi's name. The back area had a similar mess of broken glass and wine splattered on the floor. The desk drawers were tossed about in disarray. Silence filled the room while fear slithered down Joy's spine keeping her feet planted to the spot just inside the doorway. Her lungs labored for breath as she balled her hands into nervous fists.

She scrutinized the back room and ran to do the same in the front, hoping for any clue as to what happened to her friend. Resolving that nothing more could be gained, she bolted to the house and into the kitchen where she'd left her purse. This time she would involve the police.

Touching the screen on her cell phone, she found a text from Suzi's number had arrived a half an hour earlier. Joy flushed with relief until she read the message. —*Crash site. Two hours. Come alone.*—

Jester whimpered at Joy's feet as if he sensed something had happened to his master. She picked him up and hugged him close. "Don't worry, little scruff, your momma will be fine." Setting him back on the floor, she wished she could believe those words. How could she be so stupid to think Harmony might be convinced to forgive her? Right now, she'd settle for civility.

She punched nine-one-one on her phone before hitting the back button and erasing the number. If the police got involved, would she ever see Suzi again? The risk of Harmony doing her friend harm if she didn't comply with the demands forced Joy to act alone.

Checking the time on her cell, she noted she'd wasted another ten minutes. With a two-hour drive ahead of her, she would arrive over a half hour late. Would Harmony wait? Would she take out her anger on Suzi?

Joy snatched her purse from the kitchen counter, plucked the car keys from a hook by the front door, and dashed to her SUV. When she turned the key, the engine made a clicking noise but wouldn't ignite. She tried again with the same result before resting her head on the steering wheel. "This can't be happening. Not now!"

She slammed the door open and bolted into the house. Searching the kitchen and finding nothing, she ran to Suzi's room. The woman hadn't time to accumulate many belongings yet, but her purse wasn't among them. Joy rustled through the dresser looking for a spare set of keys to Daisy. They probably got destroyed in the fire. Crossing her fingers, she went back to the front entryway on the off chance her friend had adopted the habit of hanging the keyring by the door. She found a spare for her own car, the tasting room set, and another house key.

Joy checked the time and released a rare expletive to the empty house. She had no other choice. Instead of dialing the police, she called her daughter. They hadn't left things on the best of terms earlier in the day, but this was a family emergency. Petty squabbles would have to wait.

Grace picked up on the fifth ring. "Hi, Mom. This isn't a good time. Can I call you later? Owen just ran out to—"

"Harmony took Suzi," Joy rasped into the phone.

"What?" the young woman yelled.

Joy briefly explained the situation. "Can I borrow your car?"

"Do you really think I'd let you do this alone? I'll be there in fifteen minutes." She ended the call before her mother could object.

Joy redialed the number twice, but Grace never answered. With her daughter involving herself in the rescue scheme, the temptation to contact the authorities burned inside her. She couldn't risk anyone else getting hurt because of her actions of the past. But what if she called them, and they delayed getting to the crash site?

By the time Grace tore into the driveway and skidded to a stop at the front door, Joy had resolved to go it alone. She didn't care if she had to drag her daughter from the car and hijack the vehicle.

The young woman rolled down the window. "Get in, Mom."

"This is a solo trip. If Harmony spots you in the car, she might do something drastic." Joy wrung her hands.

She shook her head. "Harmony has already done something drastic, and we need to stop her from hurting Aunt Suzi. Now get in, or I'm driving away without you."

Her body tensed, and she stood her ground. "Please, just let me take your car. If you don't hear from me in two hours, you can send the police to Bellington Mountain. You've already been hurt enough because of me."

The car slowly rolled away.

"Okay! Stop!" She hurried to the passenger side door and got in when Grace hit the brakes. "You have a huge stubborn streak, you know that?"

She smirked. "And who did I learn that from?"

Chapter 37

The women barely spoke for the first hour of the drive to Bellington Mountain. Grace's cell ringing broke the silence.

Joy checked the screen. "It's Owen. Did you tell him where you went?"

She shook her head and took the phone. "Hi, honey." Silence as she held the device to her ear. "Everything's fine. Mom had a small emergency at home and needed my help."

More silence.

"No, Aunt Suzi wasn't home, and this couldn't wait." Her face screwed up as her husband responded. "We can handle it on our own. No need to come by. I'll call you when we're done."

Grace listened for another few seconds. "Love you too. See you later." Her thumb hit the end button.

With her hands fisted in her lap, Joy asked, "Did he sound like he believed you?"

"I think so. At least he won't be jumping in the car and racing to your place. I didn't think to leave a note when I tore out of the house."

"Too bad he wasn't home when I called. He would have insisted on coming."

She glanced at her mother. "Which is exactly why I left so fast before he got home. We need cool heads in this situation, not a raging bull ready to do battle. Owen means well, but he might've put Aunt Suzi at more risk by showing up."

"You came up with that all in the few minutes between my call and hopping in the car?' Joy asked.

"It's kinda like running a business—calculating all the risks." Grace punched the gas pedal speeding them along at fifteen miles an hour above the limit.

Joy gripped the arm rest on the door. "You might want to slow down for the curves up ahead."

"I got this, Mom. Relax. Just making up some time before we hit the mountain and are forced to slow down. We don't know how long Harmony will wait when you don't show up at the two-hour mark." She took a curve a little too fast and had to hit the brakes hard. Putting her foot back on the gas, she brought the speed up to ten above the limit. "So, what's our game plan?"

A weak smile came to her lips. "You sound like Suzi."

Grace shrugged. "Guess you both rubbed off on me."

"As far as a plan, you're waiting in the car. That is non-negotiable." Joy crossed her arms and jutted out her chin.

"Not happening. You are not going in alone with Harmony."

She placed a hand on her daughter's arm. "I can't put you at further risk. Besides, Harmony told me to come alone. Who knows what's going on in her mind?"

"And what happens if Cutter is there too? There's no way Harmony overpowered Aunt Suzi on her own. She may be pushing sixty, but I wouldn't want to go toe to toe with her. Would you?"

Joy laughed. "You do have a point. But I'm still going in alone. Somewhere, deep inside, I believe Harmony has feelings for me as her mother."

Grace huffed. "The only feelings she's displayed are animosity and malice. Mom, it isn't safe. What if she tries to hurt you or sicks Cutter on you?"

"I can reason with her. Let me try." She gulped before gazing at her daughter. "Promise me you'll stay in the car. If you don't, I won't tell you where to stop, and Suzi's fate is on your conscience."

Her grip on the wheel tightened. "You're serious, aren't you?"

Determination edged her features. "I can't lose you. Trust me to handle the situation."

Grace faced forward without answering. She drove the car up the twisty mountain road, braking and accelerating where needed.

"Only a few more miles." Joy nodded at the mile marker on the shoulder. The muted ringing of her cell sounded from inside her purse. Retrieving it, she screwed up her face as she read the name of the caller. "Who would be calling from my home phone?"

"This might be a trick from Harmony. Maybe she wanted you out of the house. Could she be looking for something?" Grace asked.

She shook her head. "There's nothing I have she would want. Unless…"

"Unless what? What aren't you telling me?"

With a sigh, she pulled the purple vial from where it lay beneath her blouse. "When I took Aunt Suzi to get her car after the fire, I found a necklace like this one. Except inside the substance was black. According to my father, the color has to do with the lineage of the wearer. Both his and mine are purple, while Michael's and his parents had been blue. Hybrids, like Harmony and Cutter, have black ones."

"That's fitting," her daughter muttered.

The phone stopped ringing. After a beat, the same number called again, and Joy accepted the call. "Hello?"

An exasperated breath came from the other end. "It's about time you answered your dang phone! Where are you?"

"Suzi! Are you okay? Where've you been?" she shouted into the phone.

Grace pulled the car into a turnout on the right and stopped. "Is she okay? How is she calling from the house?"

"Hold your horses! I'm fine. Where are you?" Suzi asked.

Joy held up her hand to silence her daughter. "Bellington Mountain. I got a text from your phone telling me to meet there. After seeing the mess in the tasting room, I assumed Harmony had taken you and used your phone to contact me."

"Well, the little hussy had her muscle with her, otherwise I would've knocked her block off! Cutter grabbed me, taped my hands and mouth, then threw me into the garden shed. They got away with my phone and the black necklace. Now we don't have evidence to prove they burnt down my home. Not to mention doing it with me still in it!"

"I'm just glad you're safe. Don't worry about the necklace. It might not have been enough to prove their guilt anyway. Hold on a second." She turned to Grace. "Turn around. We're going home."

"You don't have to tell me twice." With a quick check of the road, she flipped a U-turn and sped down the mountain.

Joy put the phone back to her ear. "Okay, I want you to lock all the windows and doors. Don't let anyone in until we get there."

"We?"

"When my car wouldn't start, I had to call Grace, who insisted on driving. We're a little under two hours away, so batten down the hatches and stay safe until we get there."

"Sorry to cause such a ruckus and drag her into all this," Suzi said.

Joy gripped the phone. "I'm the one who dragged you all into this. Don't apologize. And your timing is impeccable. If you hadn't stopped us, who knows what Harmony had planned when we showed up at the crash site. See you soon!"

Chapter 38

As Grace maneuvered off the mountain and hit the main highway, two motorcycles roared up behind them.

Joy watched in the sideview mirror as the bikes approached. "It's Cutter and Harmony. What are they doing? Isn't it dangerous for them to ride so close to our bumper?"

"You don't know how tempting it is for me to slam on the brakes and be done with them."

She gaped. "That's a horrible thing to say! You'd kill them both."

"Kinda like they tried to do to Aunt Suzi?" Grace snapped. "I recognize Cutter with the half helmet, but how can you tell the other rider is Harmony? She never mentioned owning a motorcycle, let alone knowing how to ride."

"I saw her in town the other day when she stood me up for a meeting at the café. At least I believed it to be her with the long, blonde braid." With a shake of her head, Joy said, "We don't know for sure if they set the fire or even knew Suzi had been inside."

"Her car was parked in the driveway. It wouldn't be hard to figure out." Rather than slowing, she depressed the gas pedal harder and put distance between them and the motorcycles.

Their pursuers sped up as well.

"Maybe if you slow down, they'll pass us." Joy

peered out the back window.

"It's worth a try. They can't hurt us as long as we keep moving." Grace decelerated and the bikes were forced to do the same. After dropping to half the speed limit, their tail remained behind the vehicle. She held their pace steady.

With a rev of the engine, Harmony crossed the double yellow line and shot past the car, nearly going head-on with a tractor-trailer hauling a load of construction equipment.

Joy screamed and braced herself against the dashboard as if they were the ones in danger.

The rider's left hand shot into the air flashing them the middle finger before she punched her speed and raced away. A few seconds later Cutter shot past them and caught up with his girlfriend.

"You want me to catch up to them?" Grace asked.

"Certainly not! Let's just go home."

Ninety minutes later, they arrived home long after the sun had set. A familiar green truck sat parked in the driveway. Joy rushed into the house calling Suzi's name.

Jester came scurrying across the tiles yapping and wagging his tail. His owner followed, along with Silas.

Joy wrapped her arms around Suzi and hugged her tight. "I'm so sorry this happened to you." She held her at arm's length. "Are you sure you're okay?"

"Stop fussing. I'm fine. It kinda reminded me of some of the wild bondage nights Nicky and I used to have the first couple years of our marriage. This one time—"

"Aunt Suzi!" Grace held up her hands while motioning toward Silas with her eyes. His face flushed a bright red.

"Right. Sorry. Sometimes memory lane comes blazing up so fast, I can't stop myself from fanning the flames." Suzi swatted the air.

"Don't worry, Grandpa. You'll get used to her sharing without a filter."

He nodded without saying a word.

Joy laughed and shook her head. At least her friend wasn't any worse for wear after her ordeal. "So what happened? How did they know you'd be in the tasting room."

"I need to sit down." She led them into the living room. "They must've been coming for another little chat when they saw me go into the tasting room. I heard motorcycles rumble up but assumed they were late tasters. When I came out from the back room planning to turn them away, Cutter and Harmony waited near the counter."

Jester jumped into her lap, circled twice, then plopped down.

"I hadn't thought to hide the black necklace, which dangled from my hand. Oh, by the way, it belonged to the little vixen since Cutter wore his."

"Why didn't you just give it to them?" Joy asked.

"Willingly hand over the only evidence we had connecting them to the fire? No way, Jose. Not without a fight." She crossed her arms and bobbed her head. "I told them just that when Cutter demanded I give him the necklace. When he took a step closer, I picked up the nearest ammo and hurled a bottle of red at them."

"Aunt Suzi, they could've killed you!" Grace sat on the edge of a cushion.

"Oh, pshaw! They wouldn't have the nerve.

Besides, I missed. Gotta work on my biceps." She flexed an arm and patted the saggy muscle. "My wimpy throw didn't come close to the mark, so I threw another." She looked at Joy. "Don't worry, I made sure it was the cheap Merlot, not the high-ticket Syrah."

Silas chuckled at the woman's account.

"Cutter stomped toward me like a deranged gorilla. I expected him to pound on his chest and howl." Suzi settled in, obviously enjoying her own embellishment of the situation. "He chased me to the back room, where we had a whole case of that spoiled Cabernet. I launched another bottle his way and missed. Then threw a couple desk drawers for good measure. At least those hit the mark, granted he stood before me by then making for an easier target."

Joy placed a hand on her shoulder. "Did they say why they'd come back?"

She shook her head. "Harmony followed with that evil grin on her face. You know the one she wore the day Owen and her boyfriend fought? Anyway, Cutter grabbed me, and she snatched the necklace from my hand. They taped my hands and mouth with a roll of duct tape sitting on the shelf, dragged me out back to the storage shed, and locked me inside. He'll be nursing a couple bruised shins come nightfall," she said with pride in her voice.

"How did you get out?" Grace asked.

"After I heard the roar of their engines fade, I scraped the tape on the edge of a shelf. It took a while since my hands were behind my back."

Joy gasped. "I heard motorcycles and thought they'd gone to the tasting room then left when they found it closed. I never imagined it to be Harmony."

"How could you know? Oh, side note—you may need a new door on your shed. They'd wedged something in the handle, and I had to whack it with a sledgehammer until I broke through. By the time I got to the house, you'd left." Suzi patted her dog on the head. "And my poor baby whimpered in a corner all alone."

Silas said, "Better to have been trussed up and left behind than to have been taken."

"I agree," Joy said. "That must've been when they stole your phone." She picked up her cell. "Since you can definitely identify them, now is the time to call in the police."

Chapter 39

Joy sent Grace home before her husband came looking for her.

Since Suzi remained home and unharmed, the police couldn't classify the crime as a kidnapping, despite her insistence. The woman even argued how *technically* they'd taken her against her will when they threw her into the storage shed. It didn't matter. The authorities refused to classify the incident as anything but assault.

Once the investigation wrapped up, Silas helped clean up the tasting room. He'd remained out of sight so as not to be involved.

"Silas, you never told me why you came here today," Joy said as she tidied the counter space.

He swept broken glass onto a dustpan and dumped it into the trash. "Didn't seem important once your friend told me what happened to her."

"The drama is over—for now. What did you want?"

"You'll need to get some kind of cleanser to remove those wine stains." He pointed to the splotches on the floor. "Vinegar might do the trick too."

She chuckled. "I think I know something I can use. This isn't the first spill I've had to mop up." Leaning against the counter, she said, "Stop stalling."

With a nod, he put away the broom. "It's not what I

want. I'm here on behalf of your mother."

The smile slipped from her lips. "What about my mother? I thought you said she returned to Celestia."

"Aye. She has. Tessa wants to see you."

"Is she coming here?" Joy moved closer to her father.

He shook his head. "She wants you to come home."

After a moment's hesitation, Joy went to the window and gazed out. "Home. That's a pretty broad term. I am home. This is where I live with my family."

"She's your family too. As am I."

Joy spun to face him. "Are you? It seems you denied that fact for quite some time." Anger tinged her voice. "You had plenty of opportunities to come to me over the years. Why now?"

Silas went through the front door and onto the path to the house.

She hurried after him. "You can't keep running away every time the conversation gets uncomfortable. Why now?"

He stopped when she came up beside him. "What would have been the point to come sooner? You didn't know who you were, let alone us. Remember I told you I'd come to visit once, and you showed not one inkling of recognition. Until your memory got sparked by those seeds, you'd have only rejected the notion."

Her father had a point. Would she have believed him if he told her she came from another planet and had left behind a child? Silas had come shortly after Joy settled into her life with Drake.

"This is a conversation for another time. Your mother will have to wait until your daughter chooses to make peace or move on. Either way, your passes aren't fully formed yet." He took off toward his truck.

"Fully formed passes? What are you talking about? Can't you give me a pass like you did when I left?" she called after her father, but this time did not follow.

Instead of answering, he got into his truck and drove away.

Frustration consumed her. How could he keep throwing out clues then leave, forcing her to solve mysteries he hinted at? Why couldn't he sit down and tell her all the information she needed to know? Now that her memory had returned, she still had gaps to fill.

She found Suzi lounging on a couch in the living room. "How're you feeling?"

"Fit as a fiddle. I don't know why you wouldn't let me help clean up the mess I made."

Joy sat opposite her. "I don't think defending yourself qualifies as a mess. But Silas and I made quick work of it."

Suzi sat up and swung her feet to the floor. "Speaking of Silas, where is he?"

"He left." She released a long breath.

"Did he mention why he came by in the first place? I almost didn't let him in when he rang the bell. It's a good thing I'd seen him the day of the fight, otherwise no amount of talking would've convinced me he was your father."

She massaged the tight muscles which had formed in her neck and shoulders. "My mother wants to see me."

"More visitors? Shall I plan a dinner party?" Suzi smirked. "Might as well make it a complete set and include Uncle Pete."

With a smile, Joy said, "No celebration. My mother, Tessa is her name, wants me to come home."

"Home? You mean like another planet home? Home to Celestia?"

Joy sighed. "That's the place. Of course, Silas couldn't leave without dropping another useless clue for me to ponder."

She perked up with eyes bright. "Oohhh. I love mysteries! What did the old geezer say?"

"He said it didn't matter right now anyway, because my passes aren't fully formed. Whatever that means. I don't know why, if they want me to go there, he can't give me a pass like when I left. I'm tired of all this cryptic innuendo."

"Fully formed? You're right, he's an odd bird." Suzi leaned into the back cushion tapping her chin. "Wait a minute! I almost forgot. Maybe we do know what he means."

Joy raised her arms in the air. "How so?"

Suzi shoved her body off the couch and grabbed her friend's hand. "Come with me. I discovered something while I waited for you and Grace to get back."

Chapter 40

Suzi dragged her into the kitchen and over to the window above the sink. "Look!" She pointed at the plants on the sill.

Stepping closer, Joy examined the flat slats sticking from the middle of each flower. She read the mostly formed words engraved on the front. "Did it say this earlier?"

"Uh-huh. It doesn't look complete, but I believe 'mit One' either means 'Commit One' or 'Admit One.' The second line that says, 'ome to Celestia' must be 'Home' or something."

"If it's supposed to be a ticket, it probably is 'Admit One.' We'll have to wait until the slat grows more to get the full phrases." Joy looked at her. "You think this is what Silas referred to?"

"Has to be!" The woman slapped the counter. "What else would he mean? Besides, it fits the fifth instruction which says to harvest. When the tickets are completely grown, you pick them."

"You've got a point."

"Of course, I do!" The blonde bobbed her head. "But how come you didn't know about these? You said your memories returned."

Joy shrugged. "I only went through the portal the one time to come to Earth. The passes in Celestia were made of a different substance, and honestly, I never knew how they were produced. I guess here, they need to be grown."

"Makes sense." Suzi rubbed her hands together. "Now, since there are two plants and two tickets, you know what that means, don't you?"

"I'll need one for each way?"

With a huff, she said, "No. It means *we* are going on another road trip."

She held up her hands. "Slow down. We don't know if it's even safe for you to go there. We don't know if it's safe for me to return after all these years. While I remember my life and everything before the accident, there may be consequences for sneaking out the way I did."

"I'm sure there's some kind of statute of limitation which you've gotten beyond. They couldn't possibly hold a grudge for over two decades, could they? It's not like you killed anyone." Suzi raised her arms in the air before slowly lowering them. "You're not on the lam for murder, are you?"

"Of course, not! How could you even ask that?"

The other woman gave a sheepish grin. "Had to be sure."

"Look, it's late, and I'm beat. All I want to do is crawl into bed and forget about everything until tomorrow." Joy walked through the living room to the stairs.

Suzi followed. "I'm gonna fix a snack. I was too spun up earlier to eat, but now I'm starving. You want to join me?"

She stifled a yawn. "No thanks. You go ahead, and we'll talk tomorrow. Good night."

"Night." Suzi waved at the dog, who watched from

his perch on the couch. "Guess it's just you and me, Jester. Let's see what we can find in the fridge."

Without hesitation, the pooch hopped to the floor and followed her to the kitchen.

In her bedroom, Joy set her phone on the nightstand before changing into pajamas. A hot shower would've eased her nerves, but fatigue weighed in more.

She awoke the next morning to the chirp of an incoming text from Harmony.

—*I'm done playing games. We need to end this. The only way is for you to meet me at the crash site. There is something you need to see. I'll be alone. I expect you to be too.*—

The time read six o'clock. Her stomach muscles bunched into a knot, as she gripped the silky sheets around her. Inhaling the scent from the rose bud sachet on her nightstand, she willed her nerves to calm. This scenario played on an endless loop with Harmony demanding an audience on Bellington Mountain and Joy refusing. Maybe the time had come to end the dance. Her response asked for a time, and they set a meeting for later this morning.

Suzi wouldn't be up for another couple of hours.

Joy changed quickly then searched for car keys to Daisy. She'd never get a service truck out this early to fix her own car, which probably needed a new battery. An idea struck her to think like her new lodger.

She slipped out of the house and checked inside the red SUV. The keys hung from the ignition.

Why hadn't I thought to look yesterday?

Hurrying back inside, she wrote a quick note apologizing for borrowing the car and stating the need to run errands. Guilt plagued her conscience for lying to the one person who'd stood by her through thick and thin. Before she changed her mind, Joy risked a few precious minutes to fill a to-go cup with coffee and left.

With no need to hurry, she drove only slightly above the speed limit. This time she didn't fret about anyone else's safety except her own. As the vehicle neared the turnout just past mile marker thirty-six, Joy pulled in and parked.

Exiting the SUV, she breathed in the fragrance of pine trees. This smell had always soothed her, yet today she remained on edge. Scanning the area, Joy didn't find another vehicle.

Did I arrive first?

She hiked back to the entry point and into the woods. Stepping over fallen logs, her boots crunched the dead leaves along the trail she blazed. With no sign of Harmony, Joy approached the cross, which had a fresh bouquet of flowers resting against it.

Kneeling, she brushed her fingers across the rough wood and traced the engraved name. "Michael, what would our life have been like, had this not happened? Would we have grown into a loving family, or would grief and sorrow consume us because of our actions?"

"Awwww, how touching." Harmony leaned against a nearby tree. "Still regretting bringing me into the world?"

Chapter 41

Joy stood and turned. "You're my child. The only regret I have is not raising you myself. I wish you could believe me. Why else would I have given up everything in Celestia and risked smuggling you to Earth?"

She shrugged. "My odds of survival did increase when you removed me from Celestia." Harmony sauntered over to the cross. "Do you know who erected this?"

"Didn't you? I assumed you'd left the flowers too."

Brushing her fingers along her father's name, much the same as her mother had, Harmony shook her head. "Silas placed this here shortly after you went off to live with your *new* family."

She winced at the callous criticism. "Your grandfather told you that?"

Another headshake. "Marla did. When Silas delivered the news about Michael, he said he'd placed a marker in case she ever wanted to pay her respects. Since my Grandpa Benjamin never knew the truth, I guess Grandma didn't have it in her to travel here alone."

"He never told me he'd been the one to put this here. It must've been Silas who found the license plate and buried it beneath the cross." Joy slumped her shoulders. "If only he'd been honest with me all those years ago, you and I could have had a life together."

Harmony roared with laughter. "You're still feeding that delusion?"

"Don't say that. I loved you and never would have willingly left you behind."

"Really? Are you sure about that?" She stepped closer almost coming nose to nose with her mother.

Joy tilted her head. "I don't understand. We'd planned to come back to you after this trip."

"So your memory hasn't returned completely? Marla told me the real reason you and my father came up here. It wasn't so you could leave the desert for a few days."

She took a step back, placing a hand on her chest. "I remember everything, and we'd come to Oregon for a little escape. We had every intention of returning."

Her daughter's eyes bugged wide. "*Escape* had been your goal. You'd heard about a hidden portal nearby which didn't require a pass. It would land you in a remote area of Celestia where you could sneak in unnoticed. You had no intention of returning for me."

Joy staggered backward, as if she'd been struck a blow to the gut. "No. Why would we leave without you?"

"Because you knew my grandparents wouldn't turn me out? Because you hated Earth and wanted to go back to your home planet? Because you couldn't stand the sight of me? Take your pick!" She stomped the ground like an angry toddler. "Either way, you and Michael wanted to be happy together with no responsibilities. Only it didn't work out the way you'd planned, did it?"

She searched her memory and came up blank. "You're wrong." With a shake of her head, she said,

"My memories have returned. All of them. The only reason I came here was to get out of the arid wasteland we'd landed in. There is no hidden portal. They're all monitored by attendants."

It was Harmony's turn to stutter with astonishment. "You're not lying, are you? You didn't know about the hidden entryway. Marla told me you and my father came here to find it. She said her son insisted it existed, and the two of you wanted to locate the entrance." She turned away and leaned against the nearest tree. "My grandmother lied to me." Her eyes focused on Joy. "He never told you?"

"Michael said nothing about an untended portal." Her legs gave way, and she sunk down, landing on a log. "He told me he had a surprise for me but died before revealing it. I'd assumed he planned to propose. It had been my dream for us to be married and spend our lives together, despite our parents' objections." With hands balled in her lap, she returned her daughter's gaze. "Maybe he wanted to verify the location before getting my hopes up. Once we'd found it, if it existed, I'm sure we would have returned to get you before going through."

"Oh, it exists. How do you think my buddy, Cutter, found his way here? His parents brought him through as a toddler."

"Where's the portal?" Joy stood.

"Mom! Where are you?" Grace's voice sounded from the direction of the roadway.

Harmony's face morphed into a scowl. "Liar! You had me going for a minute with your innocent act. To think I almost let you play me. All you wanted to do was stall until your back-up arrived. Or should I say your *real* daughter?" The young woman stormed off at an angle away from the approaching footsteps crunching through the woods.

"Harmony! Don't leave. I had no idea they would come after me. I didn't tell them about our meeting."

Chapter 42

Suzi pushed through the brush with Grace on her heels. "Running errands my ass! I suspected you wouldn't tell me if you came to meet with Harmony. Where is your evil spawn?" Her head swung from side to side as she scoped the area.

"Mom!" Grace ran and embraced her mother, who stood only a couple feet from the edge of the cliff. "Come away from there. What were you thinking?"

Joy allowed herself to be led as she sputtered. "What…how…"

"How did we know you'd be here? When Aunt Suzi found your note, she called me immediately. We both figured Harmony wouldn't give up until she got you here."

"I'm fine. I didn't want to worry you, and I'd hoped to finish this once and for all and make peace with Harmony." She looked from her friend to her daughter. "We'd almost come to terms when you arrived. I don't mean to sound ungrateful, but you should've trusted me to handle this. Now she thinks I betrayed her and planned for you to come too. She ran off when you called out."

With a hand on her hip while wielding a tree branch in the other, Suzi said, "Well, I won't say I'm sorry. You can't trust that she-demon."

Grace pointed at the cross. "This is the spot where

he…Michael went over?"

Joy nodded. "Harmony said Silas made it in case Michael's parents wanted to pay their respects. She left the flowers herself."

"Oh, Mom. With all the drama going on, I never considered how Michael's death affected you. Even though it'd been a long time, with your memory loss, you've had to relive it all over again."

She placed a hand on her daughter's cheek. "That's the way of it. Many things in life aren't fair, but you need to move on with the people still here."

The young woman smiled. "I know. It still doesn't make sense why Harmony insisted you meet at the accident site. What purpose could it serve?"

Joy related Harmony's claim about the unmonitored portal nearby.

"Do you believe her?" Suzi asked.

"She did say Cutter came through it as a child years ago. It might not even work anymore. Who knows?" Joy shrugged. "Let's go home."

Grace wandered to the edge of the cliff and looked out. "How far to the bottom do you think it is?"

An engine roared as a motorcycle careened out of the forest. With a rev of the throttle, Harmony rode straight for Grace. Her braid flapped against her back as she aimed the bike directly at her stepsister standing only inches from the precipice.

Suzi reacted first by hurling the stick from her hand as she let out a battle cry.

It bounced off the rider's helmet causing her to loosen her grip before skidding out of control. She straightened the handlebars, but the bike fell sideways sliding toward the cliff with her target in its path.

"No!" Joy forced her legs into motion and rushed toward them. A million scenarios raced through her mind and none of them ended well.

Grace bolted sideways, but the bike caught her back foot flinging her over the edge. Her blood-curdling scream sliced throughout the mountainside.

The screech chilled Joy to the bone as she raced for the spot where her daughter flew off.

The motorcycle slid toward thin air as Harmony attempted to dislodge herself, but her glove caught on the clutch. Her legs trailed behind as the bike dragged her over the cliff. Moments later, the crash of the bike hitting the base of the mountain sounded across the valley. No explosion followed, just the echo of metal smashing on rock.

"Oh, God, no!" Joy threw herself flat on the ground peering over the edge. Her sudden weight sent loose pebbles skittering down. She scoured the landscape below but saw no sign of either woman. "Grace! Harmony! Can you hear me?" Adrenaline pumped through her veins as she willed both her daughters to still be alive.

A branch cracked off to the right.

Suzi moved a few yards away from Joy and slid down to her hands and knees. The physical ordeal left her out of breath as she scanned the mountainside. Moments later she yelled, "She's alive! I can see her. She's alive!"

"Which one?" Joy asked sliding down beside her. She looked where her friend pointed.

Grace clung to a sapling growing out of the hillside about fifteen feet below. Other shrubs and wild grass bolstered the woman's position where her feet rested on a small boulder. "Mom, I don't know how long I can hold on," she said, her voice strained. Dust and debris trickled away from the rock she perched on. The roots of the tree loosened, and her hands slipped a few inches, forcing another scream before she tightened her grip around the branch.

"Hold on. We'll get help," her mother yelled. Her fingers dug into the dirt as if she could leap over and scoop up her daughter, bringing her to safety. Not wanting to take her eyes off Grace, she handed her phone to Suzi. "Call nine-one-one."

The other woman rolled to a sitting position. "I'm on it." She proceeded to tell the emergency operator to get help pronto.

Joy's eyes darted back and forth scanning the cliffside. "Do you think Harmony might have gotten snagged on something too?" She dragged fingers through her hair.

"Are you kidding me?" Suzi waved her arms in the air. "She just tried to take out my favorite niece, and you're hoping she didn't go up in a ball of flames at the bottom?"

Joy grimaced. "I don't want either of my girls hurt. It's obvious Harmony needs help. Please keep looking."

"I'm sorry, you're right. She may be psycho, but that gal was your daughter." She knelt and swept her view over the scraggly cliffside below.

"Was?" A shudder caught in Joy's throat.

Suzi placed a hand on her shoulder. "Nobody could've survived a fall like that. I'm sorry, sweetie. I know you'd hoped for more with Harmony, but she took matters into her own hands. And almost took Grace with her."

Joy's shoulders slumped. "You're right. I just can't—"

The faint wail of sirens sounded from the roadway and grew louder with every passing second.

Inhaling a large gulp of air, Joy uttered a silent prayer.

Chapter 43

"They sure believed me when I demanded they haul their cookies here in record time." Suzi puffed as she used her hands to push into a standing position.

Joy glanced nervously as her daughter strained to keep her grip. "Just a little longer, honey. We can hear the rescue units now." Quietly she muttered, "Please, God, they have to make it here in time."

"I'll guide them in," the older woman called over her shoulder as she hurried into the woods at the spot they'd arrived through.

The minutes passed like an eternity before two men and a woman wearing jumpsuits pushed their way into the clearing. As they set down their equipment, Suzi trailed behind gasping for breath. She stepped closer and waved her arms like a flight attendant indicating the nearest exit. The workers ignored her while they unpacked their gear.

"Please hurry," Joy called. "I don't know how much longer that branch will hold her weight."

The female officer moved in and assessed the situation.

"My other daughter fell too, but I don't see her." Tears formed in Joy's eyes.

The rescuer called back to her teammates, "We'll need a harness for the victim when you go down, Jacob. Her position isn't secure, so we won't have time to bring in a winch."

One of the men strapped a harness onto himself while the other secured a rope to a tree. The man gearing up said, "We can improvise." He edged to the cliff and looked at their target.

"Ladies, please clear the area so we can work," the woman commanded. "We'll get the one woman to safety first, then try to locate the other."

Joy reluctantly backed away, while Suzi had to be told a second time to move. They stood near the cross and could no longer see what went on below.

The rescuer disappeared over the edge to rappel down.

Several minutes elapsed before a loud crack sounded followed by a shrill scream.

The two observers clutched each other's hands, while the rescuers scrambled to pull up their teammate.

"Something's gone wrong." It took all of Joy's willpower not to rush to the crew's side. She'd only get in their way, but had they already missed saving the only family she had left in this world? Tears leaked down her cheeks.

Finally, Jacob's head appeared over the landing. As he rose higher, he clutched Grace to him. She coughed and wheezed as they pulled her onto solid ground.

Not being able to hold back any longer, Joy ran and fell to her knees, pulling her daughter into an embrace. She looked to the crew. "Thank you so much. Thank you."

"She was lucky we arrived when we did," the man in the harness said. "Just as I got to her, the rock she'd braced her feet on dislodged, and the branch snapped. It's a good thing she's tiny because I didn't have time to get equipment around her."

Paramedics tromped out of the woods accompanied by a state trooper. "Everybody okay?" asked one of the ambulance crew.

Joy helped Grace to her feet and led her over to the medics. She wanted her as far from the cliff as possible.

While the medical team checked over their patient, Joy rushed to the policeman. "My other daughter got dragged over when she lost control of her motorcycle. We heard the bike hit the rocks below, and she hasn't answered when calling her name. Please send help. She could be hurt."

He dispatched a unit and ambulance to locate the wreckage.

From the serious expression on the officer's face, Joy assumed the ambulance to be standard procedure and not because they hoped to find Harmony alive. When he walked away, his voice still carried to her ears as he told the operator to send a coroner's van for a possible fatality.

Luck had been on their side with the search and rescue team being in the vicinity on a training exercise. Had they not gotten there as quickly as they did, Joy may have lost both daughters.

Grace refused to go to the hospital, insisting she remained unharmed except for a few cuts and bruises. Her stubbornness didn't prevail completely when she agreed to let her mother take the wheel for the drive back.

Suzi claimed her own vehicle for the trip home.

As Joy climbed into the driver's seat, she took a moment to brush the remaining tears from her face and get her breathing under control before starting the ignition. Her fingers shook as she wrapped them around the steering wheel.

Despite her insistence at wanting to find where the motorcycle landed, the others convinced Joy it would be a bad idea. If Harmony got dragged to the base, seeing her body splattered on the rocks would only add to the sting of her loss. The authorities would contact her to identify the body once they'd processed the scene and transported her remains to the morgue.

The women went to Grace's house first, where they found Owen pacing the driveway. He'd called her during the drive back demanding an explanation as to why she took off while he slept and hadn't been answering her cell. After insisting she was unharmed, she refused to give any further details until arriving in person.

When Joy parked the car, Owen rushed to open his wife's door. He pulled her out of the vehicle and hugged her close, before eying the bandages on her arms, neck, and face. With a glare at his mother-in-law, he stated, "No more secrets."

Grace gave a sideways glance to her mom, who nodded.

"We'll leave you two to talk," Joy said. "Owen, I'm sorry to have kept you in the dark, but I guess it's time for you to know the truth about my history. Grace, call me later."

He scrunched his brows but said nothing as he led his wife into the house.

"Wouldn't I like to be a fly on the wall for *that* conversation," Suzi stifled a chuckle.

"I'll be lucky if he ever talks to me again. He'll blame everything that's happened to Grace on me and rightly so." Sadness laced her voice.

Suzi smacked the roof of her car. "Harmony's actions are not your fault. You may have given that horrible woman life, but you didn't force her to do all those awful things." She opened the car door. "Now let's go home. I need coffee, food, and doggie smooches in that order. Though I'm sure Jester will have his own agenda."

Rather than protesting at getting a free pass for recent events, Joy got into the passenger seat. Everything that'd happened rested firmly on her shoulders, no matter how much her friend tried to absolve her. Harmony's death contributed to her guilt as well.

As they pulled up to the house, Joy's cell rang. The caller ID read Oregon State Police. She wasn't up for a round of follow-up questions but answered the call anyway. After listening for a beat, she said, "Yes, this is Joy Harper."

She quieted again, opened her mouth to speak, then remained silent. A few moments later, she said, "But I don't understand. How could that be?"

The voice on the other end continued.

"Are you sure? But she might be—" She waited until the officer finished explaining. "Thank you for calling."

"Do they want you to come identify the body?" Suzi asked.

"Uh-uh." Joy shook her head and got out of the vehicle in a daze. Her movements became sluggish as if trudging through water.

"I don't understand." Suzi bolted out of her seat and followed.

With a hand on the doorknob, she turned to her companion. "Neither do I."

Suzi screwed up her face and cocked her head. "What aren't you telling me?"

"There is no body."

Chapter 44

They stood on the doorstep with neither saying a word. Joy's thoughts spun at a dizzying rate. As much as she wanted to believe Harmony could have survived the fall, the steepness of the drop made it impossible. The officer told her they'd searched the surrounding area and found no trace of the young woman. There were hundreds of nooks or crevices her body could've fallen into, all nowhere near where the motorcycle hit the rocks.

Scratching and barking from inside the house shattered the silence.

Jester bolted for his owner the moment the door opened.

Suzi scooped him up and held the pooch tight as he nuzzled her neck.

As they walked inside, Joy said, "You go ahead. I'm going to lie down for a while. My body feels as if it's weighted down with lead."

"Can I bring you anything?"

"No. I just need rest." She mounted the stairs.

"Okay. Let me know if you change your mind." Suzi set Jester on the floor and trundled off toward the kitchen.

Joy went into her room and closed the door. She stood a moment looking around as if seeing it for the first time. The home she'd known for over twenty years suddenly felt foreign. With the death of a daughter she barely knew, her whole life swam in turmoil. Where would she go from here now that she knew the truth of her life before? Would she get past the loss of a child who'd been within her grasp but slipped away?

She removed her shoes before collapsing on the bed. Sleep overtook her almost immediately.

A commotion filtering up the stairway cut her slumber short.

What now?

Yelling greeted her as she padded into the hallway. She ascended the stairs to the entry where Cutter stood toe to toe with Suzi, who blocked the doorway.

The hulking man towered over her, yet she held her ground, bracing both hands on either side of the frame. "Leave this family alone. Your girlfriend isn't here, and if you don't want to get messed up, you'd better scram!"

He stifled a chuckle. "You and what army, little woman?"

She puffed out her chest and huffed like a bull ready to charge.

The man looked Joy's way. "I need to talk to you. Tell your guard dog to back down."

"Don't worry, Joy, I can handle this clown. He won't get past me." She tightened her grip on the doorway.

Jester stood behind his master issuing a low growl.

Joy held her hands up in a calming gesture. "No need for violence. Cutter, Harmony is...she went..." The words caught in her throat as emotion choked her vocal cords. How could she tell him his girlfriend went over the cliff when she still hadn't processed it completely herself? Mustering her nerve, she said, "There was an accident at Bellington Mountain. Harmony lost control of her motorcycle and skidded over…over the edge." She walked closer. "I'm sorry. She's dead."

His expression went blank, and he quit trying to get through the door. With a narrowing of his eyes, he asked, "You see the body?"

She shook her head. "The police couldn't find her. They believe she may have…may have landed somewhere else as she separated from the bike during the fall."

Suzi backed away almost stepping on Jester, who scooted out from under foot.

Cutter dropped his hands to his sides and stepped inside. "Or maybe she survived and left without me."

Both women stared at him.

"I don't understand," Joy said.

"Tell me something." Cutter's voice grew wary. "Did Harmony tell you why it was important to meet at your accident site?"

"You mean because of the existence of an unguarded portal? She said you and your parents came through it when you were a child. Is that true?"

His face darkened. "Why do you want to know? You gonna blab to your father, so he can shut it down?"

Suzi put her hands on her hips. "Let me get this straight. You believe she survived the fall and went through the portal back to Celestia? Why would she do that?"

He shrugged. "Don't know. Maybe she got hurt and needed to heal."

"Why would she go through the portal instead of

going to a hospital?" Suzi asked.

Joy held up the vial hanging from her chain. "Injuries heal quicker there than they do on Earth. Somehow, it's tied into our necklaces, but I never quite understood the science. Another reason she needed hers back I suppose. Why was it important for me to know about this portal?"

"All she said was you might find this information valuable. Why? You leaving too?" He smirked.

"Cutter," Joy asked, "what are you doing here?"

"When she didn't come back, I figured you bailed on the meeting again, and Harmony came looking for you." He turned toward the door. "I'm tired of her games. Thought I'd give her one more chance to get away from all this and come with me."

"You're leaving?" Suzi folded her arms. "Good riddance. Don't let the door smack you in the backside on the way out."

"Wait. How can you leave without knowing what really happened to her?" Joy asked. "Don't you love her?"

He stopped and let out a laugh. "You're kidding me, right? People like Harmony and me don't fall in love. We form alliances to satisfy a need, nothing more. Sometimes we have a few laughs."

"And what *needs* did you fulfill for her other than the horizontal mambo?" Suzi scowled. "You tried to strangle Grace on the beach, didn't you?"

Cutter gave her the side-eye. "My purpose for being here was to display a little muscle backing her up. That woman preferred to do her own dirty work. She got off on it. Just like she set that blaze over at your place."

"Those accusations are awfully convenient considering she's not here to defend herself." The short woman glared. "What about when you kidnapped me? Both of you were at the tasting room before hog-tying me in the shed."

"All we wanted was the necklace back. We followed you to the winery to see if you'd been the one to find it. When you started chucking bottles at us, we diffused the situation, and Harmony decided to use it to her advantage." With a shrug, he retrieved her cell phone from his pocket and held it out. "She left this behind. I have no use for it. Consider it my one act of kindness." He sneered before pushing past her. "Believe what you want. I'm through here." Cutter stomped the few feet to his motorcycle parked in the driveway.

"We can't let him leave now! Joy, call the police so he can tell them what he just told us. I knew that lightning-wielding witch hurt our girl and tried to turn me into a crispy critter."

In a calm voice, she said, "Let him go. He'd never speak to the authorities no matter how hard we tried to convince him. Though, with all that's happened, I believe he's telling the truth. He doesn't have anything to gain by lying. With Harmony dead or missing, what would be the point in pursuing the crimes she committed?"

Cutter fastened his helmet, tugged on his gloves, and threw a leg over the seat of his bike. Looking at the women, he said, "And if that bitch ever does show up again, tell her to go rot in Hell, which is where I hope she already is!" With that, he kicked the clutch and the engine roared to life. He sped down the driveway, not even slowing before shooting onto the road.

"Guess they broke up." Suzi raised her arms in the air. "How about breakfast? I'm starving."

Chapter 45

"Guess we'll never see Cutter again." Suzi leaned on the counter as she drank coffee.

"There's no reason for him to stay with Harmony gone. As much as he protested, I believe he cared for her more than he'd admit." Joy sighed. "I can't say I'm not glad he left. Even if he didn't help with the crimes my daughter committed, his presence made me nervous."

Suzi carried her mug to the sink. As she rinsed it under the running water, her jaw dropped.

"What's wrong? You look as if you've seen a ghost?" Joy rushed to her side.

The woman pointed at the flowerpots on the windowsill. "I believe they're ready for *harvest*."

The large flowers had completely sprouted what could only be described as a thin, veneered ticket. All the words were visible for them to read. Joy gently grasped the one closest between two fingers and lifted it off the plant. She read aloud, "Welcome to Celestia. Admit One." She flipped it over and found more writing on the back. "These look like instructions on how to find the portal."

Suzi plucked the other one and scanned the back. "On the first day of the new month, find where the bilbao tree blossoms. When the guardian appears, surrender your ticket, and proceed to Celestia." She looked toward her friend. "What the hell is a *bilbao* tree?" Turning it over and back again, she asked, "Do you think this thing has autocorrect and screwed up the instructions?"

Joy chuckled. "I don't know what to think except that we've got another cryptic message on our hands. There's only one person who can explain this to us, and I don't know how to reach him."

"Silas."

She nodded. "We'll have to be patient until he shows up again."

"Patient? That's definitely not one of my virtues. I say we get in the car and scour the town for the old codger. His green truck is easily recognized. Probably as ancient as he is." Suzi laughed at her own joke.

"He could be anywhere from here to the coast if he's still on Earth. The last time he came he said my mother wanted me to come to Celestia. For all I know, he returned to see her." Joy studied the ticket. "The instructions state 'the first day of the new month.' We've still got a week until June begins, if that's even the month it refers to."

"There's no expiration date on these things. Maybe it means any month, not just the upcoming one."

She collected the slat from her friend's hand and stacked it with her own. "Well, until Silas shows up again, we'd better keep these safe. When I returned to the gift shop looking for Pete, the display didn't have any more Celestia seeds. They may be quite rare."

"Yeah. Too bad Jester ate one." Suzi narrowed her eyes. "You're very concerned about these passes, as if you've already decided we'll be going to Celestia. Should I pack a bag?"

Joy bit her lip. "I'm sorry but *we* won't be going. And yes, I've considered returning if nothing else to visit my mother. Until I get things settled, I'm not about to risk dragging you into the unknown."

"I've been married five times. Believe me, I know plenty about venturing into the unknown."

With a smile, she said, "But you've also been divorced five times. Extricating yourself from this situation may not be as easy."

"We've got time to discuss it. There's no way I'm letting you go it alone. Not after coming this far." The older woman crossed her arms as if it were the end of the debate.

Joy took the tickets to her office and locked them in the safe. She had decided to return to Celestia once she had things settled with Grace and the winery. Sadly, she'd hoped the journey would include Harmony. Before she departed, she needed Silas to confirm it wouldn't be a one-way trip. No way would she desert this daughter too. If she couldn't come back, then Celestia would have to remain part of her past.

Despite Harmony's and Cutter's absence, she still secured all the windows and doors of the house. Joy believed the man to be gone, but like her departed daughter, she didn't know him well enough to be certain.

Her curiosity almost got the best of her as far as Grace's conversation with Owen. Several times she'd picked up her phone to call, but in the end all she sent was a text verifying Grace would work the tasting room the next morning. The simple response gave nothing away about Owen's reaction.

Chapter 46

The next morning Joy didn't have to wait to find out what her son-in-law had to say about her life before Huntsville. When she arrived at the tasting room to set up, she found him sitting on the counter. His body language didn't exactly telegraph a welcoming demeanor.

"Hi, Owen. Where's your wife?" Joy asked.

"I asked her to let me help set up, so we could talk." His tone remained even, almost wary, as he hopped to his feet.

She let out a long breath. "You've got a right to ask questions. Shoot. What do you want to know?"

"Are you really an alien from another planet?"

Joy burst out laughing. Nobody had actually phrased her status like that before. "Not exactly. Yes, I am from a planet called Celestia, which has a portal between there and Earth. As far as the alien part? I'm as human as you. Our physical make-up is similar to people here."

His tough facade cracked, and the tension in his facial muscles eased. "I didn't mean to be that blunt. It's just...well..."

"I know. Hard to believe, isn't it? Until I got my memory back, I would have denied the possibility. However, my not being from this planet is true." She walked behind the counter to set out trays of glasses.

Owen followed and lined up bottles of white wines listed on the tasting board. "And Harmony really was your daughter?"

"*Is* my daughter."

He nodded once.

"When I couldn't remember my own name after the accident, she became a casualty as well. Her grandparents raised her when Michael and I didn't return. Sadly, she believed we'd abandoned her. I can't blame her for the anger she felt toward me."

"But you explained about the memory loss, yet she still pursued a vendetta against you and anyone you loved." He walked to the back room and returned with a case of Merlot.

Joy stopped. "Harmony was troubled. My people aren't *exactly* the same as the ones here. Did Grace explain the limitations when mixing certain bloodlines?"

"She did. You have a symbol on your wrist that also corresponds to your eye color."

She lifted her arm so he could see the raised markings. Pulling on the chain around her neck, she held out the purple vial. "This matches my eyes. Michael's family has a different symbol with blue eyes as well as their necklace."

"And when you mix the two, you get an evil, black-eyed child, who isn't expected to live past the age of five. Unless you bring that child here to Earth. Have I missed anything?" His voice rang with an accusing tone.

"Owen, I know you believe what I did was wrong. But wouldn't you do everything in your power to protect your child?" The words were out before she could stop them. He'd had a child, or the promise of one, before Grace had the incident on the beach.

Her son-in-law's eyes flashed with anger.

"I'm sorry. I didn't mean—"

He raised a hand. "Stop. Don't try to explain it away. It was your *daughter* who robbed Grace and me from being parents. While I can sympathize with your situation, I'm not sure I can forgive you for everything that's happened as a result. At least Harmony died on that mountain instead of my wife."

Joy bit her lip. She wanted to remain quiet, yet the man had a right to know. "It's possible she didn't."

"What?" His eyes bugged wide in his face. "But Grace said—"

"She didn't know about the phone call after I dropped her off. The search team hasn't located her body. It doesn't mean she isn't…didn't die. But there's a slim chance she survived and went through a nearby portal back to Celestia."

"Grace mentioned the possibility of a portal. Will you go back and look for it?" he asked.

She shook her head.

"So you have no intention of going back to Celestia?"

"There's other portals." She placed her hands flat on the counter and studied them a moment before looking up. "I do plan to go, but I'd prefer Grace be here for the rest of the conversation, as it will involve her too."

Owen shook his head with greater force. "You are not putting her in any more danger. She's almost died twice at the hands of your offspring. No more!"

"I can assure you, the only part she'll play in the

future is remaining here and running this winery. It's her father's legacy, and this is where she belongs."

He crossed his arms. "And you?"

"Let's wait for Grace."

Chapter 47

Minutes after finishing set-up, Grace arrived.

Before Joy could utter a word, Owen beat her to the punch. "Harmony may not be dead."

Her daughter stopped in her tracks. "What? No way. She went over the cliff. I heard the motorcycle hit bottom."

Joy's legs shook, and she leaned on the counter for support. Every time things looked to be better, they only turned more complicated. "The search and rescue team didn't find her. They scoured the area without success."

"What makes you think she's alive? Her body could've landed anywhere or gotten stuck where they couldn't find it." Grace moved next to her husband.

He put an arm around her and pulled her close. "There's no way of knowing unless she shows up to wreak havoc again."

Joy approached the couple. "Cutter believes—"

"What do you mean Cutter? When did you talk to him?" Anger rose in Owen's voice.

"He came by the house yesterday afternoon." She chuckled. "You would have been proud of your Aunt Suzi. The woman blocked the door as if she were twice his size. Anyway, he came looking for Harmony. He was leaving town and wanted to give her one more chance to go with him. I guess they parted ways, and he didn't appear happy about it. He suggested Harmony may have survived and gone through the nearby portal." She sighed. "I guess we'll never know the truth."

"Unless she shows up again, like Owen said." Grace's tone softened. "I don't mean to be hurtful, Mom. Good or bad, Harmony is your daughter, and you can't help feeling responsible for her. But she did try to kill me twice now, plus..." Grace's voice cracked as she looked down and placed a hand on her belly.

Joy's heart wrenched at the gesture. "I can't begin to list the regrets my dredging up the past has caused, but the loss of your child is at the top of that list. There's no fixing what happened. All I can focus on is assuring no additional harm comes to either of you." She placed a hand on her daughter's arm. "That's why I've decided to go back to Celestia."

Grace's eyes widened, and her lip quivered. "I don't want you to leave."

Painful tears welled in Joy's eyes. "I can't risk any additional repercussions for my actions being inflicted on the people I love. Suzi almost died in a fire. You've been attacked twice. Owen got injured in a fight, and he didn't really know why it occurred." She looked into Owen's eyes. "I know he'll protect you to within an inch of his life, but I don't want either of you put in another situation where he'll need to."

Her daughter smacked the counter. "You promised you wouldn't leave me. Now you're breaking that promise?"

"Oh, honey, when I told you that, none of this violence had occurred. I do intend to keep my promise because I will be back. My home will always be here with you. I just need to sort a few things out."

Grace sniffled. "Can I come with you?"

Owen stepped away. "No way! You are not going off to some unknown, mystical land."

"Calm down. This is a solo trip. Besides, I've only got two tickets, and you'd have to fight your Aunt Suzi for the second one."

"Tickets?" he asked.

"Grace, you have my word. I will return," Joy said. "Did you tell Owen about the plants?"

She shook her head. "It took hours to convince him about everything else. I figured it would be easier to show him the plants when we got here."

"The short version is I'll need a ticket to be allowed to travel through the portal. When I purchased these plant seeds at a gift shop while on a trip with Suzi, they sparked the return of my memories. I believe the plants came from Celestia. They've each sprouted a ticket that will grant me passage." She gestured toward the door. "Care to come up to the house so I can show them to you?"

He shook his head. "I don't need any more proof. The raised marking and necklace cemented it for me. When are you going?"

"Just like that? You'd let my mother leave us?" Grace asked.

"Have you ever known your mother to back down from a decision she's made?" He smirked. "You may not be of her blood, but the stubbornness is something you learned from her."

Joy laughed. "He's got you on that one. First thing this morning I placed a call to my lawyer about your taking over. I told him to move forward with drawing up the legal papers. Once that's complete, the only remaining mystery is where I'll find the portal."

"Wait. You don't know where it is?" asked Grace.

With a shake of her head, she said, "The instructions on the ticket are vague, like the original instructions on the seed packet. I'll have to wait for my father to turn up again and explain what they mean."

"She told me about your father, Silas. You've no way to reach him?" Owen asked.

"No. In the meantime, let's get back to work." She focused on her daughter. "Grace, you already know how to run the place, so it's down to signing the paperwork."

Her daughter grasped both her hands. "I won't argue. You've wanted to step down for a while, and I won't fight you on this. Your house isn't included in the deal, so you'll always have a place to come back to."

"Thank you." She squeezed Grace's hands before letting go.

Owen kissed his wife. "I'll leave you two alone." He opened the front door and stopped. "Hey, does Silas drive an old, green pick-up truck?"

Chapter 48

Joy bolted through the door of the tasting room and headed for the house. Silas turned from where he stood at the front door when she approached.

"The tickets are ready, aren't they?" he asked.

"How'd you know?" Joy walked closer.

He shrugged. "Just seemed about time. I suppose you don't know what a bilbao tree is, do you?"

"And I suppose you're about to tell me."

He nodded.

"Coffee?"

Another nod.

They found Suzi in the kitchen emptying the dishwasher. "Well, look who's turned up as if by wishing, you make it so." She snickered.

Joy gestured to a seat at the counter while she prepared his mug. "Care to join us, Suzi? We're about to be enlightened as to what a bilbao tree is and where to find one."

The blonde rubbed her hands together. "As if I'd miss this conversation." She plunked down on a seat and waited.

"So you've decided to come to Celestia, then?" Silas directed the question to his daughter.

"I think it's time for a visit," she said.

He leaned back. "With you having family here, I wasn't sure you'd leave at all. You plan to return to this planet then?"

Joy smiled. "Yes. Grace will take over the winery. It originally belonged to her father, and we always knew she'd take the reins. But as I said, I plan to *visit* Celestia, not stay."

"Will your other daughter be returning with you?" His face remained unreadable.

Her voice caught in her throat. She swallowed and tried again. "Harmony…Harmony is dead."

Silas gripped the edge of the counter, as if to steady himself. For a man who was usually stoic, this slight show of emotion spoke volumes. "How?"

The women told him about the events which took place on Bellington Mountain. While a slim hope remained for the young woman to have survived, odds weren't in her favor.

"Do you believe she meant harm to Grace?" he asked.

"Hell yeah." Suzi slapped the counter.

Joy winced. "We'll never know. It saddens me to have lost the opportunity to make amends for all the years she believed Michael and I had abandoned her. Despite her troubled mind, I owed her the chance to be part of my life now."

"Sounds like the young woman made her own choices. You can't keep blaming yourself." For the first time, Silas's voice held compassion for his daughter.

"There is one question left," Suzi interjected.

The man angled his head her way.

"Do I get to use that second ticket or what?" She crossed her arms and focused her gaze on him.

Both Silas and Joy remained silent. They exchanged a look, before turning back to Suzi.

Joy bit her lip. She wanted to find the gentlest way to reiterate why she had to go alone. As much as she loved her friend's company, she needed to only worry about herself this once.

Silas expelled a breath. "Well, young lady, I get your wanting to go on a new adventure. I've picked that up about you." He winked. "At some point, I believe it will be time for you to see where we come from. You wouldn't be the first one to visit from Earth. For her first trip back, I believe she'd feel better about leaving her daughter behind if you were here to keep an eye on her. Am I right, Justine?"

Joy hesitated. She'd have to get used to people calling her by that name in Celestia. Right now, it had a foreign ring to it. "Yes. Suzi, you know I love you. But I need to figure things out before dragging visitors along with me. Can you be patient?"

She chuckled. "You know that isn't one of my virtues."

"Painfully aware." Joy laughed too.

The front door opened, and footsteps came their way.

"Hi, Grandpa." Grace walked over and hugged Silas.

The man stiffened before wrapping an awkward arm around her. "Nice to see you, granddaughter. Glad things turned out well for you on the mountain."

"Me too." She held out a chain with a vial hanging from it. The substance inside was black as night. "I found this hanging off the back door of the tasting room. Do you know who it belongs to?"

Chapter 49

Every muscle in Joy's body clenched at the sight of the necklace her daughter held. Only two people possessed vials as inky black as this one. When Cutter burst in yesterday, she'd caught sight of his around his neck. Had he returned, they would've heard his motorcycle.

She could only assume the other one went over the cliff with its owner. Or had it?

Joy couldn't recall if her daughter had worn the necklace, but it could have been tucked beneath her shirt. With her knowledge of Celestia, the necklace had a direct connection to healing injuries more quickly. If this one belonged to Harmony, why would she leave it behind after going to great lengths to steal it back the other day?

Silas moved first and took it from Grace. "Well now, it seems the owner decided he or she no longer needed it."

"Is it possible to get a replacement in Celestia?" Joy asked.

He bobbed his head. "Aye. Remember, the necklace doesn't acquire its color until placed on the owner. If a person were to lose theirs, they'd be able to get another."

"Why would Harmony risk leaving it behind? Doesn't she need it to amp up her lightning-wielding abilities?" Suzi asked.

Other than a slight raise of his eyebrow, Silas gave away no emotion. "I'd heard the damage she did to her grandfather's eyes. From what her grandmother indicated Harmony hadn't been wearing the necklace at the time."

Grace let out a breath. "You're kidding me, right? That would mean she can use the evil inside of her whenever she wants."

"Another side effect of mixing bloodlines. Our laws are in place for a reason, and that extreme case further proves it." He turned to Joy. "You don't think it could have been left by her boyfriend, do you?"

"He'd have no reason." Joy walked and took the necklace from her father. "Cutter wanted nothing more to do with this situation, and I believe him. This must belong to Harmony."

"It is her style to send a message like that, as if she's thumbing her nose at you," Suzi said. "But that also means she isn't dead."

Silas stood. "I don't believe you'll need to worry about her anymore. After the events of late, I'd hoped you believed her dead. The truth is your daughter used the portal by Bellington Mountain early this morning."

"You lied to us!" Suzi bolted to her feet.

Joy held her hand up in a calming motion. "Then why ask if Harmony would travel with me to Celestia, when you knew she'd already gone?"

"I wanted to get your feelings on the situation. You've been through a lot lately and if you believed her dead, you'd move on without fear. Apparently, she had to leave a parting gesture."

"Again, you've chosen to make decisions for me

that aren't yours to make." Joy's voice held a tinge of contempt. "And how would you know she traversed the portal? She told me nobody monitored it?"

He returned to his stool. "I'm sorry, daughter, I should have learned my lesson. As far as the doorway, while we do not monitor it, we've installed a sensor. It leads to a remote part of our world, far from other civilizations. Since those who go there remain in that area, we've not found a need to close it off. However, we do need to know who may come or go."

With her tension easing, Joy said, "Then it's safe for me to visit Celestia without worrying about my family here?"

Silas nodded. "We'll know if she chooses to return and can warn you."

"Well, you'd best fill us in on this bilbao tree and where to find it." Joy sat and rested her elbows on the counter.

"You may have already seen it, though it wouldn't have been in bloom," he said.

Grace looked at her mother. "What does a tree have to do with anything?"

Joy held up a finger. "Give me a second." Leaving the room, she returned a few minutes later with the two tickets, and handed her one.

Silently, Grace read one side then flipped it over. "These say the first of the month. That's only a few days away."

Her mother nodded. "Now, Silas, is the tree around here?"

With a shake of his head, he said, "Think. Who did I tell you was the guardian before being sent back?"

"Makes sense." Joy smiled.

Suzi put her hands on hips. "What am I missing? Where is it? For once can everyone stop being so cryptic and just speak plain English."

"Remember meeting my Uncle Pete? Only at the time we didn't know who he really was?"

She narrowed her eyes. "Yeah? What's that got to do with the price of zucchini in Alaska?"

Joy grinned.

"Well why didn't you just say that in the first place? When do we leave? I could use a few new trinkets since all of mine went up in smoke." Suzi rose quickly, but then swooned, and crumpled to the floor.

Chapter 50

Joy, Silas, and Grace sat in the hospital waiting area a few hours after the ambulance delivered Suzi to the emergency room.

The attending physician from Grace's stay after her attack on the beach, Dr. Tory, approached them. "You are Miss Beecher's family?"

Grace stood. "How is Aunt Suzi?"

"She is resting comfortably. You can see her now, if you wish, but only two at a time."

"I'll wait here," Silas said.

Grace hurried toward the room her aunt had been taken to.

Joy held back. "Dr. Tory, what's wrong with her?"

"I'm sorry, but I'm not at liberty to say. It's up to the patient to disclose her condition if she wishes. Excuse me." Without another word, Dr. Tory walked away.

When she got to Suzi's room, Grace's laughter drifted into the hallway. As she entered, she found the patient poking at the bag of saline attached to the IV in her arm. "You must be okay if you've made her laugh."

Suzi grinned. "I just asked my favorite niece if she could replace this liquid with white wine. They'd never notice the difference."

Joy shook her head. "Okay, spill. What's really going on here?"

The older woman looked from mother to daughter, then back again. "I didn't want to worry you. With all the havoc your offspring decided to cause, I thought you had enough to deal with."

"Well, Harmony is gone. Grace is fine. How about you?" Joy put her hands on her hips.

"I've got a heart murmur. The doctor says it might have something to do with one of the valves needing fixed. There's some big, long, medical explanation with several multi-syllable words I can't pronounce. Bottom line is I'll have surgery, and it'll get straightened out. Easy peasy." She swatted the air. "Now, let's get outta here. I'm hungry."

During the whole explanation, Joy's face grew cold. "Back up. What do you mean surgery? As in heart surgery?"

Suzi sighed. "I believe that's the organ involved."

"This is serious," Grace said. "Aunt Suzi, how can you be so nonchalant?"

"Would you prefer panic and hysteria? The doctor assures me there's nothing to worry about. It's a routine operation with minimal risk."

Joy gripped her friend's hand. "I'll be with you every step of the way. I'm not going anywhere until you've made a full recovery."

"There is another option." Silas stood in the doorway.

All three faces turned toward him.

Joy's eyes filled with understanding, and a smile spread across her face. "Would it work with an outsider?"

He nodded. "It takes longer, but she wouldn't be the first to arrive with a condition to be cured."

"What option, Grandpa?" Grace stood straight with eyes focused on the man.

"You explain, Justine." He turned and left.

"Mom?"

Joy gave Suzi's hand a squeeze. "It looks like you'll get to use that second ticket after all. If I didn't know better, I'd say you planned all of this."

Suzi shot her fist into the air. "Hot diggity! I'm going to Celestia!"

Chapter 51

On the first of June, Joy drove into the parking lot of Toby's Treasures. Instead of pulling into one of the vacant slots out front, she drove around back and hit the brakes. On the edge of the lot in front of them stood an enormous tree sprouting huge purple flowers. "I've never seen anything like that before. Have you?"

Suzi shook her head. "Uh-uh. How is it we didn't see that thing from the road? It's twice as tall as the shop."

Shifting the car into gear, Joy parked in a spot closest to the tree.

The women got out and retrieved their bags. Neither brought a lot since Joy could always purchase anything they missed when she returned.

Jester tugged at the end of his leash as they approached the tree.

"No, Jester, you cannot mark territory on the magical tree. For all I know you might curse us for doing so," Suzi chastised then looked to her traveling companion. "Now what?"

Joy shrugged. "There's supposed to be a portal, but I never asked Silas what it actually looks like. Do you see anything?"

"Like a door in the trunk? Nope. Nothing looks out of place except the tree itself. What was the doorway like when you came to Earth the first time?"

"I arrived in the desert, and the way here had been through a cave. It didn't look anything like this and certainly wasn't beside a bilbao tree."

They walked around the trunk, which had to have been almost four feet wide. Behind it they found the attendant standing at the entrance of a tunnel carved from white stone. Jester sniffed around the man's feet, gave a low woof, then backed off to safety.

"Welcome, ladies," he said, spreading his arms. "So glad you found your way here."

"Thank you, Uncle Pete. Good to see you again." Joy embraced the man.

"And you." He motioned toward the dog. "Who do we have here?"

"This is Suzi's sidekick, Jester," Joy said.

"Well, it's a pleasure to make your acquaintance, Jester." Pete nodded at the dog before extending a hand to the dog's owner. As she reached to shake it, he gently raised her hand to his mouth and brushed his lips across the back. "This is how we greet new friends. You and I didn't have the opportunity to formally meet."

The older woman blushed and remained tongue-tied. All she could manage was a grin.

Releasing her hand, he bent down and gave a pat on the head to Jester. The gatekeeper passed muster as the dog licked his hand, then sat down panting, as if the whole event wore on his little bones.

"Well then," Pete said. "Let's get the formalities out of the way. Entrance tickets, please." He held out his palm.

Fishing into her jacket pocket, Joy retrieved two tickets and placed them in the outstretched hand. "We just go through the tunnel then?"

"Well…umm." He bit his lip.

"What's the matter?"

"I'm sorry, Justine, but every living soul counts." He remained with his hand out.

"You mean, even…" She looked down at Jester. It never occurred to her they'd need a ticket for him too.

Suzi looked up at her with knitted brows. "What's wrong? I don't understand."

"He's saying we each need a ticket."

"But we have two tickets and there's…" Tears formed in the corners of her eyes as she looked down at her dog and scooped him up. "I can't leave him."

"You won't, don't worry." Joy scratched the panting critter behind the ear. "Believe it or not, little scruff, I'm truly going to miss you. Have fun in your new world."

"Joy, I can't…" Distress covered her face like a mask. "You need to…"

"Hush now," she whispered quietly. "Like I said, little guy, I'm going to miss you, as well as your mama." She smiled at her best friend.

"You aren't coming? Jester and I are going alone?"

"You'll have friends aplenty." She wrapped her arms around Suzi, squishing Jester in between them. Looking to her uncle, she asked, "It's not my time yet, is it?"

"No, niece. I'll look in on your friends from time to time, as will the rest of the community."

Joy gestured toward the tunnel. "Can I walk her through?"

"Of course. You know, Justine, you may find another opportunity in the most likely place." He winked.

She wasn't sure what he meant but needed to send Suzi off. The sooner she arrived in Celestia, the sooner the healing would begin. Wrapping her arms around both friend and pooch, Joy gave one more squeeze. Releasing them, she pulled back and said, "You'll be fine. Besides, this isn't goodbye forever—only for now."

Suzi's tears had stopped, leaving streaks in her make-up. "You'll come soon?"

"Of course! It seems I've a few things left to wrap up here first. Come now." She tugged at the woman's arm. "Time to go."

"All right." Adjusting the bag on her arm while clutching Jester close, she squared her shoulders. "Ready for blast off!"

They walked side by side into the tunnel.

Spying the forest through the other end, Suzi asked, "Is that Celestia?"

"I'm not sure we can really see it from here. You'll find out soon enough."

"Ya know," Suzi said, "you really are my bestie. Well, after this little guy, of course." She laughed.

"I know." Joy looked toward the other woman, who'd already disappeared. "Be happy, my friend," she whispered.

After taking a moment to enjoy the beauty of the forest, she turned back the way she'd come. Pete had vanished as well. She walked toward the tree and glanced back at the entrance. Speaking quietly to no one in particular, she said, "I guess I'll find you in the most likely place—whatever that means."

Chapter 52

A few miles down the road, her low gas light went on. She hadn't expected to need the car for a while, but having remained in this world, it required her immediate attention. The road she traveled was sparsely populated. Hoping to come across a town soon, she slowed down to conserve her fuel.

Joy approached a four-way stop. Being unfamiliar with this area, she wasn't sure which direction to go. She knew going straight would lead her to the highway they'd driven on, but the next fuel stop was about fifty miles away. Her cell didn't have service, so she couldn't pull up directions to the nearest gas station. Feeling adventurous, she took a penny out of her purse and tossed it into the air. Grabbing the coin as it fell, she slapped it onto the back of her other hand.

"Heads I turn left, tails I go right," she said aloud.

Removing her top hand, the back of the coin faced her. "Right it is."

Three miles down the road, she approached a sign with neatly cropped hedges on either side. It read, "Welcome to Likely, Population 6,043."

She slammed on her brakes. *It can't be that easy.* Two blocks later she passed a residential area with a few scattered houses. They were modest in size, yet meticulously well-kept from the looks of the lawns and gardens surrounding the structures.

Larger buildings ahead appeared to be commercial properties. Passing the local grocery store, she found a gas station on the corner. With a sigh of relief, Joy pulled in.

Despite her paying at the pump with a credit card, an old man wearing navy coveralls wandered out. His name tag read Sam. "Good morning, ma'am. Looks to be the start of a beautiful day."

"Yes, it does, doesn't it?" Joy replaced the nozzle and twisted the cap onto the gas tank.

"We don't get many tourists. You visiting someone here?" His smile tightened some of the wrinkles on his face.

Joy saw no reason to hurry since it was only a couple of hours' drive after reaching the coast. She planned to stop at the same hotel they'd stayed at on the way to Toby's Treasures. "No, just passing through. Guess I wandered farther than I realized, and my fuel was near empty."

"Glad you didn't run out before you found us. We're the only town around for about twenty-five miles." He leaned on the gas pump.

Feeling a rumble in her stomach, she realized it was past eleven and she hadn't eaten anything all day. The earlier excitement of traveling to another world had left her without an appetite until now. "Is there any place nearby where I can get a bite to eat?"

The man's face brightened even more. "That would be my sister Betty's place. She runs the local café and makes the best-darned rhubarb pie you've ever tasted! Keep going for two more blocks, and it'll be on your left. Tell her Sam sent you. It tickles her when I recommend the place to folks."

"I'll do that, Sam. Thank you." As Joy drove away, she watched him in her rearview mirror waving.

Within a minute, there stood a billboard in front of a building advertising fresh, homemade pies. She turned into the parking lot of the cafe just before the building. A woman in a blue-checked waitress uniform greeted her as she walked inside.

"Welcome, honey. Sit wherever you like, there's plenty open."

"Thank you." She sat at a small table by the front window.

The woman handed her a menu. "What brings you to The Most Likely Place?"

Giving a double take, she asked, "Excuse me? What did you say?"

"How did you find us here at The Most Likely Place?"

Speechless, she read the front of the menu. The name of the restaurant was The Most Likely Place Café. Staring at the name, she found her voice and said, "I...I...stopped for gas, and Sam recommended this cafe. Are you Betty?" She looked at the woman.

"Why yes, I am. Did you know Sam is my brother?" She patted the bun holding back her auburn hair.

"He mentioned the relationship."

With a beaming smile she added, "That brother of mine is such a sweetheart sending people my way."

"I see the family resemblance. You both have a warm smile and twinkling eyes."

"Thank you. Let me know when you're ready to order."

"I will."

Betty turned to leave, but Joy put a hand on her arm. "Betty?"

The server turned. "Yes?"

"Do you, by chance, have a gift shop here in town?" Joy's mind replayed Pete's words.

"Actually, there's one attached to the café."

Eyes wide, Joy jumped up, "Really?"

"Easy, girl. Have some grub, and it will still be there when you're done."

They laughed.

"Of course." Joy sat back down and picked up the menu.

Betty went behind the counter and returned with a pot of coffee. She refilled the mugs of a couple sitting a few tables away. After checking on the other patrons, she went back to Joy. "So, what would you like?"

Joy ordered a sandwich and some iced tea. While she was anxious to see if the store sold seeds, she settled down and enjoyed her food. After paying the tab, she went next door to the shop. The bell over the door jingled as she stepped inside. She wasn't the least bit surprised by the cashier behind the front counter.

"You've found me." Pete leaned an elbow on the counter. "What you're looking for is at the back of the store."

Joy easily located the seed rack and selected a packet. Turning away, she hesitated, then went back and took two more. This was the reason she hadn't left with Suzi.

Approaching the counter, Pete said, "You've made the right choice, Justine. You know that in your heart, don't you?"

"Yes, Uncle Pete, I do." She placed the seeds on

the counter. "Why didn't you say anything when we first met?"

"Would you have believed me?"

She chuckled. "No, I guess not."

"*That's* why." He slapped the counter for emphasis. "I see you're going with three again. Covering all your bases?"

A wide grin spread across her face. "Giving a couple people their second chance. They deserve it, don't you think?"

He winked. "Yes, I'd have to agree." Pete rang up her purchases, then came around to her side of the counter spreading his arms wide.

Joy moved into his embrace.

Pete whispered in her ear, "Your mother will be waiting."

Her eyes teared up as she kissed him on the cheek. "See you soon, Uncle Pete."

****

A couple weeks later, two plants sat on the mantel. Each had a ticket sprouting from the middle of a large yellow bloom. An envelope with two plane tickets to Portland leaned against the bricks. Michael's mother, Marla, reread the notecard resting between them. "Everyone deserves a second chance. See you soon. Love, Justine."

A word about the author...

Terry Segan, originally from Commack, NY, now resides in the desert where she'll never require an ice scraper or snow shovel again. The beach is her happy place, but any opportunity to travel soothes her gypsy soul. The stories conjured by her imagination while riding backseat on her husband's motorcycle can be found throughout the pages of her paranormal mysteries. Growing up immersed in sarcastic humor and science fiction movies, Terry's goals are to cause her readers to laugh out loud, cry with joy, or cower under the covers wondering if the noise under the bed was real or imagined.

http://terrysegan.com

Thank you for purchasing
this publication of The Wild Rose Press, Inc.

For questions or more information
contact us at
info@thewildrosepress.com.

The Wild Rose Press, Inc.
www.thewildrosepress.com